Praise for Lydia Millet and *Ghost Lights*

A *New York Times* Editor's Choice

A *San Francisco Chronicle* Notable Book

"[Millet] exhibits the sweep and Pop-Art lyricism of Don DeLillo, the satiric acerbity of Kurt Vonnegut, the everyday-cum-surrealism harmonics of Haruki Murakami, and the muted-moral outrage of Joy Williams. . . . Millet is operating at a high level in *Ghost Lights*."
—Josh Emmons, *New York Times Book Review*

"Thrilling, witty, and philosophical." —Kimberly Cutter, *Marie Claire*

"[An] odd and wonderful novel." —Brock Clarke, *Boston Globe*

"With its linguistic and plot pranks and underlying moral complexity, *Ghost Lights* recalls the laconic, Lacanian novels of Paul Auster."
—Carolyn Cooke, *San Francisco Chronicle*

"Breathtaking descriptions not only of nature but of everyday minutiae mixed in with just enough drop-dead satire."
—Karen Brady, *Buffalo News*

"One of America's most daring writers."
—J. Peder Zane, *News & Observer*

"Millet's got a visionary sensibility, marked by a voice that is by turns biting and dark." —David L. Ulin, *Los Angeles Times*

"Millet [is] a writer of encompassing empathy and imaginative lyricism and a satirist of great wit and heart."
—Donna Seaman, *Booklist*

"If Kurt Vonnegut were still alive, he would be extremely jealous."
—James Hannaham, *Village Voice*

ALSO BY LYDIA MILLET

Magnificence

Love in Infant Monkeys

How the Dead Dream

Oh Pure and Radiant Heart

Everyone's Pretty

My Happy Life

George Bush, Dark Prince of Love

Omnivores

GHOST LIGHTS

a novel

LYDIA MILLET

W. W. Norton & Company
New York • London

The author thanks Maria Massie, Tom Mayer, Denise Scarfi, Amy Robbins, Nancy Palmquist, Don Rifkin, Tara Powers, Anna Oler, Ingsu Liu, and David High for all that they have done.

Printed in the United States of America
First published as a Norton paperback 2012

For information about permission to reproduce
selections from this book,
write to Permissions, W. W. Norton & Company, Inc.,
500 Fifth Avenue, New York, NY 10110

For information about special discounts for bulk purchases, please contact W. W. Norton Special Sales at specialsales@wwnorton.com or 800-233-4830

Manufacturing by Courier Westford
Book design by Chris Welch
Production manager: Anna Oler

Library of Congress Cataloging-in-Publication Data

Millet, Lydia, 1968–
Ghost lights : a novel / Lydia Millet. — 1st ed.
p. cm.
ISBN 978-0-393-08171-8 (hardcover)
I. Title.
PS3563.I42175G49 2011
813'.54—dc23
2011026502

ISBN 978-0-393-34345-8 pbk.

W. W. Norton & Company, Inc.
500 Fifth Avenue, New York, N.Y. 10110
www.wwnorton.com

W. W. Norton & Company Ltd.
Castle House, 75/76 Wells Street, London W1T 3QT

1 2 3 4 5 6 7 8 9 0

GHOST LIGHTS

1

The walls were kittens and puppies. Like other pet facilities he had seen—even the Humane Society, where he had taken Casey when she was six to pick out a kitten—the kennel trafficked in a brand of cuteness he could not endorse. He had nothing against pets; in theory, the more pets the better, although he personally did not own one. Not in the sense of unchecked proliferation, feral cats mating all over the place, etc., but in the sense that cats were good, dogs were good. No argument there.

But he did not see why this high regard for pets, his or anyone else's, should be represented by photographs of puppies with word balloons emerging from their mouths—balloons that contained supposedly witty sayings that were, in fact, stupid. There was no call for dachshunds dressed up as the Blues Brothers.

Susan's name had been on the list of emergency contacts for

this particular dog. When its owner failed to pick it up after several weeks the kennel had finally called her. Instantly she felt guilty; she should have thought about the dog far sooner, she told Hal. She had forgotten the dog, forgotten all about it.

What was *wrong* with her? she asked him insistently.

Now here they were, come to pick up her missing boss's dog—the dog of a man who had vanished many weeks ago into a tropical jungle—and the woman at the front desk was worried for the dog. Not for the absent owner, no. She was interested only in the dog's situation.

Hal glanced over—surreptitiously, he hoped. She was a heavy, lank person with bleached hair showing black at the roots and a kind of jowly gray pallor that bespoke ill health. Neither dog kennels nor the Humane Society were typically staffed by so-called beautiful people, in his experience. They were staffed by committed pet lovers, and frankly these committed pet lovers put less than average value on appealing physically to their fellow men.

Or maybe they sought out the company of pets in the first place because they did not enjoy the company of said fellow men. It was understandable—a form of relaxation, perhaps. Even if he himself was not a committed pet lover per se, a committed a.k.a. professional pet lover, he could appreciate that. As to the lank half-dyed hair, greasy pallor, etc., they were probably caused by a philosophy. Hygiene and style were aimed at winning the favor of others, after all, and the committed pet lovers already had the respect, or at least the gratitude—which might even be preferable, in the eyes of a committed pet lover—of peers and strangers alike. They were monks and nuns, in a sense. Monks and nuns of the pets.

The dog woman held up a rubber banana printed with a smiley face and squeezed it. It squeaked.

"She's not eating well. I recommend a chew toy. It could ease the transition."

Susan, on the other hand, was worried not about the dog but for the dog's owner, her boss. She was fond of this employer far beyond the livelihood he provided, which might no longer be forthcoming since he was gone from the United States and possibly also dead.

She had confessed she was afraid of this. She had leaned over in bed and whispered her fear in the small hours of the morning. She was afraid her employer, to whom she had grown close—in the kind of unequal, crypto-friendship for which such relations occasionally allowed—would never return from the tropics, where he had disappeared some weeks ago while ostensibly conducting some routine business.

Hal was strongly ambivalent about the employer, known for some no-doubt-pretentious reason simply as T. For starters, he refused to refer to the guy using a single letter. He called him by his last name Stern, though seldom to his face. But Susan would brook no criticism. Ever since the boss guy's girlfriend died—for which Hal had sympathy, of course, but which still did not sanctify him—he could do no wrong in her eyes. To her he had become almost a son surrogate.

"Just sign these and we'll release her into your custody," said the dog woman abruptly, and shuffled papers. Susan was shaky, emotional, and clearly the dog woman was uncomfortable with this display. She handed Susan a clipboard and a pen. "She's all up to date on her shots, see? Two months ago, 08-05-94 it says here. And the leg's healed pretty well where it was amputated. The name and number of the vet he uses are on the card here. Wait a minute and I'll make you a copy."

She turned and disappeared through a doorway.

"It's a *three*-legged dog?" he asked Susan.

"She was run over."

"I didn't know it was a dog amputee."

Susan seemed to be trembling. He pulled her closer and held her. First the man let his dog run around in the street till she was hit by a car, then he flew off to Central America and left her in a kennel.

Quite nice.

After a minute Susan pulled away. While she busied herself rummaging around in her purse he wandered over to a door marked RESTROOM. He often escaped to bathrooms when he was in public, stood at sinks and gazed into mirrors. Bathrooms were the respite. What would he do without them? From when he was a boy, gangly and shy, he had found comfort here.

Slowly he washed his hands, let the warm water run. On the wall behind him was a mural of clouds, with stylized dogs and cats jumping among them. In the mirror he saw himself with a flying poodle over his head.

The three-legged dog deserved to be happy, as did they all. But a three-legged dog was not a four-legged dog. A three-legged dog had to mean more upkeep, with the addition of pathos . . . of course, this right here was the kind of impulse Casey despised. She hated pity and railed against it, in particular the presumption that pity implied and the way it had of raising one person above another, subjugating the injured and then elevating them to make up for it. Injury is not a moral state, she had said to him once when she was angry. People think disability makes you a better person—on the inside you must be some kind of martyr, they figure, since on the outside you're wrecked. But losing the use of your legs does not make you the Dalai Lama, she said. So the pity, which people usually reserve for things that don't threaten them, is bullshit.

He accepted this, from her perspective, but pity was a fact of life when it came to dogs with amputations and when it came to the paraplegic. There was nothing in his life that had hurt him more than what happened to Casey, the shock of which would never fully recede; so he and Susan already had, occupying the central space in their lives, a victim—the only victim, the closest victim possible. They did not need a canine victim too. They were decent people but they were not cut from the same cloth as the kennel employee. They were not caregivers first and foremost; they didn't wake up in the morning and say, "Hey! Let's go nurture something."

They were only parents.

Other parents, whose children had not been hurt, could never know how parenthood could be extended infinitely on the heels of such an event and become a domed universe, a closed universe beneath the opaque dome of the accident. Even the stars were not visible anymore.

The Milky Way, he thought suddenly. The Milky Way was out there. Not only that—a hundred billion galaxies, some with a trillion stars.

Shifting away from the blurry spiral arms that could not be fathomed, he gazed at the tiles on the wall beside him, their creamy blandness. At a certain moment—oftentimes at the crossroads between youth and adulthood—a change of position occurred between the self and the world. As a child and even a teenager he had felt small, looking up at the rest of it all as a monument, but then suddenly he was older and part of the architecture, its tangibility and the impulse behind it, its failings and its strengths. The heavy installations had lost their majesty and seemed temporary, even shoddy, with a propensity for decline.

At the same time he had felt himself fading in and out of the installations like patterns of sunlight or lines of insects; according to his mood he might be a partner in their solidity, a detractor or an opponent, but he had passed from outside to inside and become culpable for the world.

That was the price you paid for the feeling of inclusion: the buildings, the grids of cities with their roads and subways, their storefronts and systems turned approachable, even trivial. The two of you were locked in an interdependence in which you were both always decaying . . .

He had been bred to feel like an insider, no doubt—had grown up in an affluent Southern California suburb in the wake of the war, though the fifties and sixties were the time he remembered. It had been a pleasant blur of a youth. Sun on the lawns, his mother and father sitting at a thick pine table in the evening by lamplight. Braided placemats, soft butter in a dish and green beans in a bowl. The gentle sheen of the wood.

Time was like the table when he tried to recollect his childhood—vague but solid, fingerprinted and warm.

"Hal?"

It was Susan, on the other side of the door. She often lost him in bathrooms.

"Coming. Just a second," he said, and dried his hands on a soft paper towel. He had read a pamphlet that said the softest and thickest towels and toilet rolls were made not from woodchips but from the ancient giants: you wiped your ass with the history of the world . . . what was different for him and for Susan too, for anyone whose life had been interrupted, was that after that ascension to the citadel he had suddenly been ejected again. He'd been ejected from that communal life of achievers, the life of regularity. He had found himself there, in the span of the arches and the rise of the walls—that quick belonging, those years of lockstep—and then, with the accident, he was outside again forever. His own childhood and Casey's merged in his recall, encased in a golden glow; at the moment of her paralysis the childhood turned into a lost paradise, and so it would remain—for as long as he lived he would not be able to shrug off the sense of this loss. It left him with the sear of heartbreak and the pressure of resentment.

You worked, of course, to get clear of that resentment, to give it up like an offering. But it was a struggle that did not end. One day you felt it rise from you and disperse, you felt an upsurge of freedom, but the next day it settled on you again.

He existed, in fact, half in the moment of her childhood, suspended for all time. The memory dogged him with such persistence that he wished he could replace it with one that was less glowing, more tarnished and scuffed. The shine of her lost joy was blinding.

Of course the memory was not the childhood itself but a

vision of it he had created without wishing or trying to—a memory as unchanging as the accident itself, formed almost at the same moment, or at least at the moment when he was told, in the hospital, that the damage was permanent. At that instant a barrier was thrown up between what was and what should have been, a future for his little girl that had never been permitted. The childhood memory was a bridge between them, between then and now, which had to stay separate to be bearable. But there it shimmered, with a deceitful, sly nostalgia.

The dog woman came out from the back office trailing the dog on a sturdy brown-leather lead. No cheap and functional nylon for Thomas Stern. But Hal had to admit he took to the animal right away. She walked gamely, hopping with her hindquarters; she wore an attentive expression and wagged her tail.

He glanced at Susan: her eyes were filling with tears.

"Let me," he said softly, and reached out to hold the leash.

Susan knelt down and petted the dog, put her arms around it.

It was all Stern's fault. Stern had been an imposition on the family from start to finish. First he was an imposition on Susan, demanding her full-time loyalty as the caretaker of all the most trivial details of his gainful enterprise; into their quiet home had come long discussions of his youth and conscientiousness, even his overpriced wardrobe and alleged charisma. The latter of which was a myth Hal saw no reason to believe.

As a husband he had been forced to endure this intruder in his house constantly—not his physical presence but the daily, dull news of him. Many times he had wished that Susan was employed in an office with more personnel, for the sake of a little variation in her bulletins from the workplace. He himself was stationed in an office whose very size kept him from getting on oppressively intimate terms with any of his colleagues.

Then he had imposed himself on Casey—who knew how, Hal did not open his mind to the permutations, but he and Casey had been close, briefly—and now, missing, possibly even deceased, he was imposing on all of them.

• • • • •

The mutt sat in the back seat of the car, her ears forward, watching and listening. Hal drove.

"If she sheds a lot we can spread out a blanket back there," he said.

Susan gazed out the windshield.

"Casey might want her," she offered after a few minutes.

"Maybe she could have the dog some days but not all the time. That would be easier."

But strangers might laugh at them. Someone might laugh to see the girl in the wheelchair, walking a tripod dog.

He did not say this, of course.

They lapsed into silence until he turned into the grocery-store parking lot. They had to buy dishes and dog food.

"I'll stay with her," said Susan, so he rolled down the windows, crossed the lake of pavement and went into the store alone.

In the dry-goods aisle, where he gazed at brands of dog food, hypnotized and vacant, he felt himself floating back. It was the chief pitfall of any time he spent alone, anywhere from minutes to long hours. At work he did not drift so easily, because work occupied him. It commandeered his attention in a way that offered relief.

Casey had picked out a white kitten at the Humane Society and that was the last time he remembered being in a pet food aisle—although he must have bought cat food in the succeeding years, of course, after the kitten had grown into a cat, but he did not recall this. The cat had finally died shortly before the accident, of a kidney infection. But the first day of the kitten, with his six-year-old Casey in her blond ponytail, he had walked up and down an aisle indistinguishable from this one—it might even have *been* this one; they might have walked here together—holding her small hand.

He looked down at his own hand, which had flexed suddenly as though feeling the imprint.

Casey had gazed up at him and asked him why kittens didn't eat people food. His thoughts flicking briefly over slaughterhouse by-products and rendering and bone meal and carbolic acid and what "gourmet lamb entree" was code for, he told her smiling that kittens just liked cat food better.

Such was the duty of fatherhood, he had thought to himself, neatly satisfied at a simple task well accomplished, and reached for a bag of Purina.

Standing in front of the bags again, red backgrounds with head shots of golden retrievers, cocker spaniels, he wished it had all been so easy, even if it was a lie and a facile one too. What he would give now to be able to hand her such a lie in place of the life she had. Anything. He would have no qualms at all, not one.

He would lie through his teeth if it would do any good. If only lies would suffice.

* * * * *

There was a libertarian in his office. It happened fairly often.

This one believed carmakers should pay for all roads. He was a hefty man in his thirties and his face was red with anger as he sat in the seat across from Hal's desk; understandably, in a way, since his house had been seized by a revenue officer.

The case was closed, but he had hammered on the bullet-proof glass door.

Hal made a gentle case for public roads—a gentle and inoffensive case, he felt—but still the libertarian looked at him through narrowed eyes as though he were a damnable liar.

"The way I see it, the tax system is what *gives* us our freedoms. The freedom to move, for starters. I mean, what would happen if every man had to build his own roads? Or if every single mile of road was a toll? You could try looking at it that way."

The libertarian's narrowed eyes were already glazing over. Tax protesters liked to talk, often, but once someone else took a turn at talking they felt a nap coming on.

Roads were easy as a soapbox because no citizen could cling to the belief that roads were built for free. On the roads where they drove they *felt* free, of course—they drew in a sweet breath of independence and let it out again happily. Americans loved to drive, discovered in driving both a splendid isolation and the shimmering mirage of connectedness.

But how did they come to drive on those roads, those slick long roads that gave a view of mountains or valleys, of suburbs or cities? They paid for their vehicles, of course. Hal had never yet met a protester who believed the cars themselves should be free, handed out like candy at Halloween to all and sundry from a benevolent car-giving source. A typical protester did not blame car manufacturers for charging money, for he held private enterprise in high esteem. He blamed the government for charging for its myriad services, but private operators could rob him blind in broad daylight, all in the name of liberty.

Hal's own father had been wary of government programs. Possibly this was why Hal had an affection for libertarians, albeit patronizing. Most of them had a chip on their shoulders, a heavy chip. It was as though, when they were young, a schoolyard bully had terrorized them, and in the memory of that bully an idea of Big Government had come to be encoded.

But government is only a bully, he liked to tell them, when it needs to be for the common welfare . . . crime was another arena where government took a stern and paternal hand, and most tax protesters did not mind this a bit. When it came to crime—a matter far more serious, in the eyes of your average protester, than say education or poverty—protesters were all about government. Also they had no argument with the government when it came to the commissioning, manufacture and deployment of vast arrays of weapons, both conventional and nuclear.

According to your typical tax protester the potential oblivion of all things living was rightly the province of government, but not so a measly ten- or fifteen-percent garnishment of their salary.

It was not the mandate of the Service, of course, to psychoanalyze or proselytize. It was not the purview of the Service to take taxpayers under its wing and baby them. It was the task of the Service simply to evaluate, assess and finally collect. But Hal often chose to engage personally despite the fact that, under the law, he was not required to do so or even, frankly, encouraged.

In truth, no matter what facts and figures he marshaled to defend government, the protesters were never converted. Simply, they cherished their right to direct fear and loathing at government bureaucracy. It was a God-given right, and one they insisted on exercising to the fullest. All he could give them, in the end, was an impression of having been listened to and reasoned with. Though they stoutly resisted reason—it was another God-given right to be unreasonable, indeed to hate reason almost as much as they despised government—they might not forget that he had made them a cup of coffee.

"Let me get you some coffee," he said to the libertarian, who was jiggling one foot. "Milk? All we have is that powdered dairy creamer."

While he was in the hallway pouring the coffee the libertarian might notice the pictures on his desk, of Susan in a dress and Casey in her wheelchair. Casey hated the picture and accused him of pandering, but he genuinely loved it and in any case could not bear to have earlier pictures of her around.

His coworker Linda came up behind him at the coffeemaker.

Her large round earrings were like Christmas tree ornaments. "Hal," she said, reaching for a tea bag, "the papers room is a mess. Where are the 433-D's?"

"New stack," he said. "Beside the obsolete forms? Second shelf. On your left."

Protesters often rejected reason without even pinning down what it was they rejected, he thought as he tapped in the dairy creamer. They understood in the most nebulous terms the difference between argument and debate, or even raw unquestioning instinct and rigorous logic. Finally what they cherished most, he thought—and he made these generalizations only after decades of service—was their relationship not to morality or individualism but to symbols.

The symbols had about them an aura of immanence, and to the symbols many protesters cleaved. It was often not one symbol for them but many—say a flag, say an eagle, say a cross; say a pair of crossed swords. The symbols were richly pregnant, pregnant with a meaning that would never be born.

It never needed to be.

Against a symbol there could be no argument.

"Here you go," he said, in his office again, and handed over the coffee mug.

•

His colleagues in general were not believers like him but cynics. They were cynical about their jobs and cynical about the tax code; they were cynics about human nature and about civil service. Indeed his own deep convictions on the subject of taxes and government would likely have been objects of their ridicule if not for the fact that, due to Casey's paralysis, he often got a free pass on everything.

And it wasn't simple pity either. Everyone came to know illness in the course of their lives, everyone came to know death, and somewhere within this grim terrain was the situation of Casey, Susan and him—a situation in which people beheld the inverse of their own good fortune. In Casey they saw a lamb on the altar: there others suffered for their sin. If they did not believe in sin they tended to be superstitious at least, believing her affliction filled some kind of ambient bad-luck quota that might otherwise have to be filled by them.

He reorganized a taxpayer file idly. The dog had slept at the foot of the bed last night, where she'd whined until lifted, and left short white hairs all over the red quilt. He did not like these hairs but he had liked the feel of the dog on his feet while he was falling asleep. In the morning, as he was pouring coffee into his travel mug before leaving, Susan had called Casey from the wall phone in the kitchen. "We have his dog," he heard his wife say, watching the dog lap at her new water bowl, and then, "No. Still nothing."

A knock on his office door.

"Come in," he said.

It was Rodriguez, who wore his pants belted high.

"Hey, man," said Rodriguez.

"Hey."

Often a single habit of an otherwise unremarkable person, such as wearing high-waisted pants, struck Hal as tragic.

"So you coming to lunch? It's Linda's fiftieth."

"Fiftieth," said Hal. "Whoa."

With the pants tightly cinched right below his rib cage, Rodriguez limited his options. Figuratively speaking, Rodriguez shot himself in the foot every time he got dressed.

"Who woulda known, right? She doesn't look a day over sixty-five," said Rodriguez, and laughed nervously.

"Thanks for thinking of me. I have an appointment with my daughter at lunchtime, though," said Hal regretfully. It was his standard excuse, but in this case a lie and thus in need of fleshing out to have the ring of truth. "She's in the market for a new car. I have to go with her to a dealership to talk about conversion. You know—hand controls, wheelchair loader. You'd be surprised how many of those mobility-equipment folks try to rip off paraplegics."

"Oh man," said Rodriguez, looking pained. "You kidding?"

"Yeah," said Hal. "I am. They're all right. But she needs help with the process."

Rodriguez was not a real cynic but wore the guise of cynicism to fit in. His attempts at sarcasm had the air of a strained joke, and from the rare moments when he allowed his actual persona to reveal itself Hal suspected he was secretly and painfully earnest. The earnestness and the high-waisted pants were connected, of course. Intimately. Anyone could tell from looking at his beltline that the cynicism was a juvenile posturing. But Rodriguez was a guy who could watch comedians on TV make fun of nerds simply by wearing their pants belted high and laugh heartily along with the crowd, never suspecting that their target was him. Essentially he had a blind spot—as everyone did—but Rodriguez's blind spot was in the public domain, like Casey's paralysis.

"Sure, man. Too bad though. We're going to that place with the kickass enchiladas."

Hal had a weakness for Rodriguez. And he presumed that his own sincerity—mainly his devotion, which had become known to his colleagues only by dint of their collective involvement in taxation, to the quaint idea of a wise and kindly government—would look practically jaded next to the near-cretinous gullibility of Rodriguez.

But this genuine, earnest persona of Rodriguez, being kept in lockdown, was never allowed into Gen Pop long enough for Hal to be certain.

"Eat one for me, OK?" he said in what he hoped was a tone of finality. "With New Mexican green chiles."

"No way," said Rodriguez. "Those chiles'd be repeating on me."

"Jesus," said Hal, and waved him away. "Enough said then."

Rodriguez retreated with a swaggering manner, as though his remark about vomiting into his mouth placed him firmly within the pantheon of the suave.

•

At one o'clock Hal drove west, partly because he was committed to his fabrication and partly because he wanted to pay his daughter a visit. Casey had recently relocated from her Soviet-style tenement in the Marina to a pleasant building dating from the thirties or forties, rare for Santa Monica, with large, airy rooms and arched doorways. He was delighted with the move, which signaled a rise out of apathy. Calla lilies grew in profusion beneath the front windows.

She had a new job in telemarketing. Difficult to see how selling timeshares in Jamaica could satisfy her in the long run, but for now at least she had a steady income. He should have called before he left but if she wasn't home, fine: he had to get out of the office anyway.

The freeways were open and before long he had parked on the street and was walking around to the back door. Through an open window he heard her voice—"Uh huh. And what do you want me to do then?"

The tone struck him as wrong for telemarketing. Of course she was a novice, she might not have it down yet. Casey had a nice voice, low and husky, which to him had always seemed tomboyish. It occurred to him she was probably, in fact, talking to her new boyfriend, a man from the support group, and he felt sheepish. For the so-called differently abled, privacy was a chronic problem.

He rapped on the window and waved to her inside; she turned, wearing a telephone headset, smiled, and mouthed at him to wait. He nodded as she rolled into the next room and out of earshot.

He was used to waiting: he waited for her often. Sitting down on the ramp, he gazed out at the backyard. Behind a small patch of grass, the usual deep and lush L.A. green that looked fake but in fact merely represented an extravagant level of water use . . . but here she was, already.

"I hear you got yourself a new cripple," said Casey from the back door. It was automatic and had swung open silently. "I'm so jealous!"

"Hi, sweetie. Hey, you meet any of the neighbors yet?" he asked, and stood.

Good if someone close by was looking out for her.

"Dad, please. I mean I know your little girl is coming out of her shell finally, every day is a blessing, rise and shine and like that, hell, I'm full-barrel on the positive attitude. But I didn't get a lobotomy. I don't roll around to the neighbors smiling and doing the meet and greet."

"A lobotomy wouldn't have that effect," he said, and went up the ramp and inside.

"So the three-legged dog thing, it's like a classic empty-nest syndrome, child-surrogate deal. Am I right?"

She went ahead of him through the kitchen, where an electric teakettle was whining. She switched it off and poured.

"You want a cup of tea? I'm having peppermint."

"Thanks. I'll just get a glass of water I think," he said, and moved around her.

"I knew this couple that when their basketball-playing kid went away to college—and this guy was like seven feet tall—they went out and got a dog two days later. Thing was though, the dog was a hundred-and-sixty-pound English mastiff. Came up to their chest level. True story. Remember Cal Shepard? From Samo?"

"The kid that drooled," he said, nodding.

"Cal Shepard did not drool. He was a popular jock. That was Jon Spisiak."

"A kid that drools in high school," he mused, shaking his head. He stood at the open refrigerator looking in. It was almost empty. "You don't have bottled water?"

"And I wouldn't even say Jon drooled per se," she said, and gestured at a white watercooler in the corner. "It was more like he had extra saliva. Oh. So Sal's coming over, by the way."

"The new boyfriend from group? This is great. I can submit him to the rigorous screening process."

"He'll fail. I have to warn you."

"Of course. They always do."

"But more than usual. Trust me."

"What. Is he a protester? A militia member?"

"He used to be a cop. Now he wears fatigues and sometimes a balaclava."

"Guy wears a balaclava in L.A.?"

"He took me up to Tahoe once. He wore it then. A black one. He looked like a paraplegic ninja."

He was following her into the living room, where a leather couch and chairs surrounded a low glass table.

"What, he wants to keep his face hidden?"

"I dunno, Dad. Ask him yourself."

"I can't ask him about the balaclava if he's not wearing it."

"OK. I'm like officially tired of this subject."

"Touchy!"

She spun her chair slowly and stopped, picked her mug out of the cup holder. He sat down opposite.

"I'm sorry," she said.

"Anyway. I look forward to meeting him."

"So T. still hasn't been heard from."

"No. And I think it's time your mother moved on."

Casey blew across the surface of her tea.

"I realize she's loyal," he went on. "But who knows what's happening with him. You know? It could be anything. Maybe he had legal trouble she never knew about and a secret account in the Caymans. Right? Change will be good for her. Something new."

Casey nodded and sipped.

"It'll be hard," he went on, and drank his water, "for her to know how long to wait before she makes key decisions, lets people go. There's that young guy that works there, that she hired a while back. And then the financial situation. I say find a good lawyer and pass the buck."

"She filed a missing persons report," said Casey softly. "And she's been calling the embassy every day."

"The U.S. embassy? In Belize?"

He heard the front doorbell ring.

"That'll be him. The father of your grandchild."

"What?"

"Kidding."

"I'll get it," he said, and rose.

As usual she was right; as soon as he pushed the button to open the door he knew the guy was a loser. Tamped-down anger, free-floating rage.

"Hey, welcome," he said affably, and stood back.

"Who are *you*?" asked the guy.

"My father," called Casey from within. "Hal, meet Sal."

"We rhyming," said Sal flatly, and rolled past him with no gesture of greeting. Hal had seen his share of bitter disabled guys and was inured to it—more or less preoccupied with this new information about Susan, he realized, turning from the door as it closed. His wife who was consumed with anxiety about the real-estate guy. The extent of her affection for Stern, the transparently maternal attachment, if examined by a professional, would likely prove rooted in some psychopathology related to the accident.

"I should get back to the office," he told Casey, and extended a hand to Sal. "It was nice to meet you."

Sal did something with his own hand that looked like a gang sign. A poser, thought Hal, as he stooped to kiss Casey's cheek. Understandable, but hardly deserving of respect. Before he was paralyzed he had been a cop, likely a swaggerer and a bully since almost all of them were, but now that he was spinal-cord injured he identified with the same underclass he used to dream of bludgeoning.

Outside Hal passed the suitor's conveyance, a battered hatchback in gunmetal gray that featured a bumper sticker calling for the rescue of POW/MIAs. It was parked half on the driveway and half on the lawn, and the right-side tires had ripped up a fresh track in the turf.

Law-enforcement officers were not his favorites among the varied ranks of persons who chose a career in public service. He recognized that the job carried with it certain personality requisites, such as a predisposition to violence, and that the demand for violent enforcers was embedded in the system, as was the supply of violent offenders. By some estimates, one out of twenty-five Americans was a sociopath.

And that was higher than anywhere else on the globe: this great nation was a fertile breeding ground for psychos. Or rather, as the economists would put it, the U.S. of A. had a comparative advantage in antisocial personality disorder.

And hey: these guys had to have incomes, just like everyone else.

At the very least one in fifty.

Casey, of course, could not be dissuaded from her choices,

having become stubborn and intractable after the accident—a development he had come to accept for the strength it lent her. This boyfriend choice, like the others, had to be left to play out. Still it was difficult to believe she had been on the telephone with the cop-turned-homeboy using that tender voice. Slipping behind the steering wheel, Hal repressed a shudder.

Remember: she is grown up. He often had to remind himself.

Also, she carried pepper spray when she went out at night. She had taken a course in disability martial arts.

Susan had to be frustrated, he reflected, driving. She likely felt responsible for what had happened to Stern. This feeling of responsibility was completely irrational, of course, but he knew it well. When regret was strong enough, guilt rose up to greet it. Maybe she thought she should have kept Stern from traveling alone; maybe she thought she should have persuaded him into therapy or grief counseling. Not that this would even have been possible.

They should talk more, Hal and Susan. They lay down to sleep at different hours, they rarely went out, lately there had been more distance between them than he wanted.

An old lady with a walker stepped out in front of his car; he swerved and hit the curb hard.

• • • • •

The car had to be towed. He called Casey, and Sal came to get him.

"I appreciate this," he told Sal, mildly humiliated.

Sometimes a sociopath helped you out.

They drove together to a rental car agency, Hal shooting sidelong glances at Sal's hands on the controls. The fingers bore small tattoos between the knuckles, which he was relieved to see were small plantlike designs rather than, say, LOVE and HATE. Looked like pot, possibly. There was a stale smell in the car—sweat, grease and cigarettes. He cracked the window, then rolled it all the way down. The dash was covered in stickers: rock bands, possibly, to judge by the graphics. Of course the names were unfamiliar to him. Blood, skulls in cowboy hats, sheriff's badges and guns, tigers and poppies and roses and faux-Gothic lettering.

Some of the paraphernalia was Mexican, some American, but all of it was equally encoded. Loud music played, a polka beat with electric guitar and an accordion. A *narcocorrido* if he was not mistaken: he had learned about these on National Public Radio. They celebrated drug kingpins.

Sal was moving his head to the beat and seemed to be muttering the lyrics.

"So your Spanish is fluent?" Hal said loudly, and smiled.

Sal nodded and flicked his fingers against the wheel, still mouthing.

"You grow up in L.A.?"

"East. I used to be police," said Sal. "L.A.P.D."

"Casey told me."

"She tell you I got shot by a friendly?"

"She didn't tell me that part."

"Yeah. This little kid, his first day on the job."

"Jesus," said Hal, shaking his head. "That's . . ."

"Fucked-up shit," said Sal, and went back to hitting the steering wheel and jutting his head forward in an embarrassing rhythm. Thankfully they had already reached the car place.

She has to be kidding, thought Hal as Sal screeched out of the lot touching his forehead in a mock salute.

He called the office from the car-rental counter. He had to take the rest of the day off, he said: car accident, and half the afternoon was already gone. Then he tried Susan's office and got the answering machine.

He wished he could go back to Casey's apartment, but that was inappropriate and would come off tedious and doting. Also very possibly Sal had gone back there also. No, he had to make his own entertainment. He would drive home in the rental and relax, take the dog for a walk.

•

His street was silent—neighbors dispersed to other parts of the city, in their compartments of earning. The branches of trees were still, there was no breeze at all, and pulling into the driveway in the rental car he had a curious impression: nothing was moving.

The car shifted into park, he sat beneath a giant maple. The leaves had turned red. After he turned the key to shut off the engine, even he was still. He concurred in the stillness of the scene, half by choice, half by temperament. There was a kind of soft suffocation in it . . . time, he thought, passing forever in front of him and not passing at all.

A young man was coming out the front door. It was Robert, who worked with Susan, shrugging on a jacket as he closed the door behind him.

"Robert!" he said, but since he was inside the car the sound of his voice was trapped. He opened the car door and Robert glanced up from his feet, startled briefly before he smiled. Hal stepped up and shook his hand.

"Hey," said Robert. He was handsome—far nearer to what Casey should have for a boyfriend than, say, Sal was. Although Robert, like Tom Stern, erred on the side of a prep-school caricature. No doubt he had rowed for Yale. "Hey! Yeah! So how you doing, man? I'm here on courier duty. Susan's working at home today."

"You looking for a new job yet?"

"I am. I wish I wasn't."

"I know. Unfortunate."

"It's a tragedy, is what it is."

"You don't think maybe he, you know, chose to leave? Numbered accounts, like that?"

"Hey, you gotta think that way. Right? Being the IRS and all."

"Occupational hazard, I guess."

"Seriously, I considered it for a minute or two. But nah. He's basically a good guy. And I mean there are projects we're right in the middle of. I'm talking, with him not being here? Like literally millions of dollars are getting washed down the drain."

"Have you met my daughter?" asked Hal, aware this was a non sequitur. When he hit the curb something had jarred him—he thought the shock of the crumpling fender had torqued his neck, possibly. Suddenly he was feeling lightheaded.

"Casey? Sure. Why?"

"Oh, I don't know . . . ," said Hal vaguely, and all at once they were awkward. "Anyway. Good luck with the job search."

Inside he heard the shower running. A sealed manila envelope lay on the dining room table, along with the mail. The dog must be upstairs with Susan. But climbing to the second floor, he shivered with a passing chill—the house felt wrong. He and Susan needed to go away somewhere, he thought: since the accident they never traveled much, fearing Casey would suddenly need them.

"Susan?" he called, and the dog came galumphing out of the bedroom.

"In here," came her voice, and he went into the bathroom, where the mirrors were steamed.

"Ran into Robert on his way out," he said to the shower curtain.

"Uh huh? What are you doing home, honey?"

"Car accident."

She pulled back the shower curtain. Her face was flushed; she looked lovely.

"You OK?"

"Maybe a little headache. No big deal. But I have a rental."

"No one was hurt though?"

"Zero casualties." He reached out and kissed her. "You smell so good."

"It's the shampoo."

He wanted to go to bed with her. He held her and kissed her more, water falling on both of them.

"Oh, Hal, not this second," she said. "I'm all wet."

"That's fine with me."

"Later. I promise."

He let her go and stepped back, his hair plastered.

"You look cute," she said, and swatted the wet mat of it before she pulled the curtain closed again. He gazed at the blur of her form through the blue plastic, which was covered in raised dots. He could barely tell what she was doing. One of her arms stretched up and back again. Had she put a hand up to adjust the nozzle? Her movements were shrouded. Equally she could have been reaching for a razor. She could be anyone, seen through this filter, doing almost anything. She was unknown to him.

"So what happened, exactly?" she asked through the curtain.

"I swerved to avoid a pedestrian."

He turned around and went into the bedroom, sat down on his side of the bed. The stillness from outside was with him here, ongoing. In the doorway stood the dog, watching. Their bed linens were still wrinkled and mounded from the morning; the triangle of sheet he sat on was warm. She must have been napping. But then, when Robert arrived, she would have risen. Why was it still warm now?

Maybe the dog had been sleeping there.

Hal's stomach felt nervous.

In a minor panic he pulled back the coverlet, checked the sheets. Nothing, of course. Paranoid.

Usually—only on weekends of course—she took a brief afternoon nap on her own side of the bed, just as they kept to their own sides at nighttime, but it was warm on his side today. Still, it was a trivial anomaly. A young man coming out of his house at midday and for this he was suspicious? He had turned into a middle-aged cliché. Suddenly a blip in the routine had become a conjugal violation.

He stood and began to straighten the blankets, unthinking.

The dog lay down, head on paws, in the hallway. He finished with the coverlet and the pillows, hospital corners because he kept on perfecting them mechanically, at the same time struck by the phrase: *cuckold*. But someone had to do it. The bed had to be made. A bed unmade in the afternoon seemed decadent, even ugly.

When it was accomplished he turned toward his nightstand. The alarm clock had fallen on its face; he set it upright again. Otherwise the order was usual—all of it familiar except for, wait, a very small piece of plastic.

It was minuscule, a triangle maybe three millimeters long with a couple of scallops along the edge, and shiny black or maybe even dark green. It could be anything. He thought about this, his heart racing. He held the dark piece of plastic between thumb and forefinger. A small scallop, a small serration.

He was paranoid. He should seek help.

In the meantime, it was an itch that had to be scratched.

With difficulty he deposited the fragment on the nightstand again, careful not to drop it on the carpet and thereby lose it, and went back to the bathroom, to the nearest trash can. Susan had the shower radio on—a song about coming to a window, which he seemed to recall was sung by an annoying yet strangely popular lesbian.

The air was hot and moist and heavy and he couldn't see even her blur through the curtain now. Good, for his purposes.

Quickly and furtively he pulled the can from beneath the counter and looked inside. Balled-up tissue, mostly; a Q-tip was visible. To stick his hands in the trash can would be openly desperate. Yet he did so.

Nothing hidden in the wads of tissue but an empty aspirin bottle. He put it down and washed his hands, let his breath out softly.

Still.

He went back to the bedside table and carefully picked up the fragment. He did not let it go.

"Going out for a soda, back in five," he called out.

He stepped over the dog and took the stairs two at a time. There was a drugstore on Wilshire. He kept the fragment pressed between the pads of his fingers, pressing it hard even as he grabbed his keys with the other hand, strode out the front door and got into the rental car. He pressed it hard all the way there, strode purposefully to the back and was face-to-face with a wall of condoms.

But his findings were inconclusive. The piece was small, its color indeterminate. It might be one brand with certain specifications or it might be another. He held it up next to the packages and leaned in close, squinting despite the fluorescents in the hope of seeing more precisely. It might be none of them. Plainly. Abruptly he smelled something familiar from antiquity—what was it? Yes: benzoyl peroxide.

A pimply boy leaned past him and grabbed a single Trojan.

Science, he scolded irritably as he made his way up the aisle, could easily discern the answer, with a microscope and maybe one or two more instruments. Science could plumb the mystery, could discern, for example, whether this had been part of a foil packet or simply plastic.

He was not a scientist, unfortunately.

What other form of packaging would there likely have been, in that location on the nightstand? Kleenex? It was not a piece of a Kleenex packet, though. Too thick, too solid. Crackers? No. Also no. The fact that she had been taking a shower right then, the warmth of the sheets . . . he could ask her himself, but regardless of the answer it would be humiliating. Even the suspicion was destructive. He knew this. Better simply, on his own recognizance, to know. One way or the other. Robert: maybe he would test him. Go into the office tomorrow. Find a pretext to discuss marriage? Casually, in passing. Few specifics. Confide in Robert, ostensibly, about the pluses and minuses of marriage? The costs and benefits it might bring? On Robert's face, as he listened, he would catch any sign of shame.

But this would not happen.

When he first met Susan, he remembered, stepping through the metal detectors and out into the parking lot, she was almost a hippie. The year was 1966. She was a teacher back then. Though she did not engage in politics much or smoke marijuana she had honey-colored long hair, wore all-natural fabrics and believed in free love. Shortly after they met she announced a plan to move into an intentional community called "The Eden Project" up in Mendocino. He had to work hard to dissuade her. She was young and idealistic and more than that she was romantically inclined, with a tableau in her mind of fresh air and fields of strawberries. A pure life, etc. He was idealistic too, but wary of stereotype and quite certain of what he wanted, namely for her not to move into an intentional community with a lute player named Rom.

In the end he won her over by arguing that the intentional

community was elitist. He added to this an insinuation that it was also racist.

He smiled ruefully at the memory, recalling his earnest youthful idiocy and the forcefulness with which he had prosecuted his aims. He could still hear the discussion, at a party on the beach. She wore faded cutoff jean shorts and her legs were tan and slim. He had held her wrists in his hands and argued passionately that for her to move with the other well-meaning hippies to Mendocino would mean a "renunciation of society" that would lock her into a "white, upper-middle-class cultural ghetto" and ultimately augur "an abdication of personal responsibility."

After that they had moved into a one-bedroom together—in a white, upper-middle-class neighborhood, of course. She cut her hair and he finished his accounting degree. Eventually the free-love notion faded.

Possibly now, however, the free love had made a resurgence.

He tried to remember how the free love had ended. They had argued about it on and off, but not with great engagement; Susan had always believed it more in theory than practice. She was shy by inclination and reluctant to let others see her naked. But she said the usual things the hippies liked to say back then about the limits of monogamy, such as "Why should the intimacy and joy of sex be reserved for one relationship?" and "People are not property." Once, almost to prove her point it seemed, she kissed another man at a foreign movie—an individual she barely knew who was French, had body odor and smoked cloying cigarettes. This had provoked a minor drama in the relationship. But in due time the Frenchman retreated, as they were wont to do.

Still, he had never, he reflected, actually asked her formally to renounce the free-love idea. There was nothing contractual, there were no stipulations. He had merely assumed she had grown out of it. In a certain sense it seemed ridiculous now that the matter was unclear to him; most marriages did not allow for such ambiguity. Did they? On the other hand this was not ambiguity, exactly, rather it was an element they had forgotten, a corner left untucked . . . it was like a religion that receded, leaving a vague memory of faith but few practical details. The religion had been overtaken by the day-to-day.

He had to admit: there was the possibility that quietly, in a private realm, she was still a believer.

The fragment was imprinted into the pad of his right thumb. He stood beside the rental car and flicked it off with his forefinger. It disappeared instantly; it was too small even to watch flitter down . . . to tell the truth, he thought, unlocking the car door, Susan was probably right, or at least had been more honest back then than he had. He had been looking out for himself, frankly. He had known she was too good for him, but also felt that, having attracted her, it was more or less his sovereign right to retain her. Like a lost-and-found coin.

They got married, had Casey and were happy, the three of them. Time passed; the events were not important, only the feel of it. Then the accident happened. Somehow after the accident he had assumed they would always stay as they were, exactly.

In his own case he loved Susan steadily and took for granted that he always would. He had believed until now that she felt the same way. Also, when couples lost a child they frequently divorced, but something like the accident tended to lock you together like clenched teeth. At least that was what he observed in the parents' groups. Sitting in pairs around the circle, on those hard, awkward chairs, many wives and husbands seemed to share nothing more than a sloping and gray defeat.

When he considered it, though: since the boss man went missing her interest had been diminishing. He had not taken it personally. He had believed she was preoccupied, and this, he thought, was still true. For whatever reason, he had seen, he was currently on the periphery of her life, or at least at the periphery of her attention. By itself this was not a problem; he was comfortable in the background. He often thought of himself on the sidelines, not at the center of the action, and the image was not unpleasant. For a long time there had been more pressing matters than his own needs or preferences; there was Casey first and always and then there was Susan's job, where she considered her boss a virtual prodigy, a kind of urgent cause that required service.

Why the cause of real-estate profit should now command her fealty, when it had never before done so, he had not seriously questioned. Her sense of professional obligation seemed grounded in the personal, chiefly.

Backing up in the rental car—careful now, careful; he could easily have two accidents in one day—he considered the possibility that her preoccupation had been due not to Stern's absence, as he had previously reasoned, but to the new chemistry of her small office in the awareness of that absence, a small office now inhabited solely by her and Robert.

2

The mother lived in a small townhouse not far from their own near the Venice–Santa Monica boundary, connected to other units around an open yard. She was not much older than Susan or Hal but apparently somewhat *non compos mentis,* since she required a live-in attendant. He was not clear whether she suffered from early-onset Alzheimer's, presenile dementia or some other condition, and Susan did not enlighten him.

They met to visit her at lunchtime, pulling up to the curb at the same time from different directions. Susan had spent the morning at her office, of course, no doubt closeted with Robert, whereas he himself had spent the morning at his office closeted with Rodriguez, who picked his teeth with a plastic cocktail sword. When they stepped out of their cars Hal leaned in to kiss her and breathed in her sweet smell; he also scrutinized her face closely, trying to detect the vestigial presence of the free love.

But there was nothing out of the ordinary. Still his suspicions hovered as he followed her up the front path.

A busty, squarish woman opened the door, a woman with a large mouth and bulbous nose. She had a thick accent, possibly from eastern Europe. She led them in and seated them on a sofa, where a large china cabinet dominated the view.

"You're lucky. It's a very good day for her. Clear, you know?"

As they waited Hal gazed through the glass diamonds of the breakfront at a large, Asian-looking soup tureen in faded pink and green, trying to discern what scenes it depicted. He was deciding whether to rise and inspect it more closely when Susan grasped his hand with a sudden fierce need.

"I'm not sure how to tell her," she whispered. "Even though I practiced."

He leaned his shoulder against her, but before he could say anything Mrs. Stern came in smiling, wearing white slacks and a linen blazer. A good-looking woman, if a little weak-chinned—thin and pale-blond and somewhat patrician, as though born into wealth and then faded from it.

"Susan," she said warmly. "It's so good to see you again."

"Angela," said Susan, and rose to embrace her. "This is my husband Hal."

"A pleasure. And what a wonderful daughter you both have."

"We think so," said Hal.

"We used to do jigsaw puzzles, the two of us. I had to give it up though. It's my vision—I need cataract surgery. Can I get you a drink? Iced tea or coffee? I have a fresh pot brewing."

"Oh. Sure. Thank you."

"Yes," said Hal. "That would be nice. Thanks."

Roses and leaves and very small Chinamen.

The term was out of favor.

"So what's the latest," she said, as she moved into the kitchen. They were separated by an island with barstools. Susan got up nervously, followed her and leaned against it.

"We—we still haven't been able to establish contact," she told the mother with some hesitation, and he felt certain that only he could hear her voice waver.

"Milk?" asked Angela. "Or sugar?"

"Just a little milk, please," said Susan, and nodded distractedly.

"No thanks, not for me."

"I check in with the embassy on a daily basis," went on Susan. "But there's nothing they can do, on the active side. It's quite a small facility. They don't have resources. All they can do is relay any reports that come in."

"Oh, yes," said Angela, nodding as she poured milk into both of their cups. Hal considered waving a hand to prevent her, but then gave up. "The boat man worked for them, didn't he."

"Pardon?"

"I think the man who called about the boat worked for the embassy."

She put Susan's cup in front of her on the counter and walked around the island toward Hal. At the same time Susan turned to both of them, wide-eyed and deliberate. He accepted his cup and smiled gratefully.

"What boat?" asked Susan, with a hint of alarm. "What do you mean?"

"The man called about a boat he was in."

"I had no idea," said Susan. "Oh my God."

She wandered back to the couch and sat down heavily. Angela glided back to the kitchen, oblivious, and poured her own coffee.

"Oh yes. The little white motorboat. They found it."

Susan gazed at her agape as she came back in, holding her cup delicately, and perched in a chair opposite.

"Tell us the details," said Hal carefully. "Won't you? Susan has been very, very worried."

"There was a little white motorboat he was in? With a native guide, you know, a tour guide doing the driving. Then the other day they found the boat, but there was no one in it. It floated back down to the beach, and there were some people fishing just then, or someone there was a fisherman . . . ? Anyway. Do they fish there? Something about fishing."

"Just the boat?" asked Susan.

She seemed to him to be entranced, breathless and possibly fearful. He reached out and rested his hand on her shoulder.

"A man from the embassy called me, I thought he said. Or wait. Maybe it was the United Nations. Don't they also have policemen?"

Angela crossed her legs gracefully and cocked her head, as though idly wondering.

"Uh," said Hal slowly. "Are you sure they called you?" She was beginning to show her lack of acuity; for all they knew the boat story was a full-fledged delusion. "Did you, for instance, get a name from this informant?"

"It was the hotel where Thomas was staying," said the attendant from the doorway, and Angela sipped her tea. "The resort hotel. They made an inquiry and then they called us."

"Of course," said Susan faintly. Her cheeks were flushed, Hal noticed, but he could not tell whether she was upset or excited at the news, whether it chilled or encouraged her.

"They have not seen Thomas yet," said the attendant.

"No," agreed Susan, and shook her head. "I do know that much." She went to pick up her coffee cup—for something to occupy her, Hal guessed—and gulped from it thirstily, looking away from them.

"You take care of his business," said the attendant, and smiled at Susan. "I know because of the paychecks!"

"Yes, I do," said Susan. "But we may need to change that. It's one reason I came. Mrs. Stern? If you have the means, you may find it easier to pay Vera's wages out of your own accounts for a while. T.'s finances are in transition. With all this confusion. Will that be a problem?"

"Oh? Oh. No," said Angela, and waved a hand dismissively at Vera. "My checkbook is in there," and she gestured toward a small writing desk.

"I am already paid for last week," said Vera. "No problem. OK. Excuse me."

"I would also like," said Susan slowly, as Vera disappeared down a corridor, "to hire someone. I want to take *action,* I want to step in. I owe it to him. We all do. And to his business, which needs him. We're losing money daily."

"Someone?"

"A private security firm. To investigate what happened down

there. I can handle it out of our petty cash fund at first, and draw on his other accounts later, if it starts to drag out."

Angela nodded but Hal thought she was hardly listening.

"You know, to fly down and be in-country. Have a team on the ground. A search party actively looking for him. I would do it myself, but I have to handle things at this end."

"Whatever you think, dear," said Angela. "But don't worry too much. He doesn't really need them."

"Them?"

"You know. Policemen."

There was a pause, during which Angela recrossed her legs and smoothed her slacks over one thin thigh. From the apartment above them Hal could hear a bass line thudding. The rhythm was powerful but the melody indistinct. He tried to attune himself to the music, in case of recognition. In the meantime he was conscious of the quietness in the room, the soup tureen with its outdated homunculi in their robes and black topknots.

He had a sense of the rapidly cooling coffee in his cup, which he could not drink because he did not like coffee with milk, and the uncanny calm of the mother, which settled on her like a soporific . . . was she indifferent to her son, his well-being? Or was she absent?

"I hope you're right," said Susan to Angela, and smiled tightly.

"That boy has always landed on his feet."

"But this is . . ."

"Trust me."

After a few moments Susan consulted her watch.

"Well. I should probably be getting back," she said, and Hal placed his coffee cup on the end table, relieved to be rid of it, and rose. "Do you have a couple of photographs I could take with me? To give them for the investigation?"

"Oh!" said Angela. "Certainly."

She handed Susan a white and gold album off a shelf, and Hal waited impatiently while Susan paged through it, slipping snapshots from beneath plastic.

"It was good to see you," said Angela when Susan gave it back. "Thank you for visiting me."

She stood beside them at the door, benign and passive as they filed out. Susan was agitated, almost distraught. For his own part, all he was thinking as they left was: So, about the free love.

He wanted to ask her but he knew the question would seem irrelevant, pathetic in its smallness and its self-interest. There was a man's life at stake. She was thinking only of that. The specter of death trumped the free-love worry.

"I should have done it before," she said, shaking her head as she strode ahead of him toward the street. "I should have followed my instincts."

For him, however, there was no specter of death, frankly. For one of them, there was the specter of death; for the other, only the specter of free love.

"I should have hired someone right away, but it's not the kind of . . . I mean who thinks of that? You know?"

"I do know," he said, with what he hoped was solemnity.

"I'm going to call them today. All it takes is picking up the phone and a credit card. A couple of photos . . . but why would they call *her*?"

"I'm sorry?"

They were standing at her car, facing each other.

"That hotel. They had explicit instructions to call *me*. I had to authorize the charges to his card, finally . . . she can't do anything with the information, you saw how she is."

"I did. It's just she *is* his mother."

"Still. It's unprofessional that they didn't call *me*."

"Maybe the language barrier. A misunderstanding."

He wondered if she was close to discerning his near-complete indifference to these questions, if she could discern the fact that he was hiding the real worry. What about the free love.

"OK. Anyway. Thank you for being here, honey. Sorry I'm so scattered," she said, and opened her car door.

He was due back immediately—it had been two days now of distraction and not attending to his workload—but he did not go back. Instead he let her car disappear down the street and then drove toward her office himself.

He pulled into a parking structure close to the Promenade, from which, if he went to the third floor and gazed southward, he could see through the windows of her suite. She had pointed out this feature to him when she first began working for Stern—how from the west windows of the office you could look over a few white rooftops to the Pacific Ocean, and from the east you had almost nothing in view save the hulking gray levels of the parking complex.

He made a few circuits before a space opened up in the right location. He wanted to be able to stay in the car as he watched, unseen. He had become a stalker.

He was almost sure he had the right window, and gazed at it expectantly, but the rectangle stayed dark.

For a few minutes, idle and slightly anxious, he listened to the squeak of tires as cars rounded corners in the structure behind him. He tried to rethink his position. Give this up, this adolescent fixation; return to doing your duty.

He was not quite willing to leave, but still he had his hand on the keys in the rental car's ignition—disappointed but also a little relieved—when the light in the rectangle flicked on. He saw Susan. She leaned over a cabinet. He could not make out her facial expression or even her features, only the lines of her silhouette. He wished he had a pair of high-end binoculars. She could be a bird, he thought, and he could be a birdwatcher. He had always thought there was something furtive about birdwatchers, mainly the ones who kept "life lists"—something voyeuristic and calculating in how they observed and catalogued their quarry.

The young man Robert stood in the room also, further away. His head moved slightly: he must be talking, Hal thought. He turned and opened a file cabinet. The free love. The free love.

But no: the free love was not yet in evidence. Wait, he told himself. Only wait. The free love was bound to rear its head. Eavesdroppers heard no good, or something. Almost because he was here, his wife had to be guilty.

Susan and Robert were currently in Stern's office, which was large and stretched from the east, or back, side of the building to the west. The main window in that office was the ocean window, a large picture window, he thought. He had been in the office several times, though rarely when Stern was. The large metal cabinet backed up beneath this eastern window, out of which Stern had probably seldom deigned to look, was a little lower than shoulder-height. It contained large flat drawers for large maps and the like. Hal felt he was fortunate the vertical blinds were not down; they might be, so easily. No one needed to look out this eastern window. And yet if Susan did so now, she might see him watching, if she could make him out in the dimness behind his windshield.

The young man was behind Susan now as she looked down at something, possibly something in a drawer she'd pulled out. Look up, thought Hal, but she would not—there it was. The young man Robert was facing the window as Susan turned; their heads were aligned. Hal could see the back of her head and this obscured the young man Robert's face completely. Jesus Christ. Were they kissing?

He had asked for it—at this point he believed he deserved it, even—but still he resisted. He sat there feeling a scream rise in him, trying to suppress it. Robert's hands were up on either side of Susan's head, blurs, moving. His own hands shook. He waited for Susan to turn, to adjust how she stood. They could be conversing face-to-face, having a close discussion. It was by no means a foregone conclusion. . . .

Suddenly their heads went lower. He could barely see them beneath the upper edge of the cabinet. Robert's head, of which chiefly a sweep of dark hair was visible, seemed to be gobbling, aggressively gobbling up his wife's lighter-brown head; the two blurred ovals, conjoined, sank even further as he sat without taking a breath—not believing, refusing to credit the sight. He could barely move. Now they sank down below the cabinet edge and were gone.

He felt queasy. He touched the steering wheel: his fingers were clammy on its grainy plastic. It traveled his mind that he had wanted to set up Robert with Casey. Sickening.

Guy rowed for Yale, went through his head, though it was a phrase he had constructed himself in the first place and had no concrete relevance. For all he knew Robert had attended community college. He was a paralegal, after all, not a lawyer, barely even a white-collar professional. He must be a faux-preppy, come to think of it: an impostor. A guy who rowed for Yale would not end up as a paralegal. Likely he *aspired* to be seen as Hal saw him. Hal had given him the benefit of the doubt, WASP-wise.

He had never read Robert's résumé, of course. It struck him now that he should have insisted on seeing it. There must be something there he could wield against him, some indication that he was wrong for the job, that he was far, far from qualified.

On the other hand it might be better to be cuckolded by a Yale guy, in a sense. A level of exclusivity, at least. Better a Yalie than a guy off the street. Wasn't it?

The paralegal got up again, was standing looking down, then turned to walk away from the window. His torso was all pale now; his jacket must have come off. Then the yellow rectangle of the room disappeared. He had flipped the switch.

Hal felt a stab of outrage. Susan was doing this right when she pretended to be so concerned about the specter of death. Here she was simulating an oppressive, pervasive concern, going to great lengths to demonstrate her worry about her possibly deceased employer—crying at dog kennels and getting choked up in the homes of Alzheimer's ladies, when really all she wanted was to sink down on her back and get it on with a good-looking guy in his twenties. It was the duplicity that gnawed at Hal. Because it was not free love anyway, was it, if you hid it, if you went around sneaking and concealing, if you lied and lied and covered up and were devious about it. It was not the hippie style of free love then, but something sleazy.

He could drive right to Casey's and tell her what he had seen. Right? Right? And how would Susan feel then?

But no, of course. Never. Not ever in this world.

He needed to get away: in place of the prurient need to know he felt only a disgusted, almost frightened proximity.

He backed up the car and found himself in a contest with Robert, a contest for Susan's loyalty—actually priding himself on the fact that it was still he who had been chosen to go to Angela Stern's house, that it was still he, the husband, the worn shoe, the swaybacked old mule, who fulfilled this supportive function—who had, in fact, been expressly chosen for it. Since Robert worked in the office with Susan she could easily have asked him to go with her to see Mrs. Stern: it would not, by itself, have been inappropriate.

But no: she had asked *him*. Him Hal, husband. The sacred trust was still there in these small gestures . . . he had been with her to hold her hand when she was nervous, hold it without saying anything (and while holding it to gaze steadily in front of him at the Chinese soup tureen, in tacit understanding). What *was* the understanding, exactly?

The strength you had when you sat there, a couple for many years now with all the landscape of a shared history, predictable glances, your own language sewn together of habits and tics and old jokes . . . it was the strength you had of knowing that you were not alone—the solid, indestructible knowledge of the otherness of others.

And come on. Please. Robert the Paralegal was, after all, what pop culture referred to as a *boy toy.*

Then again, it was always said, wasn't it?—that women were incapable of sex without emotional involvement. This was held up as common knowledge. It relied on a conception of the weakness of women, that much was obvious, how they needed soft sentiment over the hardness of gratification, and further how childish and self-indulgent this was on their part. Women, you were led to believe, were seldom inclined toward physical intimacy without a projection of attachment—some association of their partner with an ideal or a fantasy of escape.

Was this empty? Or was there a core of truth to it?

He almost lost his grip on the wheel as he rounded a sharp corner, descending through the levels of the parking complex in a giddy spiral. There was the whole of life between him and Susan, the familiarity with each other that gave them meaning through time, but of course that whole life—that very same shared life and shared history—had removed his candidacy for objectification. At first the removal was slow, he might even have lost track of it, but now it was complete. He was not Robert and Robert was not him; she chose Robert, she wanted to fuck Robert.

What weighed him down, what was a heavy, awkward knowledge, was that it was exactly the quality of being known, of being yourself, that desexualized a person. It was time that all of them—all of them! In their millions!—stopped deceiving themselves and openly admitted what they knew: Love was not sex, sex was not love. They went together out of convention only, because the best sex came mostly before knowing, before real love was even possible.

He was angry as the yellow arm raised at the parking structure exit, as he drove beneath and made his right turn into traffic. A history of losing, he thought: he and Susan knew all about each other's defeats and defects, the rifts and cracks, the craters—and understanding those losses, they had realized long ago, was not erotic. Not the kind of loss they knew, anyway, of atrophy and defeat. Still, he thought they had put it aside, or put it aside enough. Hadn't they?

But for his *loss* to be held against him, he thought—cruel. He couldn't help that loss.

They had gone on anyway, they still had sex fairly often, and it was decent. Tender, familiar. He liked it. But it was not glamorous, that much he had to admit, not epic, not breathtaking.

He was the third man, pathetic—a paper-pusher, a dim gray shade. Faded from relevance.

Heading in a dull haze back toward the freeway entrance off Lincoln—he had directed the rental car back toward his office without thinking—it dawned on him that he could not confront her, that all he had of his own was the secret of this knowledge; that he would have to take a new road, strike out and away, and like his wife command a private dominion.

Of course it hurt him. It was a cut, and sitting behind the wheel, staring ahead, he felt the lips of the cut stretch open.

3

They were due at Casey's apartment for dinner that night. She cooked once a month for them and a few of her friends, a new routine since she'd moved into the place with the wheelchair-adapted kitchen. Sal the sociopath would be in attendance this particular evening, among more seasoned guests.

Before the incident with the paralegal Hal had considered the prospect and winced; it would be awkward and tedious to sit next to the guy for a whole long meal, the cop turned homeboy with his finger tattoos and his bogus argot of the ghetto. But now he felt relieved at the idea of Sal. To sit next to Sal instead of Susan would be liberating. He was more or less neutral when it came to Sal: Sal was impersonal, Sal had nothing on him. He was distasteful, sure, but distaste was such a trivial emotion—superficial, even. Hal could be generous to Sal, if only because Sal was not Susan. In his distance from Sal there was a beautiful freedom.

It was Susan's betrayal that occupied his full attention now, from which tense attention he needed a break. It was keeping him anxious; the tendons in his neck hurt. He was worried by how different she might look to him in the light of his discovery, and by exactly how he might go about concealing this silent revolution. Because she knew him. He was not a cipher to her. And without concealment he would have nothing left.

He would be late, first off, he would be late because he would go to a bar beforehand. He seldom entered such establishments, seldom drank much at all, but the occasion called for it. She had momentum, she had velocity, she *did*. He did nothing. He existed, simply, going along as always. He had to keep pace with her, had to seek out events.

He found a place that was dark and mostly empty and quaffed two whiskeys in a short time, watching a television screen where a colorful cartoon raged of a fat, bulgy-eyed family with strange hairdos. He watched TV only at Casey's instigation—always it was her choice what they watched and she did not watch this particular show—but he knew the program was popular. The sound was not on, which was frustrating at first but finally just as well. He watched slack-jawed, the whiskey dispersing in his bloodstream. Colors in my eyes, he thought, fields and fields . . .

He let the picture blur and then sharpen again, blur and sharpen.

Did this mean he was getting cross-eyed? He tried to see his own eyes in the mirror behind the bar, but there was no room for his reflection between the bright libations.

He did not want to be stumbling drunk at Casey's so he downed two large glasses of water in a row and drove slowly and carefully the few blocks to her house.

"Sorry. Office birthday party," he said, when she ushered him in. This would explain his buzz, if it was even noticed. Others sat around in the living room, he saw, but Susan was not among them.

"Where's your mother?"

"Bathroom," said Casey, and went into the kitchen.

Of course she might be engaged in a devious activity there—the removal of a diaphragm, say.

Such thoughts were unworthy.

And anyway, they used condoms.

"We're having a Thai soup," said Casey. "Chicken coconut. Tom Ka Gai."

"Sounds delicious."

"I don't know. Wait until you taste it."

While she hovered at the stove he wandered into her living room, greeted her friends. There was a woman named Nancy who was also in a wheelchair and a tall man Casey knew from a class she'd taken at Santa Monica College, thick glasses and a receding hairline though he was only in his mid-twenties. Hal forgot his name every time: Adam? Andy?

"Addison," said the man, obliging, and shook his hand.

"Can I get you a drink?" asked a voice behind him.

Susan.

Turning to look at her, he was surprised: she looked the same in her features but invisibly separate, as though she was cut off from him by a membrane. Instantly he superimposed the figure of Robert the Paralegal on her image—it happened without premeditation, almost violently, as though the guy had burst into the room.

Then the picture was gone, thankfully.

"Sure," he said, and cleared his throat. "Just a beer. Already had a double at the office, so—thank you."

"What was the occasion?"

Behind her Sal was in the doorway in his chair, chewing gum. He blew a large bubble and popped it.

"Linda's birthday," mumbled Hal, as Susan turned.

"Sal!" she said warmly, and Hal had a vision of her straddling him.

"Oh," he said aloud, inadvertently. "Excuse me."

He went to the bathroom, locked the door and sat down hard on the toilet seat. Grabbed the cool rail next to him and breathed deeply. Ridiculous. He was seeing her everywhere with spread legs. It had to be the whiskey. He was not used to drinking.

When he ventured out again the guests were gathering around the table, pulling chairs out, organizing. Susan was standing near the head of the table—the dark angle of her black sweater, the rusty, autumnal orange of her slacks. He recalled how they clung to the backs of her thighs, which had always had a nice slim curve of muscle . . . it shocked him to think of someone else clutching at them. He was still shocked, when he thought about it—as though surfaces were falsehoods and the vigor inside them, which could never be seen, had a purpose to it, a purpose that was slyly hostile or at least secretive.

It could take a while for the dinner guests to get settled at the table, since several of them were in wheelchairs. The shifting of chairs, the discussion of positions . . . he shrank back past the doorjamb. He could not show Susan he did not wish to sit beside her. On the other hand, he did not wish to sit beside her. It was too soon and too public. He would hang back until others seemed to make the choice for him.

Casey was still in the kitchen; he could help her bring the food in. A pretext. But he would keep hidden till the last moment, even from her, in case the whole crowd had not taken their seats yet.

Lingering in the hallway next to the kitchen, he heard Casey talking to someone and hung back again: the food was not ready. There would be nothing to occupy him. He did not want to hover awkwardly; he would hide here, safely unseen.

He glanced down and picked a framed photograph from a bookshelf, to be doing something in case someone saw him. It was Casey with Stern's dog, when the dog still had four legs. Must have been taken by Stern, thought Hal, when the two of them were spending time . . . Casey was sitting on the beach in her chair, smiling, and the dog was standing up, her front paws on Casey's knees. Mostly the dog was featured: you could barely make the person out behind her. Casey did not like pictures of herself.

Nancy was in the kitchen with his daughter. From his hidden position against the wall he could see one of Nancy's bony shoulders and part of the back of her chair; its netting contained knitting needles and several large, bright skeins of yarn—red, orange, yellow, pink and purple.

A garment fashioned of those colors could only be an abomination.

"You told them tele*marketing*?" asked Nancy in a stage whisper, and then chortled.

"What else? They know it's a phone job."

"But I mean what if they ask you about it? The timeshare thing?"

"I have a spiel. I once actually did try selling timeshares, for like three days. It was hell on earth, I'm not even kidding."

"And this isn't?"

"You know what? I kind of like it. I do. Maybe it's still the novelty, but I like it, Nance. That's my dirty secret."

"You *slut*!"

"I'm a ho. Hand me the oven mitt, would you?"

"I'll take the rice. I can get it."

"You sure it's not too heavy?"

He could not enter the kitchen at all now. He could not present himself. He was falling apart. He crept back to the bathroom. Familiar refuge.

Did she mean what he thought? He tried to recall what she had said on the telephone yesterday, not knowing he was there: "What can I do for you," or words to that effect. But the tone had been sultry. He shivered.

1-900. Phone sex.

This was his family. Susan on the carpet. Casey in the chair. Doing that.

He breathed deeply in and out for a minute, bent over the sink and splashed cold water on his face. When he straightened he reached for a washcloth and then stared at his reflection in the bathroom mirror. He had once possessed a certain angular handsomeness, or at least he had been told this once or twice—a lean, affable appeal. Then again, most people received compliments on their appearances now and then, even those most egregiously victimized by genetics. It was standard. If he allowed for the margin of error created by social niceties, he would have to guess he was average-looking.

His eyes were blue but it seemed to him now they had faded, were more and more watery. He half-expected himself to start crying just looking into them—he was on the brink of tears already. Did he look like this all the time? He saw the parallel horizontal lines on his forehead, deeply etched, and thought the eyes disappeared beneath them. He had a full head of hair, small mercies. But he looked unremarkable.

He disappeared, he thought, against any background; he blended, he faded in.

How she and Susan must see him: an old man. But he was not old. He was only fifty.

"Daddy? Are you OK in there?"

"Yeah. Headache is all. Be out in a minute."

"There's ibuprofen in the first cabinet. Also acetaminophen with codeine."

"Thank you, sweetie."

The phone-sex men probably called her that. And far worse.

•

At the table, where he was seated between her and the four-eyes named Addison, topics of conversation included Rwanda and a dead rock star in Portland. Or Seattle. Some rainy city. Casey had played a few songs for him once by the rock star in question.

There was something to it, something genuinely interesting in the tone, he had thought at the time—he never liked to be dismissive of Casey's taste in music, about which she was painfully sincere and impassioned—but the vocal track was a problem for him. Frankly the guy sang like he was trying to force a B.M.

He was distant, nursing his beer, vision grown hazy. He did not attend closely to the chitchat. Something about the angle of a shotgun and whether the dead rock star had in fact been murdered by his rock-star wife, who was widely disliked as a loudmouth attention-seeker though as far as Hal could tell this was her legitimate job description. Then someone said primly that the shotgun angle was not dinner talk, was it now.

Across from him Sal ate his soup quickly and noisily—it was spicy—and wiped his running nose on his sleeve. Hal averted his eyes at this revolting display. The man was rudimentary. Nor was he well-liked, it seemed, by Casey's other friends: most of them avoided even looking at him, much less stooping to conversation. Even for Casey, he was a departure. It was difficult to imagine them together. Little affection seemed to pass between them. Luckily.

During the main course, yellow curry with rice, Hal noticed Susan and Casey were talking in lowered voices about the visit to Angela Stern—a good, safe subject for them, he decided, as Susan would probably not choose to discuss other elements of her workday with her daughter, such as fucking the paralegal on the office floor.

". . . they give an opinion?" asked Casey. "I mean what does it mean, I mean, did they analyze the boat or anything?"

"Analyze it?"

"Forensics. Were there blood traces?"

"You been watching too much TV, babe," said Sal.

"I don't think so, honey," said Susan, compounding Sal's offense against Casey with her own patronizing tone. "I mean first of all it's a small village in Central America. They're poor. And they just got hit by a tornado."

"Hurricane," mumbled Hal, correcting. "Different. Very."

An image came to him: an old motorboat, paint peeling, beached on the sand, listing. Seagulls cawing and swooping. He saw the silver braids of a river delta fan out in brown sand far beneath him, as though he were high up in the air. Susan had mentioned a tropical rainforest—that when Stern disappeared he had been headed upriver into the jungle.

Mistah Kurtz, he dead.

He could barely stand to hear Susan talking, he had to admit it. Every word had a tinge of disingenuousness, as though she could say nothing that was honest.

"Did you hire them?"

"First thing tomorrow," said Susan. "It's just, you know, I don't exactly—I just don't know anything about security. Private investigators? I don't know how to screen them, how to check their references. It's a big blank to me. For some reason I have a block around it."

"I'll do it," said Hal.

It came out abruptly. Around the table faces turned toward him, and the guests were waiting expectantly. Except Sal, who went right on eating. Hal gazed at him blurrily as he slid a whole wet bay leaf out of his open mouth, tongue lolling, and dropped it on his placemat.

"You'll research investigators for me?" said Susan.

"No. I'll go to Belize," he said. He picked up his beer bottle and took a deep swig. It was warm now, and now it was gone. Yes. He saw a chance and he took it.

Change. Freedom.

Robert the Paralegal would not do this.

"What?" said Casey.

"You'll—what are you *talking* about, Hal?" asked Susan, and smiled uncertainly.

"I'm going," he said. "I'll fly out as soon as you can book me a flight. Don't have to speak Spanish—see—English is the official language there. Former crown colony. British Honduras. Used to be called. As I'm sure you all know."

He had weeks of vacation days coming to him—months, very likely. He could use all of it if need be. He risked a brief glance at Susan's face: astounded. Almost stricken. He had blindsided her. He felt a surge of elation.

"Hal, that's . . ."

"Come on, Dad," said Casey. "What do you know about missing persons?"

"Actually a fair amount," said Hal. His eyes were dry and his head was almost spinning—or would be if he lay down—so he was gratified at his own lucidness. "I've been tracking down delinquent taxpayers for years. It's part of my job."

He mainly supervised the process these days, of course. A technicality.

Sal was picking all of the bay leaves out of his leftover soup and placing them one by one, with a wiping motion, on his placemat. Hal found himself captivated by the process. Its repugnance was bold. Practically courageous.

Was Sal insane, actually?

"Honey, we should talk about this," said Susan.

"You need someone you can trust," said Hal, a bit severely. He knew himself for a liar, because she could not trust him now, not when he was angry. Not at all. But *honey*? The nerve of the woman. "You need a known quantity. There's nothing more to discuss."

There was a silence, the guests chewing their food. Possibly they were simply bored. Hal noticed again that his beer bottle was empty; at the same time Nancy reached for a saltshaker and knocked her wineglass over. Red wine flowed and then dripped over the edge of the table.

"I'm getting up anyway. I'll get something to clean that with," said Hal.

"Daddy, I think it's brave of you," said Casey softly. "I do. Volunteering like that."

He felt a rush of tenderness toward her as he rounded the end of the table behind her chair and looked down at the golden cap of hair on her head, neat and small and shining—but then she too was deceiving him, albeit to a lesser degree. From now on, in his nightmares, she would say "I'm a slut" . . .

Not words to reassure a parent. No indeed.

It was settled: he would fly away from all of it and that would leave the field wide open, he reflected as he went into the kitchen. He had already forgotten what he came for . . . a rag? A rag for cleaning up the spilt wine. And a beer for drinking. He didn't care if he drove home at all; he would be happy to fall asleep here. Too drunk to drive would be, the more he thought about it, a very neat solution . . . of course Susan had her own car, but he could claim he did not want to leave his here, didn't want to have to come back for it in the morning. He would get so goddamn drunk no one could reason with him.

Then he would get into a plane and leave the field wide open; the field was crammed with paralegals, all of them stoutly armed with condoms.

Possibly, he reflected, Susan and Robert had an Oedipal relationship. She was, after all, twice his age.

Here also he would leave the fat, ugly men on phone-sex lines, grunting and jerking off as they listened to his baby girl.

It was all crumbling. No one had his back anymore, no one was with him. Not a single person. All he felt at his back was a cold wind, a falling-off into nothing. As he left, an abyss yawned behind him. He'd nearly been swept in.

Before him, the ground would be more solid. Anyway there was nothing more Susan could do to him once he was far away—nothing she wasn't already doing.

His own bed, slow and lavish afternoons.

• • • • •

Although she made the arrangements for him dutifully he could feel Susan's shock reverberate throughout the day. It was gratifying, in a minor way. She had not let him pass out alone at Casey's as he preferred to, had insisted on sleeping alongside him in the guest room. But still he had crept away from the dinner early, three glasses of wine and two rapidly quaffed beers under his belt behind the two whiskeys, and collapsed on the edge of the bumpy futon. He slept so heavily he did not even register her presence when she came in later, and in the morning he got up stealthily, leaving her fast asleep with her back turned to him. He rinsed his face, brushed his teeth with toothpaste on a finger, and kissed Casey's forehead before he left, stopping at a gas station to chase three aspirin with a can of V8.

He was glad of the shock. He would not like to see Susan get comfortable with his gesture, adjust to it easily. He wanted her to recognize this as a private venture whose meaning was locked up to her and out of sight, a gesture belonging solely to him.

He drove home and packed a suitcase with a few changes of casual clothing, a shaving kit and some work boots. All he had for sneakers were worn-out Converse hightops, probably fifteen years old. He packed his passport, which he was relieved to see was still good, a phone card, a cheap camera. The dog regarded him patiently as he ordered the items in the case; he felt a stab of affection or regret, hard to say which.

But Susan would take good care of the dog, he did not need to worry. In fact the dog would probably be right here, watching calmly and every so often blinking, as she and her boyfriend thrashed and moaned on the bed.

Would the dog observe a moving tableau, slow and graceful with soft shadows and a gentle light—and therefore chilling to Hal if he saw it himself? With the dog as his proxy, would he have a connection to this? Or maybe the dog would see a labored, awkward contact, something Hal could watch with contempt or disgust, almost entirely unmoved. Would a dog perceive any difference?

Dogs had the habit of watching when you did it. Cats, not so much. Dogs were bigger perverts.

Foraging in the hall closet, he found outdoor supplies left over from camping trips taken in the seventies: a windbreaker, a small bottle of iodine, a safety blanket, a bandage and a lighter. Who knew where he would have to go? It could be anywhere. And he could buy what he needed when he knew what that was, but it pleased him to think he might have an urgent need for these simple objects—objects that in his house, in his disused closet, seemed both commonplace and completely irrelevant. It signaled the possibility of a great departure from his life's routine.

After that he drank water and black coffee, popped some more aspirin, pet the dog on the head once or twice, heaved the suitcase into the back seat of the rental car and drove to work.

•

He was standing over his deck, parceling out files into separate piles, when Rodriguez came in and asked him where he was going.

"It's so sudden," said Rodriguez. "Like, *¿qué pasa, hombre?*"

"Family matter. Helping my wife with a problem," said Hal.

"But like where you headed?"

"Central America. Her employer went down there and now no one can find him. I'm going down to see if I can suss out what happened."

"Holy shit," said Rodriguez.

"Yeah well," said Hal, and picked up a pile. "Here you go. And this stack here is Linda's. Can you ask her to come in and see me?"

"Oh, man. You gave me all the TDAs, didn't you."

"Do your worst."

"Huh. Going down *south,*" said Rodriguez, lingering. "You da *man.*"

"The man. Yes."

"Palm trees, margaritas, all the sexy señoritas . . . you need a sidekick? Hey! I got vacation days coming too."

"Thanks for the offer. Think I'll try flying solo this time."

"Send us a postcard, homes."

"Will do."

He called Casey to say goodbye. He would not talk to her about what he had overheard. She said again that she was glad he was going, that she admired him for following through on what was clearly an irrational impulse.

"I just wouldn't have thought it," she said, and he felt a twinge. It occurred to him that she had, for a long dreary time, basically been bored of him, her *boring old father,* and that this unexpected and sudden turn was possibly a rare opportunity for redemption. Spark-of-life-in-the-old-geezer-yet. "I never would have thought you would take it on. Like, I couldn't personally do this. I mean, even if I could, I couldn't. But you know what? I'm glad that you're stepping up. I'm glad one of us is looking out for him."

He almost asked why she and Stern were not close anymore. There was a time the two of them had got together almost every weekend. He had assumed the relationship was purely platonic, but that assumption was rooted in fatherhood and, if he had to be honest, also her condition. She would not appreciate a question on the subject. Not in the least.

Anyway he thought of her in the kitchen with Nancy and did not wish to know the details.

After they hung up he was torn: possibly she attributed noble motives to him where there were none, maybe he was lying to her by letting her think this was some kind of generous act. Then again she was not too interested in nobility, as a rule. She was interested in honesty, and also some other quality that sometimes seemed like courage and other times bravado, but she was not interested in altruism; she thought it was beside the point. Maybe she was just relieved to discover he could be spontaneous.

He had to talk to Susan next, there was no helping it. He had to get information from her: contact numbers, addresses, copies of photographs to show around, his travel itinerary. Reluctantly he called her office, praying Robert would not pick up instead.

"I got you a flight out this evening, believe it or not," she told him, a bit breathless. "The travel agent's next door. You know, Pam? It was either tonight or early next week."

"Fine with me," he said, and waved in Linda, who stood hesitating in his open door. Her frizzy hair descended from her head like a flying buttress, or a wedge not unlike the headdress of the Giza Sphinx.

The effect, sadly, was less regal.

Then he felt a stab of guilt, or sympathy. Both. Linda was a self-effacing, kindly woman. He picked at the flaws of his coworkers because he could never get at his own, he knew they were there but could not easily identify them—save for one, which opened before him like a hole in the very fabric of space, bristling with static. Bad father, father who let them hurt his baby.

It was transparent, but no less a habit for being so obvious.

He felt sorry for all of them, the coworkers and himself. He barely listened to Susan, who seemed to be nattering on about logistics. This lack of attention was a victory of a sort, a victory over her. Or his love for her anyway.

Meanwhile Linda sat down self-consciously in his guest chair, shifting in the seat as she crossed her wide legs.

"Is there a copy of his passport? With the number on it?" he asked Susan, mostly to sound official.

"I'll look."

"That would be helpful. Other than that, the hotel, his own itinerary, flights, cars, whatever records you have of the travel. His Social Security, just in case. Business credit-card numbers. All that."

Linda shuffled her feet back and forth in their sturdy brown shoes and fiddled with her watchband, waiting. He caught her eye and mouthed that he was sorry. The gesture was too intimate for her, however. She looked down, embarrassed.

"I'll have it ready in a few minutes. You fly out around six, so you should leave the office by four," said Susan. "You'll be staying the night in Houston before you do the international leg in the morning. I got you an airport hotel."

"And you'll need to return the rental car for me. It's parked in my space. Linda will have the key."

"I'll send a runner over with the documents. And your ticket. And whatever."

"Excellent."

"But Hal? You were drunk, honey. OK? You really don't have to do this."

"I want to."

"You don't realize how much this means to me. At least to know, finally. But I worry."

No doubt.

"Last-minute things to work out here, sorry. Gotta go."

He was relieved to have Linda with him, grateful her presence had given him an excuse to say nothing personal.

"I'm sorry to keep you waiting, but there's good news. At least, I hope you think so. You'll be Acting while I'm gone," he said, and saw her face light up.

•

When he left the office at four, slumped in the soft vinyl seat of the taxi and watching the buildings float past, he was by turns worn and eager—sunk by the loneliness of his position and then, as he let the defeat dwindle behind him and rushed onward, almost exhilarated. He sensed a kind of freedom and looseness in the air—in the things of the world around him, in the long low land and the height of the sky. It was a dream of running, running away.

It *was* running away. But he was not ashamed. He could not care less. It was what he wanted.

4

He had to hire a car from the airport, a four-wheel-drive taxi in the form of a mud-spattered jeep. When he got in, vaguely remembering film-noir detectives, he rummaged around in his case and brought out a picture of Stern to show the driver. This opened the floodgates, apparently, and whenever he was beginning to drift off in his seat, whenever he thought that maybe, by dint of the long moments of contemplation and engrossment, he was on the edge of coming to a new pass—a discovery or at least a mental accommodation about him and Susan, or more specifically him and Susan and Robert the Paralegal—the driver would interrupt his train of thought with a question of triumphant banality. Then when Hal grunted out a minimal acknowledgment he would offer up a few words about his country, words so flat and devoid of content that Hal drew a blank when called upon to answer. "Beautiful." "Nice weather, you know?" "We got beaches. You like the beach?"

There was nothing to say to any of this, though each remark seemed tinged with the expectation that Hal would answer with great and sudden enthusiasm.

Susan was a natural at responding to empty phrases, though she did not enjoy it either. He had watched her on occasion, dealing with, say, a person in a service transaction who was inclined to chitchat. She made soft murmurs of assent, often, nodding her head and smiling as she listened and, in a gesture of fellowship, asking questions so minute and tailored to the other person's mundane interests that he could barely believe she was expending the calories to produce them. It was an exhausting effort for no clear payoff.

Casey, on the other hand, never did this. She would go so far as to rudely announce that she didn't do small talk. And because of the chair, would be his own guess, she got away with this without blame or comment.

Twice the car stopped unexpectedly at a gas station and the driver got out, then loitered talking to other loiterers with no apparent purpose. Meanwhile Hal waited in the car, impatient and unmoving, full of rising resentment, until ten minutes later the driver got in again without bothering to proffer an explanation. A Caribbean cultural practice, possibly. Possibly Hal would be rewarded one day for broadening his cultural horizons.

It was three or four hours at least to the resort where Stern had been staying—first on a two-lane highway that meandered up and down hills with a view of the sea, then on a long red-dirt road down a narrow peninsula. Most people flew directly to one of the resorts on the coast and landed on a private airstrip, skipping the inland road where barren fields and dirty urchins with stick-legs would dampen the holiday mood.

Whenever settlement hove into view it was shacks with graffiti on them, snarled wire and molding, flimsy pieces of particle-board in place of fences and walls. There were fields of dirt where nothing grew but bald tires and garbage, smoke rising from ashcan fires, and no cars or trees or vegetation outside the hovels either, only bare expanses of soil with an occasional weed. Sometimes a woman or child or dog could be seen wandering through, emaciated; one old woman he saw through a fence with a ragged, open sore on her calf. He caught a glimpse of some skinny kids playing soccer outside what was probably a schoolhouse, which cheered him a bit until he also noticed, beside the stretch of baked earth where the boys were playing, a corrugated-metal rooftop. Underneath it two other boys were carving up a dead animal. He could not tell what it was.

Here and there a bedraggled brown palm tree struggled to look exotic. Forests must have been felled, for sometimes he caught sight of a clump of shiny-leafed bushes and trees in brief straggles of green against the backdrop of dirt and rust, with stumps around them that looked like they'd been hacked at with machetes. Once he saw a column of smoke on a low hill in the distance.

"When will we get to Placencia?" he asked the driver.

"Not too long, not too long," said the driver unhelpfully.

The peninsula had been hit hard by the storm. There were still power lines down, and here and there a telephone pole lay tumbled in wire beside the road. It was strange to him, the poles left where they fell—as though there was no machine here to move them and make the roads safe again, no vigilant authority.

The sky faded into a velvety dusk as he watched it through the window, thinking: I came here to escape my wife. My wife who may not love me after a quarter of a century.

Now he was far away from her, in a strange place. He was almost nonexistent; he was nowhere and known by no one.

• • • • •

It was only the next morning that he got a look at the hotel grounds. Out his window he could see the ocean, a few small boats without sails, and near the dock white-skinned guests sitting atop the glittering water in colorful kayaks. The water, he thought, was gray-blue, not what they led you to expect in commercials for Hawaii or the Bahamas—not the emerald or turquoise transparence of a kidney-shaped pool. The color was less stunning, more familiar. Crews worked in the gardens, making flowerbeds, laying turf and digging. There were many of them, men in straw hats with shovels and wheelbarrows.

He would eat, take a walk. It was safe to admit it, since no one was listening: he was not here to find anyone. Not here to exert himself, but rather here to melt down, settle, coalesce, and rise in a new form . . . still he could occupy himself a few hours a day with a search of some kind. That was fine. It would give him something to do.

At his table in the restaurant, which overlooked the pool and beyond it the sea again, he gazed out the window. Children played in the pool, spitting long gouts of water out of their gap-toothed mouths. He watched a little boy bounce on the diving board and could not help seeing the boy's head split open as it connected with the concrete bottom, spinal trauma and then, as usual, Casey. It was a sign of his partial recovery that he was falling back into his old habits of thought again, the worn ruts of his neural circuitry—back to Casey and her injury instead of Susan.

But then even this flicker of Susan opened up the whole scene again. She and Robert in the bedroom or on the floor of the office; himself, papery and sad in the blurry distance.

So there was no recovery yet, after all.

He should not think too much. As a rule he set too much store by thinking. Or at least, complacent in the knowledge that thought was the most useful tool available to men—and one so often neglected by his fellow Americans—he relied on it to the exclusion of other ways of filtering information. Thought was the act of conscious cognition but there were alternative processes of the mind that could work around or alongside it, processes of slow and growing awareness that did not register until they were complete, or the accretion of vague ideas that suddenly produced a form.

Thinking alone had not given him an answer to Casey's situation and it would not give him an answer to his and Susan's either. That was his prediction. He should walk on through his day and let the passing of time mold him; time would go by and he would see what to do. This was a vacation—and after the four long years of aggravation that Stern had given him, all the grating secondhand descriptions of his mini-malls and cookie-cutter subdivisions, it was right that Stern should receive the final bill.

Eggs arrived, with a slice of papaya to remind him of his location. Lest he mistake them for Hackensack eggs or eggs in Topeka, the papaya came along to announce they were tropical eggs, to remind him that congratulations!—he was on a tropical vacation.

He ate the eggs and even the papaya, which had an overly luscious, sweaty taste. He went to a rack and picked out a newspaper, then came back to read and drink his coffee. It was a day-old copy of *USA Today*. This was not a newspaper he chose to read at home—too many colors on the front page, for starters—but it was nice to let his eyes rest.

Sometimes he glanced out the window, past the pool at the stretch of beach: a few of the ubiquitous palms, a hammock, some beach chairs and umbrellas, flapping a bit in the breeze, a pile of upside-down red and purple kayaks and a man raking sand. This was less opportunity, he thought, than the simple end of something. Pebbles and sand and waves softly lapping. For their vacations, people liked to arrive at the end.

He himself would have chosen something with height, cliffs or mountains—something with grandeur and scale. Sure, the water was mild here, and there had to be a coral reef or two. But he saw mostly a blankness, a place that was less a place than an erosion into nothing. That was what he had seen when he stood on the shore that morning—the flat ocean lapping, the flat sand beneath his feet. Maybe tourists came here because they actually missed flat blankness in their daily lives. The flat blankness was possibly a reminder that there was an end to everything, a reminder they lacked while they were going to work and running errands in their suburbs and cities, where they were constantly required to answer the stimuli. Maybe they yearned to be in a place where there was little to see but a line between water and air.

He went back to the paper and listened to a conversation behind him as he scanned the headlines. He could not see the speakers, a man and a woman, could not turn to look at them without being noticed, but he could tell they were young.

"You can do the scuba class but I'm not doing it. No way."

"Come on! Come *on*. Do scuba by myself?"

"This one guy I read about who's a diver in the Marines or something? He got the bends and he ended up with these little pockmarks all over his face. Like bad acne. Plus he got double vision."

"You won't get the bends, OK? This would be at maybe twenty feet deep. They call it, like, a resort dive or something. To show that it's basically for wusses that would sue them if anything happened. The risk is like *nothing*."

"It can also hurt your brain. Or you can choke on your own vomit. You know who choked on their own vomit?"

"I'm getting the Belgian waffle. What are you getting?"

"Hermann Goering. Little-known fact."

"What are you *talking* about? The guy took a pill! Believe me. I saw it on the Hitler Channel. He was going to be executed like a few minutes later."

"May I take your order?"

"I'd like the egg-white omelet? With mushroom and tomato?"

"And I'd like the Belgian waffle."

"Very good, sir. Coffee?"

"Wait. Does that come with like just regular fruit or that jelly-ish, bright-red fake-strawberry stuff? Know what I mean?"

"Seasonal fruit, sir. Today it is fresh blueberries."

"OK. Yeah. OK then, I guess I'll get the waffle."

The woman addressed the waiter.

"Sorry. We're on our honeymoon. He's not usually so picky."

"Are you kidding me? Picky? That stuff is like fluorescent. It's full of Red Dye Number Three. Erythrosine. Heard of it? It's a known carcinogen. It causes cancer in mice. They feed it to those little tiny white mice and then the mice sprout tumors the size of a cantaloupe. Man. They can barely even walk lugging those things around."

When Hal got up to leave he saw they were pale and thin and black-haired—out of place in the resort, where most of the families were blond, overweight and Midwestern-seeming. Temporary refugees from SoHo, possibly. In fact he had not been to SoHo since the early 1970s but he imagined young people there might resemble these two.

•

"Excuse me," he said to the clerk at the front desk. "You have a Xerox machine, right? I'd like twenty copies of this, if possible."

He passed across Stern's photo.

"One moment, sir," said the clerk, a lofty woman with prominent cheekbones and beads in her hair, and went through a door. He would be expected to check in periodically with Susan—every couple of days, he thought, and wondered how he could get around it. He would fax her reports, that was it. Cheaper than international calls, was how he could justify it, and people liked to receive or send a fax. They liked to say the word *fax,* said it with abandon. No doubt its moment would be brief.

Personally he preferred telegrams and mourned their passing. He could remember getting one from his father when as a college student, traveling in Italy, he had called his parents in a panic and asked for money. His father had wired it to an American Express office and sent a telegram to Hal's youth hostel to tell him this. It contained only the AmEx address and the words *Next time beg sooner.*

"There you go," said the clerk, and smiled with white straight teeth. "Twenty."

"Bill it to my room, would you? Thanks. 202," he said, and as he went out thought she resembled an African queen.

It flashed through his mind that he, too, should have an affair, if only to prove he could, but then he knew this for a juvenile impulse.

He stopped in at the manager's office and left a message with the secretary. He wanted to hear what the hotel knew about Stern's trip up the river and what had become of the belongings from his room. He handed his business card to the secretary as he was leaving and she smiled at him sweetly.

At home the card struck fear, or if not fear a kind of casual contempt.

In the hotel gift shop he bought a local map, a baseball cap against the noonday sun, and what appeared to be a child's backpack—they had none for adults and damned if he was going to carry his briefcase like a stodgy old fucker. The backpack was emerald green, festooned with frogs and lizards. He slid the photographs into the pack and ordered a taxi at the front desk, where the queenly woman had been replaced by a thin man with a pencil mustache. He had the address of Stern's foreman in the papers Susan had given him and he gave this to the driver when he stepped in.

The road was deeply rutted and the jeep had no suspension, so he bounced on the hard seat as they drove. Out the window he could see restaurants in rickety buildings on stilts, named after animals and painted in pastel colors. They had a temporary, slipshod appearance and were often combined with homes or small convenience stores; faded soda logos graced the storefronts and fluttering laundry hung on clotheslines out back. The thin walls would only suffice in this warm, mild place, where no protection from the cold was needed.

There was a garish, yellow-green color to the palms and other trees, gaudy and somehow translucent. He did not believe in the permanence of the trees any more than the buildings. He had read that many of the trees and flowers here had been shipped in from far away—Tahiti and Australia.

The peninsula was a glorified sandbar, he thought, waiting to be washed away by a towering swell.

As the jeep jerked along in the ruts he saw debris collected against the base of palms, clustered along hedges—food trash mostly, cardboard and plastic, but also netting and newspaper and old shoes and wrinkled pieces of mildewed rug or fabric. They turned left at what seemed like a construction site, many small shacks going up all over the place on the slick, muddy ground.

It was like a minefield of outhouses, he thought.

"Seine Bight," said the driver.

"This?" asked Hal, before he could stop himself.

"Rebuilding," said the driver, nodding. "You know: it was all knocked down. In the big storm last month."

They drove between the shacks, not on a road at all as far as Hal could tell—bumping over the corrugated curves of culvert pipes, weaving and tipping sideways. A white bird, duck or goose maybe, flapped out of the way and children ran alongside the car. He was enraptured by this, stared out the window at the flashes of light on skin, the kids' stretched and laughing faces. Then quickly the field of shacks was behind them again, the beach and ocean not so far ahead, and on their right in a grove of palms was a colorful small house with a nice garden.

"Here you go," said the driver.

"Please wait," said Hal, even though they had it all pre-arranged. "I won't be long. Maybe fifteen minutes." He recalled the driver from the airport, how he had randomly stopped at service stations and once leaned against a wall, doing nothing but gazing at the ground. The driver had kept up the pose so long that it seemed he was dutifully observing an officially appointed function.

The contract between driver and passenger here was a loose one.

He walked up to the house and knocked on the door, thinking he wished they had a telephone so that he could have called to warn them, but god*dammit,* while he was standing there waiting he heard engine noise and turned and sure enough there was the taxi pulling away again. He had the urge to run after it screaming—half-turned from the front door to do this, even—but then figured maybe the driver needed to use the toilet or some other mild embarrassment. Surely he would be back in fifteen.

Still. Couldn't he have said something? What was it with these people?

Impatient and a little anxious, Hal waited until the door opened. It was a short woman, her black hair tied back with a red ribbon. She was dull-eyed and barely looked up at him.

"Excuse the interruption," he said. "I'm looking for Marlo?"

"He is out working," said the woman.

"Can you tell me where I can find him, then? It's about Thomas Stern. His disappearance."

The woman nodded vaguely. "He's at the big hotel. The Grove."

"Oh you're *kidding,*" he said, exasperated. "I just came from there. It's where I'm staying."

She nodded again, unsmiling.

"All right," he said lamely, and turned to go. Then turned back. She was already shutting the door. "Listen, could you tell him I'm looking for him? If we miss each other again? My name is Hal Lindley. Here, here's my card. Wait, let me write my room number on it. He can stop by whenever. Room 202." She had to open it wider again for him to stick the card into her fingers. "Thank you."

After she closed the door on him he stood there for a long moment letting the foreignness absorb him. He had an impression of being out of place: that was what it was, ever since he got here. Even more now, near the village that was in ruins, than at the hotel, of course, since the resort was populated by people he could just as easily have run into on the streets of Westwood.

He looked down at the details of the doorknob—a cheap brassy color—and the frame, which was painted purple. Marlo's house was not an American house: nowhere in America would you find a house like this. The difference might be in the physicality of the doorframe, the stucco, he couldn't put a finger on it. Possibly it was more asymmetrical than he was used to, or the lumber was a tree species unknown to him. But somehow there was an irregularity, a foreignness. It seemed to discourage him, imply he was not natural here. He was an intrusion.

Or maybe he had forgotten, over time, how familiar elements everywhere had a steadying influence. At home there was the security of known formulations and structures all over the place, in window fastenings, in the door handles of cars, gas pumps, faucets, sidewalks, restaurants, shoes. Products and habits were so deeply linked it was hard to separate them. And their reliable similarity helped keep him on an even keel, apparently, had given the world a predictable quality that made passage through daily life calm and easy: he glanced around when he was out in the world and he recognized everything. There was almost nothing that jolted him, almost nothing in the landscape that broke him out of his reverie of being.

He had not considered it before, this effect of mass production. Could it be that the very sameness of these commodities, these structures both small and large that gave the physical world its character, afforded a certain freedom from distraction? The ill effects of their sameness, of this standardization and repetition were talked about and studied—how their homogeneity devolved the world and denuded it of forests and native peoples and clean water and difference. But now that he was far from all the standard objects and dimensions what he noticed was how they also gave a feeling of civilization. In their reassurance they conferred strength on the walking man—strength and the illusion of autonomy.

On his way down the garden path he noticed the skull of an animal. It was stuck on a fencepost among flowers—a goat, he guessed from the horns. It still had a little meat on it.

His taxi was nowhere in sight. He stood for a few seconds, waiting, and then started walking back along the troughs of baked road-mud to the village.

• • • • •

He could not find Marlo on the hotel grounds and soon he gave up looking, found a lounge chair beside the pool and ordered a midday beer. He planned to sleep afterward, and was looking forward to it with a kind of greedy anticipation, when the manager of the resort bent over to talk to him. Hal blinked at the blinding light of the sun, saw the man's broad face recede as he sat up.

There was a small valise of Stern's clothes, the manager said, which he would have brought up to Hal's room. Beyond that he feared he could not be helpful; he knew nothing but the name of the town where Stern had rented his boat, and what he had already told Mrs. Stern. It was a very small village at the mouth of the Monkey River, so small it made Seine Bight look like a crowded metropolis. You could only reach the town by water, said the manager, which was why it was so small. There were no roads overland.

The boat itself, said the manager, had come floating back downriver to Monkey River Town during the night. He had told Mrs. Stern all of this. The boat had struck a dock and become wedged underneath, and kids had found it in the morning. They had noticed nothing out of the ordinary. It had been cleaned and tied up but that was all that the manager could tell him. If he wished to learn more Hal could visit the tour guide's brother, who was not reachable by telephone.

Hal nodded, drained his beer glass and hoped the manager would give up. The double bed was calling, with its bleach-smelling sheets and blessed privacy.

But the manager persevered. "There is a family," he said. "Other guests. They are from Germany. They are renting a boat to go on a day trip up the river."

To get to the river Hal would first have to take another, larger boat to the town, he went on. You took one kind of boat to travel down the coast over the ocean, to reach the river delta; then you disembarked and walked to a smaller dock, where you took a different boat to go up the river. Hal could tag along with the Germans if he liked, said the manager, as far as the delta town where the guide's brother lived. The Germans were taking an afternoon cruise up the river themselves, however; he would have to wait a few hours for the return trip.

So without his rest in the double bed, and slightly disgruntled, Hal met the German family on the dock where they were waiting for the first boat. He shook hands with them and smiled quickly. There were four of them, a mother and father and two young boys, all tall and tanned and lovely, with shining hair in shades of blond and golden-brown and perfectly molded biceps visible where their short, well-ironed cotton shirtsleeves ended. To make matters worse they seemed resolutely cheerful. They radiated something akin to joy. Such Germans were irritating.

On the one hand they were an unpleasant reminder of Vikings and Nazis, on the other hand you envied them.

He, by contrast to the Germans, was a low creature. He was not sleek and limber as a tree, but hunched and preoccupied; he was not shining and tanned, but dim and pale despite the fact that he hailed from Southern California, where movie stars and surfers reigned. He wore a baggy windbreaker and clutched his green-reptile backpack; he was a tired assemblage of imperfect elements. Protruding from his jeans pocket was a wallet messily stuffed with small bills and old receipts.

He watched the Germans file into the powerboat ahead of him, and in particular the two blue-eyed, tow-headed boys, who reminded him of a horror movie he had watched with Casey called *Children of the Corn*. It struck him that he had been picturing himself in a movie ever since his arrival. It was a movie of his life, which had suddenly become interesting in the way only a story could be, with hills and valleys of plot like a rollercoaster. There was much to laugh at in this posture, certainly, but the feeling of cinematography lingered. He was still half-dazzled by the warm beer.

All of them sat on a bench at the prow, touched by the clean spray as the boat thumped over the waves. No one spoke, though they were all quite close together, perfect strangers, side by side. The Germans, he sensed, felt no awkwardness at this. Probably they were content just to Be.

Though the kids, at least, were now rummaging impatiently in their bags.

"My wife's employer disappeared on one of the Monkey River boat tours, just a few weeks ago," he announced.

The boys ignored both him and the scenery. They had found what they were looking for; frantically they pressed buttons on their handheld video games. Beadily concentrating. This was a comfort since it showed they were as venal as regular U.S. children.

"We think he's probably dead," he went on.

There was something about the Germans and their seamless tans. He felt like shocking them.

"Oh my God," said the German woman.

She seemed earnestly concerned. The husband held her hand and nodded, also looking worried. Not only were the Germans beautiful and cheerful, they were also capable of empathy.

"What do they think happened?" asked the husband.

Hal was faintly gratified to note he had the typical German accent, endearing because it was also quite foolish-sounding. A slight but recognizable *z* sound on his *th*'s.

"No idea," said Hal, a little too breezily perhaps. "The boat came floating back empty." He turned and dipped into the back-pack, handing over one of the photographs.

"When was this?" asked the husband, studying it.

"A few weeks ago. I'm here looking for him," said Hal.

"But there aren't any rapids," said the woman, peering over

her husband's shoulder at the picture. "It couldn't have been a drowning accident, or?"

"Maybe there were mechanical problems," said the husband. "If you are going to see this boat, you should check the outboard motor."

"Cannibals," said Hal.

They looked at him blankly. No doubt alarmed at his callousness. But they had a point. It wasn't witty.

"The truth is, we don't know what happened," he went on quickly, to cover up his inane remark. "That's what I'm here for. I'm here to find out."

He caught himself wanting to mollify them. The Germans should not think ill of him, after all. They were not unlike superheroes. You might mock them for their stolid, self-righteous attitudes and overly muscled chests, but still you wanted to remain in their good graces.

The three of them sat in an ambiguous silence for a few moments until the Germans turned and said something to each other in discreet, low tones in their guttural language. He imagined it was along the lines of "What a pig this guy is," or "Americans are stupid." He faced into the spray and closed his eyes, but then he felt a soft hand on his arm.

"Let us know," said the German woman gently, "if there is anything we can do to help you."

He found he was blinking back tears. It came on him without warning. He tried to smile at her, at the same time turning away a little to disguise his emotion. Ahead of them there were a few boats out on the water, and to the east a low, blurry line of trees on a far-out island.

What about him and Susan? Once, when they were young, they could have passed for Germans. Couldn't they? He was unable to look at the Germans to verify it. They might see the tears that stood on his lower lids. But if he could look at them, he would see statuesque beauty. See what humans could be: weightless and straight, beautiful in their purpose and their autonomy. The sun shone down on them and the breeze whipped back their light clothing.

But he and Susan had both aged out of that splendid independence, or the illusion of it. Whatever it was that young, beautiful people had—people who were young and strong, who could scale cliffs and toss their heads back in laughter, whose cheekbones caught the sun. Their own outlines were not so fine, their shoulders and profiles not so elegant.

Was it worse to have been beautiful once and not be beautiful anymore? Or to never have been beautiful at all?

Because he had never been a German.

And poor Casey had never been the blond boys.

She was better, his love said—better! She was everything.

But briefly it twisted him with sadness, this matter of never having been German.

•

It took a long, dull while to find the man he was looking for once he and the Germans parted company. He sat in a small restaurant with wooden floors, where they served nothing but fish with too many small bones in it and no discernible seasoning and rice and beans and warm soda. He waited. These were his instructions; another man had told him the first man, the tour guide's brother, was on the water and would come in later.

He had tried waiting outside the brother's house for a while but there was nowhere to sit, only a patch of dirt beside a screen door hanging off a single hinge, and eventually he had wandered back to the restaurant and told the hostess he would like to wait at a table, please.

Once or twice he got up and walked around, stretching his legs. In the back of the restaurant, on a small, dusty table, they sold folk art of a heartrending ugliness.

The Germans were coming back at four-thirty, when he was due to meet them at the ocean pier again for the ride back to the hotel. He consulted his watch frequently and worried that the brother wouldn't show up by then, that he'd come all this way for nothing. Finally he fell asleep with his head on his arms on the table, and a man came and tapped his elbow. He jerked his head up in startlement.

It was an older man, dark-skinned with thinning hair cropped close to his head.

"Mr. Lindley?" he asked, and Hal nodded, still sleep-addled, and gestured at him to please sit down, and could he get him something to eat or drink.

When they both had grape sodas in front of them—the only thing available in a bottle besides beer—Hal said he understood the man's brother had taken Stern on the boat, and only the boat had come back. The man said it was his half-brother Dylan, and that yes, the boat had come back but not the men.

At first, when the boat was discovered, no one was sure whether to do anything. After all the men had been headed out on a cross-country backpacking trip. The loss of their boat would be a handicap, but only when they returned to the trailhead at the river and found it missing. No one knew when to send another boat looking for them. They had taken enough supplies for a couple of weeks, and Dylan knew the braids of the river well and could bring them back down without the boat. On the other hand, if their food was entirely depleted by the time they discovered the boat was missing, that could be a problem.

Hal remembered what the German had said and asked about the boat's outboard motor. The brother said it was broken, one of the blades had snapped, but it was not clear when this had occurred, whether it was before or after the boat had been separated from the men. It was more likely, said the brother, that it had happened when the motor was running. But this made little sense, because Dylan would not have abandoned the boat. Under no circumstances. He had bought it himself and rebuilt it with his own hands.

In any case, said the brother, they had to assume, at this point, weeks later, that the men were not returning.

He would never have thought it could happen. The Monkey was a slow, muddy river; the only possible human predators in the rainforest were jaguars, and in many generations none of these had harmed anyone. There were venomous snakes like the fer-de-lance, but it was unlikely a snake would have bitten both men. Possibly they had been attacked by thieves or guerrillas wandering the jungle, but that too was extremely far-fetched.

He was confused. He was mourning his brother but it was an odd, uncertain mourning.

"If I needed to find out more," said Hal, "what could I do?"

"I don't know," said the man, and finished his grape soda. His way of speaking had a kind of Creole lilt, or maybe Caribbean generally. It was melodious.

"Should I go up the river myself? Pay an outfitter or another guide to cover it, take along some rescue workers? I have a budget."

"The problem is," said the brother, shrugging, "there's too much ground up there. It's only jungle and mountains. We don't know where they went. One day I looked around where my brother used to go, this one place where there is a hiking trail, but you know, the rains already came then. There were no tracks or anything. I did a couple of walks with some guys from the village here, you know, but we never found anything. None of us."

"So it's a dead end," said Hal.

Then the Germans were at the screen door, looking fresh and invigorated with wet hair. Hal was surprised to see them until he recalled this was the only eating establishment in the town. Before he could say anything the man and woman were sitting on the rough bench on either side of him, their kids standing in the middle of the room toweling off their blond heads and then snapping the towels at each other.

"Did you find out good information?" asked the husband.

"There isn't any," said Hal.

"You know where the boat came from?" asked the German woman, looking at the brother.

"I know the trail he used," said the brother, and shrugged.

"Here, look," said the husband eagerly, and pulled a map out of a clear-plastic sheath. It was a topographical map, Hal saw, far better than anything he had. Trust the Germans. "Where is this? Show me, if you please."

The husband and the brother bent over the map, tracing their fingers up the line of the river. Their heads blocked the view and after a few moments Hal sat back, feeling superfluous.

The wife reached out and took his hand, squeezed it briefly and let go.

"We went swimming in the river," she said, smiling. He noticed her white teeth and the youthful, sun-kissed sheen of her skin. Her hair was caught back in a golden-brown braid. He could picture her in a blue and white dirndl, gaily performing a folk dance.

Too bad he couldn't have sex with her. But he was not an old lech. Not quite yet. He wouldn't wish himself on her even if she would have him.

"Aren't there caymen? Or piranhas or something?"

"Sure, crocodiles," she said, and laughed lightly. "But you know, very small. The water was so refreshing! We didn't see the crocodiles. Too bad. But we saw beautiful herons."

Germans always thought water was refreshing. They ran down to the water and plunged in boldly, welcoming the bracing shock of it as some kind of annoying proxy for life.

"Here, see here, Mr. Lindley?" asked the husband. Hal was surprised his name had been remembered. He leaned over the map, obliging. "Here is where Mr. Palacio says his brother would usually start the hikes. You see? There. I marked it with the pencil. Back at the Grove you can make a copy of this."

"Thank you," said Hal a little faintly.

Once they were back on the powerboat, the boys hunched over and pushing buttons on their handheld games again and the German couple became caught up in the momentum. They were enthusiastic.

"You must contact your embassy in Belmopan," said the husband. "They have military forces! Maybe they would help you."

Germans. They thought you could just call in the army.

"My understanding is, the U.S. embassy there is a very small facility," protested Hal, but they were already shaking their heads at this trifling objection.

"This is what they are here for," said the wife. "To help the citizens!"

"Technically I think they're here to prop up the Belize Defence Force," said Hal. He had skimmed a passage on the local military in his guidebook. "Which boasts about six soldiers."

"But also humanitarian assistance," said the husband, and the wife nodded in affirmation. They believed in the logic of cooperation, the good intentions of everyone. That was clear.

"They must have, what do you call it, Coast Guard," said the wife. "To do rescues in the ocean. Like *Baywatch*."

"*Baywatch*," said the husband gravely.

"Exactly," said the wife.

He had no idea what they were talking about. Possibly it was some kind of wholesome Krautish neighborhood-watch thing. He nodded politely.

Would he like part of a granola bar, asked the wife, with peanut butter in it? She divided one into three parts and they shared it.

The husband was some kind of electrical engineer, he learned, and the wife was a kindergarten teacher. They were living in the U.S. recently for some job of his. Their names were Hans and Gretel. He hadn't caught that at first. He asked if they were joking and they gazed at him with wide eyes and shook their heads.

He told them he worked for the IRS and they were practically admiring. That was a new one on him.

• • • • •

In the hotel business office, his third whiskey in hand, he composed a fax for the clerk to send to Susan. It was in telegram style, though he had a whole blank sheet to write on.

RAISING AN ARMY WITH GERMANS.

5

He woke up in the morning with a splitting headache once again. Thankfully the drapes were closed and he was safe in dimness.

His bedside telephone was blinking, a red message light. He did not want to reach out and touch it so he lay there, long and heavy on the hotel bed. Susan and Casey had both visited him. He hadn't dreamt much but he remembered them both spinning around him like tops or bottles, either angry or worried, with white and yellow ribbons streaming from their hands. Now he had the taste of peanut butter and iron in his mouth . . . the peanut butter he could remember from yesterday, when Gretel had made him eat granola, but where did the iron come from?

When a woman like Gretel offered you a piece of something to eat, you took it. You put it in your mouth. You barely noticed what it was. Personally, he never chose to eat granola, in bars or other formats. He banished granola from his sphere. But when Gretel broke off a piece and handed it to him, he ate the granola. Readily.

He had almost no memory of lying down. It could be he'd put his mouth on the bathroom tap, though you were cautioned not to drink the water. That could account for the iron. Or blood. Had he bitten his tongue? He stuck a finger into his mouth but it did not come out red.

Was it Susan who had called the room? Probably. Few others had any interest in him. He lived a life that was neither broad nor open. Only a few days ago he had ascribed this narrowness to the committed pet lovers, but like all of his nitpicking criticisms it was, in reality, merely his own view of himself. Projection or whatever. You didn't have to be a Sigmund Freud to see that.

He had believed, once, that somewhere outside in posterity was an impression of him—the collected opinion of the rest of the world, in a sense. The way he was seen by others was out there like a double, not his real self but a view of him that might have more truth, or more style at least, than his own. But now he knew there was nothing like that at all. You did not exist in the mind of the world as a whole person, there was nothing out there that represented you. There was no outside ambassador.

All you were to the rest of the human race was a flash or a glint, a passing moment in the field of the perceived. Parts of you struck them, parts of you did not; the parts formed no coherent image. People had few coherent images of anything. Even simple concepts, small words like *dog* or *tree,* were confusing to them: a thousand trees might pass through their memories in the split second of invocation—the white of birch or red maple or palms or small pines with golden angels holding Styrofoam trumpets.

Or all the dogs in the world. What room was there for you in this panoply?

People were like dogs and this was why they took pity on them—dogs alone all the hours of their days and always waiting. Always waiting for company. Dogs who, for all of their devotion, knew only the love of one or two or three people from the beginning of their lives till the end—dogs who, once those one or two had dwindled and vanished from the rooms they lived in, were never to be known again.

You passed like a dog through those empty houses, you passed through empty rooms . . . there was always the possibility of companionship but rarely the real event. For most of the hours of your life no one knew or observed you at all. You did what you thought you had to; you went on eating, sleeping, raising your voice at intruders out of a sense of duty. But all the while you were hoping, faithfully but with no evidence, that it turned out, in the end, you were a prince among men.

•

Someone was knocking on the room door—knocking persistently. He had dozed off again, a glass of water on the nightstand beside him. The red light was still blinking. The knocking would not let up.

"Hold on. Hold your horses," he struggled to say, resenting the interruption. "I'm coming, dammit."

He stood at the door in his skivvies. He opened it, realizing in the same instant that he had powerful morning breath.

In front of him were Hans and Gretel in skimpy trunks and a

flowery bikini, showing their tan, smooth bodies and cornflower-blue eyes as they smiled at him.

"I have contacted the Coast Guard," said Hans proudly.

"Sure, right," said Hal. "Right. Sure."

"Good news!" said Gretel. "They will send a task force."

"Very funny," said Hal, and wondered if they would allow him to go brush his teeth. From the second he met them, he had basically been their captive. Even in his own room he could not get away from these eager Germans.

"No, but seriously," said Hans. "The Coast Guard has a boat in these waters currently. I was put through to them. Also there are some local cadets they are helping, a mentoring exercise. The Americans are training them in search-and-rescue, so it will be like a practice."

"I don't . . . give me a second, I have to splash some . . ." He was mumbling as he retreated, but still they stepped into the room after him.

Gretel pulled open the drapes with a certain exuberance.

"You need some fresh air in here, Hal Lindley!" she said.

Probably to let out the morning breath.

Germans were not known for their sense of humor, he reflected as he brushed his teeth, the flimsy bathroom door shut carefully behind him. Their idea of a joke was not his own, that was all. Cultural barrier. Not uncommon. But he could have used another hour of sleep.

Let them stand there in all their terrible beauty. He was secure here in the bathroom, with a toothbrush and a tap and a clean toilet. In the end there was not much more a man truly needed.

But it could not last forever. Breath freshened, head aching, he stepped out again. There was no helping it.

"They will arrive tomorrow," said Hans. "The Coast Guard and also the cadets. All of them."

"Ha . . . it isn't that funny, though," said Hal. He hoped the fly on his boxers was not gaping. Couldn't risk a downward glance, however. He was already playing the buffoon in this particular comedy. Where were yesterday's pants?

He bent down and grappled with the bedcovers.

"No, but really, really," said Gretel, and smiled again. "It is a special task force! There will be approximately twenty persons."

"That's impossible," said Hal flatly.

He felt around under the bed for the pants, found them collapsed in a heap.

"Hans was just talking to his friends," said Gretel. "It's not a problem."

"Hans has friends in the Coast Guard?"

"Actually they are working for NATO," said Hans, nodding. "The Supreme Allied Command Atlantic. In Virginia?"

"He consults for them on the avionics systems," said Gretel.

"I called in a small favor," said Hans.

Hal shuffled away from them to pull the pants on. When he zipped up and turned back, their heads were backlit by the window and their faces indistinct; he saw them for a second as leviathans. They might be slim and standing there in their G-string swimwear, which had an all-too-floral tendency and made them look far more naked, even, than him. But in the strength of their Teutonic conviction he put his finger on what it was about them.

They were machines of efficiency, purposeful. Even in the

simple act of unwrapping a granola bar there was the sense of a necessary fueling.

•

"I'm afraid you may be drinking too much," said Susan.

She had him paged in the dining room while he was eating his breakfast. Because the Germans were sitting at the table with him, believing him to be a family man who was close to his loving wife, he could hardly refuse to take the call. Reluctantly he had followed the waiter to a telephone at the end of the front desk.

"Not at all," he said.

"What was that fax about, then?"

"It was accurate. There's a task force involved. Something to do with NATO."

"Come on, Hal. I don't get how you're acting, these last few days. I'm asking you please just to be serious."

He had brought his coffee cup to the phone with him and took the opportunity to sip from it with a certain poised nonchalance, his telephone elbow braced on the high, polished wood of the counter.

Robert the Paralegal could not raise a task force. A Trojan perhaps, but not a task force. None.

"What can I say? I met Germans with connections. Germans who refuse to take no for an answer, I'm guessing."

"See? This is what I mean, Hal. You just don't make that much sense right now."

"I'm telling you, Susan. Either there's a twenty-man task force trained in search-and-rescue that's arriving tomorrow to look for your friend Stern, or the Germans are conning me. It's possible. As history has taught us, Germans are capable of anything."

She was silent for a few static beats. He sipped his coffee again.

"Really, Hal? Honestly?"

"So they tell me. We'll see."

"But that's amazing, Hal. Amazing!"

"The jury's still out on it. OK? Keep you posted. I was right in the middle of a hot breakfast, though. Do you mind if I get back to it?"

More static. He had hurt her feelings.

"Not that I don't want to talk. Just a rush here—hectic. Wreckage, repairs. Aftermath. Hurricane. You wouldn't believe the scene."

He gazed out over the tranquil dining room, where lilies stood in tall vases on the white tabletops. Hans waved out the window to the boys in the pool, and Gretel, her long, languid legs crossed, was peeling an orange and licking the juice off the tips of her elegantly tapered fingers.

"OK. But keep me informed, OK Hal? Tell me everything that happens."

"I always do. We've always told each other everything, haven't we?" He was feeling a pinch of malice. Speaking with a dangerous transparency. He told her goodbye, hung up and downed the tepid dregs of his coffee.

• • • • •

There was no reason, he found himself deciding, not to enjoy himself while he waited for the armed forces. The day was still young, he had hours to kill before the night came on, and Hans and Gretel had invited him to go scuba diving.

Fortunately the children of the corn were too young to qualify for the scuba course and had resigned themselves to playing ping-pong.

"For the whole boat trip? They're going to play ping-pong for five straight hours?" he asked Hans, when he saw the boys hitting the ball back and forth at the table beside the pool. They were steadfast and tightly wound, their lips compressed, eyes darting only a fraction to the left or right with a predatory glint as they followed the bouncing ball.

"At least," said Hans.

"One time they played for two days, stopping only to sleep," said Gretel. "Of course it was a weekend."

They said goodbye to the boys, who ignored them studiously. Then a resort employee led them down to the dive shop, a kind of bunker with wet sand and footprints crisscrossing the rough concrete floor. There were wetsuits hanging on a rack and fins and masks arrayed in wooden cubbies along the wall; the ceiling was low and the walls were painted a deep, gloomy blue inside, maybe to simulate the ocean. The divemaster shook their hands and welcomed them.

Before they went out they had to sit through a safety lecture. Hal tried to listen attentively but was distracted by the presence of half-naked Gretel in her bikini, smelling delicately of coconut oil, and also by the belated arrival of the young bohemian couple hailing presumably from lower Manhattan.

The bohemian couple appeared skeptical of the lecture by the divemaster, bored and skeptical despite the fact that they had never been diving before and, if their breakfast exchange of the previous day was any indication, were also hypochondriacs. When the lecture ended and the divemaster began to choose gear for each of them, asking shoe sizes and moving along the row of cubbyholes searching, the bohemians raised an objection.

"This says we don't have the right to sue if we suffer injuries on the dive, up to and including death," said the man.

"Yes," said the divemaster politely. "It is a required legal waiver. I am very sorry but it is not possible to go out on the resort dive if you do not sign it."

"I don't know about this," said the woman, shaking her head. "I don't do waivers, normally."

"It says you can't go if you've ever had a lung collapse," said the man.

"I've never had a lung collapse," said the woman. "Have you had a lung collapse?"

"Not that I *know* of."

"It's something you would probably notice," said Hal.

The bohemian man ignored him.

"I had bronchitis one time in college," said the woman. "Is that a risk factor?"

"Or smoking. It says here you can't be a smoker."

"I did have that one clove cigarette at Dinty's. At that New Year's thing?"

"It was clove? Clove cigarettes are the equivalent of seven regular cigarettes."

The rest of the group stood waiting for them to sign or not sign the waivers, gear slung over their shoulders, fins hanging by the heels off two crooked fingers.

Hal felt impatient. He was irked by the bohemians. Previously he had been irked by the Germans, now it was the bohemians who irked him. Although the Germans had become his allies. What if the bohemians fell into line also? Would the bohemians also befriend him?

No. A bohemian was not a German. Socially speaking a German turned outward, like a sunflower toward the sun; a bohemian turned inward like a rotting pumpkin.

"Why don't the rest of you go ahead and get into your wetsuits," said the divemaster, and smiled affably.

When they came out of the restrooms the bohemians were also wetsuited. All of them stuffed their clothes and shoes into cubbies and walked barefoot down the beach toward the dock, the bohemians broadcasting a sense of glum foreboding. Or perhaps it was terror. Hal hypothesized that one bohemian had blackmailed the other into the scuba diving excursion, possibly with threats of poisoning via Red Dye Number Three.

Hans and the divemaster walked at the head of the pack discussing reef fish and Hal listened to Gretel tell him about swimming with stingrays in the Grand Cayman, how she had gently stroked their soft pectoral wings. He nodded without saying much, smiling in what he hoped was a beatific fashion and meanwhile wondering if, in the black wetsuit, he in any way resembled Batman. Was his torso, for example, slightly triangular? Just slightly, he didn't mean any big bodybuilder-type-deal. Did it descend just a bit from broad shoulders to a narrow waist, creating an impression of virility?

Squinting down at himself he noticed the wetsuit was in fact a very dark green. He was disappointed. In the shade of the dive shop he had thought it was black. Gretel's was black, as was Hans's. They gave the Germans the black wetsuits; him they gave the dark-green, the color of spinach slime. He suspected he most resembled the animated character Gumby, which as a child Casey had watched on TV with barely suppressed delight.

"Out at the caye," the divemaster was telling Hans, "where we will stop between dives for a late lunch and snorkeling, you will see lemon sharks. Some people feed them, although it is technically forbidden. Small sharks. Pretty. They swim around at your feet."

In the boat Gretel sat beside him and asked him about Stern. "This is the man who is the boss of your wife?" she asked.

"The boss of my wife. Yes."

"And he is a seller of real estate, you said before. Like a small Donald Trump."

"Better hair, though."

"That is very funny."

"I notice you're laughing hard."

"But you must be very close to him, yes? To come all the way here looking. He is a friend of the family, maybe."

He considered telling the truth but dismissed this as rash. And in fact Stern was a friend of his family, both his wife and his daughter, though not him personally.

"It's difficult," he said, but nodded.

She reached over and squeezed his wrist in sympathy. So easily misled.

•

He would not have come scuba diving if Gretel had not lured him with her kindness and beauty, he thought resentfully as he sat on the edge of the boat, his tank hanging heavily off his back, waiting to roll over backward into the ocean. He did not want to roll over backward into the ocean. Who was he? He was a middle-aged IRS employee, a father and a cuckold. He was an idiot.

He had let Hans and Gretel go before him so they would not witness his tomfoolery. He anticipated some kind of choking, spasming incident. But it was time. He had to follow Hans and Gretel, for they were his dive buddies. If he waited too long he might lose them. The pressure was on. This was it. The divemaster was staring at him expectantly. The neurotic bohemians were also watching. Their scrutiny was a grudging challenge.

He had hoped the neurotic bohemians would go before him, but they had found reasons to fiddle with valves and masks almost endlessly. Now there was no more excuse for delay. He could not see the expressions of the neurotic bohemians through their masks, but he imagined they were white-faced and trembling.

Middle-aged employee, or tax man? It was all in the wording. He was the tax man, by God.

He felt off slowly, even limply. He grappled. Then he was in. Sinking. For a second he panicked. Then: breathe only with the mouth. It was OK. He was doing it.

He heard his breath, the slow in-and-out like Darth Vader. There were white bubbles around him as he sank, a screen across everything, and then they cleared and it was light blue and placid. He looked down: beneath the black fins on his feet were rocks and yellow- and gray-striped small fish. He raised his head again and saw Gretel ahead of him, moving toward a wall of coral. She was lithe and graceful with her fins moving back and forth; her long hair floated behind her and caught the light, a stream of warmth in the cold water. It rippled.

Off to the right at a slight distance was Hans, at greater depth. He had announced on the boat that he had two goals: sea cucumbers and moray eels.

Hal did not share his goals.

The fins felt good, powerful. He propelled himself forward, hastening to get close to Gretel. It was nice down here, lovely. It was a cathedral of light and softness. Down here you probably couldn't even tell the difference between a black wetsuit and a dark-green one.

The dive would last about a half-hour, they had told him. He would stay close by her. She would point at things.

As they held steady side by side about fifteen feet beneath the surface he found himself entranced, not only by her but by the corals and the fishes. Beneath them and around them—he had to be careful not to brush up against the coral, hit a sharp urchin or a stinging anemone—there were formations like brains and antlers, sponges and intestinal tubes and lace and leaves of lettuce. Among them the fish swam, some hunkering low and inside, others flittering lightly along edges. Gretel touched his shoulder and they looked down together at a speckled, dun-colored fish on the bottom half covered in sand, bloated and with spikes on it. Some kind of blowfish or puffer, he guessed. They ate them in Japan. Flat, tall fish that were a deep purple-blue with a line of bright yellow moved past him in stately elegance.

He thought how Casey would love all this. He would describe it to her when he got home. She had seen photographs, had watched Jacques Cousteau and the like, but she would never know how it felt to be here, the buoyancy. How everything seemed to move slower, with a silence that changed the world. Time, even. He felt a quick wrench of longing, worry and regret—what he always felt, when he recalled her and was not in her company. The guilt for not being there, actually, among other impulses . . . not that she wanted him there. He was only a father.

When they were small you were everything to them, then they grew up and you dwindled into next to nothing . . . she liked underwater scenes, had drawn them often when she was a little girl. He remembered her pictures in felt-tip pen: mermaids hovering beside straggly green seaweeds, mermaids with dots for breasts and large scales along their tails and yellow hair. She had believed that underwater was a kingdom where she would be welcome—where she could move like a fish, move like fluid itself.

She would have seen Gretel back then, when she was six years old, and thought she was beholding a mermaid.

Hans was also still in view, though just barely. He was always diving, scouting, always searching for something. Hans was not content to float and look, unlike Hal and Gretel.

Hal was watching a fish nibble at the coral, listening to the sound of many of them eating, like the *pop-pop-pop* of milk in rice cereal, all over in the background, when she suddenly grabbed him by the upper arm and turned him. They were surrounded by silver, or at least there was nothing but silver in front of them. It was a vast school, thousands. Small, moving in silver flickers, hundreds of them switching angles in the same pulse of motion, instantly. He was astonished by it, how hundreds or thousands moved in a flash, as one body. It seemed impossible.

Then he was startled, almost breathed through his nose feeling Gretel's hand move over the arm of his wetsuit with something akin to tenderness—was there intent in the touch? He could almost believe it. But it was through the wetsuit. Most likely she had just forgotten to let go. Both of them gazed at the flanks of the fish—the gleaming, moving-as-one legions. He thought they could never be like this, people. Never. Was she thinking it too? With her hand on his arm. It was the two of them, suspended, the rest of the world far above and in the dryness of air—nothing like this below, these silver thousands.

Finally the school thinned and dispersed, left them gazing out into a fading blue abyss. At some point her hand was gone from his arm, which he also regretted. He felt cold despite the wetsuit.

It was not their place, after all. They were here only by the grace of machines.

He had forgotten to check his tank and lost track of his oxygen, but luckily she was on top of it. She showed him her gauge and made a thumbs-up signal, which he thought at first meant everything was OK. In fact it was the signal to return to the surface, which he recalled a second later from their safety lesson. She was already rising slowly, and he watched her for a while before he went up too.

•

On the island where they went to eat lunch there were too many tourists crowded onto a slight, barren finger of sand. Many small boats were anchored, wave-slapped and bobbing, on the windward side, while on the lee side all he could see was a field of snorkels sticking out of the shallow water, black and day-glo yellow and fluorescent pink. Seagulls had splattered white onto the rocks and benches all around; there were bathrooms and some low shelters over picnic tables. On one end of the island were a few tall, thin palms, scraping and flapping their dried fronds in the breeze.

The neurotic bohemians found the last empty picnic table in the shade, unwrapped the packed lunches the divemaster handed them from a plastic cooler, then talked in low voices about how there was nothing in them they could stand to eat. The woman was a vegetarian, the man was lactose-intolerant.

Hal sat at the other end of the table with Hans and Gretel. He was ravenous. He wanted to order the neurotic bohemians to hand over their portions; he wanted to tower over them and scoop up their sandwiches into his gaping maw. Instead he quietly ate his own ham-and-cheese and listened to Hans enthuse to the divemaster about a sea cucumber.

Apparently, when alarmed, they could extrude their intestines.

Gretel was impatient to see lemon sharks so after a minute Hal got up from the table, left the neurotic bohemians and Hans and the divemaster and followed her with the final crust of his sandwich in hand as she walked along the lapping edge of the water. You could walk from one end of the island to the other in five minutes and soon they found the sharks, circling again and again in less than a foot of water. They were small, just a couple of feet long, and being fed by tourists, who tossed in fragments from their own bagged lunches.

Gretel shook her head, worried.

"It is not natural," she said.

Germans hated it when things were not natural. Hal remembered this from college philosophy. Heidegger or something.

"Sharks have strong stomachs," he improvised, straining to recall any actual facts. Natural history was not a strong suit, despite his years of watching *Nature* with Casey. "Great whites have been found with oil barrels in their digestive tracts. Rusty engines. I doubt a few Fig Newtons are going to hurt them."

"But these are not great whites," said Gretel, and squatted down on her haunches to see them more closely. "Look! They are like little babies."

A few paces away the divemaster was already gesturing at them: it was time to head back to the boat. Gretel left the so-called baby sharks reluctantly.

On the windward beach again, lagging behind the rest of the group, Hal looked out beyond the boats and saw a small skiff cruise by, a thin, bearded man standing in the front of the boat leaning into the wind with raised binoculars, one bent leg braced against the prow like a sea captain in books of yore. Hal tried to recall where in the hotel he'd run into him. Then the bohemian woman screeched. She was barefoot and had stepped on a bottle cap.

"You could get lockjaw," said the bohemian man.

• • • • •

Back at the hotel the Germans pressed him into service for dinner also, as though he could not be trusted to be left on his own. Their two boys left the table in a rush once they had bolted their kiddie menus, running outside to continue the ping-pong tournament.

"We must get organized for tomorrow," said Hans. "We have the map. I have made many copies. We have many copies also of the photograph of Mr. Stern. The hotel is having them laminated."

"Nothing left for me to do then, really," said Hal. "Is there."

He had a cavalier attitude; he was drinking a margarita, which Gretel had encouraged him to order. She drank one also and her bright-blue eyes were shining.

"Does Mr. Stern have any medical conditions?" asked Hans.

"Not that I know of," said Hal.

"You should find out the blood type, in case he is located and is injured and requires a transfusion. Also a medical history."

"Huh," said Hal, nodding vaguely. "My wife would probably know." He had ordered the snapper, which was overcooked and too fishy. He decided to leave it mostly uneaten. The margarita tasted far better.

"Also, does his insurance cover helicopter evacuation," Hans was saying.

Hal was already at the bottom of his glass, and at the far end of the dining room a band was setting up. He was thinking how pleasant it was to be drunk, that he had been missing out all these years in not being drunk far, far more often.

Couples gathered at the edge of a dance floor. There was a drum flourish, bah-da bum. A woman singer in an evening gown said something husky and incomprehensible into a microphone.

Lights sparkled. Yellow and golden in the dining room, now a ballroom. Beyond the large windows, the pool, the chairs, the deep-black sky, the ocean. A room full of people and golden lights, and outside the whole dark world.

Tequila, he thought, made him sad—was it sad, though? Anyway, melancholy. Youth had flown. It wasn't all bad, though. You couldn't move as well as you used to, you didn't look as good, you had either forgotten the dreams of youth or resigned yourself to their disappointment.

But at least you could see more from your new position. You had a longer view.

"Come on, Hal. Why don't we go dance a little?" asked Gretel, smiling, and cha-cha-cha'd her shoulders. Hans was pushing buttons on a calculator, which seemed to have appeared from nowhere. He waved them to go dance, got up and headed off. Hal watched him buttonhole the maître d', nod briskly and start dialing the restaurant phone.

"He's really taken this on, hasn't he," said Hal. "This whole search-and-rescue thing."

"Hans does not like vacations," said Gretel. "He gets bored. He always needs to have something to do. He's some kind of genius, people tell me. With his electronics. You know, and he talks to me about his work? But actually I don't understand it. But always he likes to keep busy."

"I noticed," said Hal.

"Dance with me," said Gretel. It was cheerfully platonic, but he took what he was offered.

"With pleasure," he said, and set down his margarita glass. The stem of the glass was green and in the shape of a large cactus, the kind you saw in cartoons and Arizona. A margarita was not a manly drink. But more so than a daiquiri.

Heading for the dance floor, he was recalled to reality—the reality that he was a flat-out embarrassing dancer. Among the worst. He had almost forgotten. He was a finger-snapper and a head-nodder. He had no other moves.

"Wait. Only if it's a slow song," he added, and hung back. "I'm really bad."

"What's important is to have fun," said Gretel, taking him by the arm. "*Express* yourself."

"You don't want to see that, believe me," said Hal, feeling the silkiness of her fingers. "Self-expression is a young man's game."

"Oh, come on," she said.

They were on the dance floor, other people around them. She started to move, a couple of feet away. Lithe and elegant, as would be expected. He could not do anything. He was stuck. Then desperation washed over him. He had to cling to some self-respect. He reached out and grabbed her, clamped her to his person.

"Sorry," he said into her ear. "This is all I can stand to do."

She drew back, a bit confused, and then smiled. After a few seconds she balanced her arms on his shoulders and let him hold her and sway.

Leaning into her he let himself believe, for a moment, that others caught sight of them and assumed they were a couple. Yes: he was a party to this assumption, he welcomed it. Possibly they surmised he was some kind of businessman and Gretel was his trophy wife. Only for a moment of course, for a fraction of a second. As he felt her back under his hands, the swell of breasts on his front. Then the gazes passed over them and fastened elsewhere. But it was better than nothing.

Hans was tapping his shoulder officiously.

"Susan wishes to speak to you," he said. "She is waiting on the telephone. But do not worry, I have the blood type. Fortunately, Mr. Stern is O-positive."

Gretel stepped back from him and took Hans's hand with a light, casual gesture, twirled herself around as she held it. Hans danced with her, stepping primly back and forth; plainly his heart was not in it. Hal's own heart had been in it, very much so.

As he wandered listlessly toward the phone, which the maître d' was holding out to him, he could not recall ever resenting Susan like this. Not when he had seen her in the office with the paralegal; not even when they were young and interrupted by Frenchmen.

"So it's really happening," she said, when he picked up the receiver. "You're going to find him. I know you are."

"Maybe," he said. "Don't get your hopes up, though."

"Casey sends her love," she said. "She's here with me."

He softened, feeling homesick.

"Can I talk to her?"

"Daddy."

"Case. How are you, sweetheart?"

"An army? The Coast Guard or something?"

"Apparently."

"You're my hero."

•

Later the cornboys came running in from ping-pong, the smaller one bleeding from the head. In a doubles game with two other kids the wooden edge of a paddle had cut him upside the eye socket. Hans and Gretel were not overly worried, but Hans plied a white linen napkin to the wound, filled it full of ice from a nearby table's champagne bucket. He got the kid to hold the ice against his temple and then announced it was the boys' bedtime. Putting his hands on their shoulders to steer them to the room, he looked back at Gretel, but she shook her head and grabbed Hal's arm. She would be there in a few minutes, she said, but she was going to take a walk on the beach before bed, and Hal would escort her.

Hal was tired and ready for bed himself: he felt slack and let down. After the last drink he had turned a corner. There was an art to drinking and he had not mastered it. But Gretel was determined; she tugged at his hand, so he shrugged and agreed to go along. After all, due to the Germanness there would likely be a midnight swim, a shucking of clothes and plunging into the waves. It would not surprise him.

A vicarious thrill in it anyway, or at least a view of her naked ass. He could pretend there was more, that it was for his benefit.

"Leave your shoes," she urged, when she took off her own. Obediently he discarded them, balled up the socks inside the shoes and left them beside her sandals underneath a hammock. She walked a few paces ahead of him.

There were few stars—no visible cloud cover, but still the stars were obscured and the moon was high but not bright. He followed her, hearing the wash of the tide as the small waves curled in and feeling the water on his feet. They passed a dock and left it behind, passed a row of canoes on the sand. His jeans got wet at the hems and he bent over and rolled them up. If Susan could see him, walking by moonlight with a lovely young woman. Along a seam of the Caribbean.

"Look out for jellyfish," he said. "Washed up I mean. You wouldn't see them."

"I'm going to go swimming. It is so beautiful!" she cried, and idly he gave himself points for predicting.

"Of course," he said.

"You have to come in with me!"

He was flatly opposed to this. He would be cold and wet. He had no interest in it.

"OK," he said.

Wearily and without haste he took off his clothes. Who cared, after all, who would ever notice or give a shit? No one. Gretel herself wasn't even looking. The air was black around them and the blackness gave them a loose kind of privacy. She stepped out of her own skirt as though it was nothing, pulled her shirt over her head and dropped it on the sand too. No brassiere. He had a glimpse of pertness, the sheen of skin.

She left the clothes in a pile without casting a glance at them, bounded forward into the surf and dove. Submerged.

He watched the water, holding his breath. Shivering. Now he had to go in after her. That was how he was with the Germans—he acceded to their demands and then he had to summon the wherewithal. When in fact he did not have it. He was afraid of dark things in the water, surging up from the deep.

Where was she? She should have resurfaced by now. He waded out, up to his knees, up to his waist. Where was she?

She came up with a splash, laughing and shaking the water off her head.

"I love it!" she cried.

"Nice," he agreed, nodding, and dropped in up to his shoulders, dog-paddling. She went under again.

He remembered a scene from one of the British nature shows featuring famous, avuncular naturalists—wry, witty men who casually stepped down from helicopters in the African veldt and talked companionably to the camera in their Oxbridge accents as they walked through the tall, waving grass in their safari outfits. Such men were at home with the animals, picked them up and showed them to the camera as though there was no trick to it. They said *this little fella* as they described a mating behavior or trotted out a surprising factoid. But the scene he remembered had been part of an episode devoted to bioluminescence. They had shown deep-sea fishes that looked like spaceships, myriad lights rimming their graceful, pulsing bodies. Marine biologists had descended in a bathysphere like something out of Jules Verne. In the depths near the Mid-Atlantic Ridge, in the bathysphere's headlights, they caught luminous creatures undescribed by science.

Casey had cried when she saw that. But she hid it from him. She pretended she was crying for another reason, pain probably. She was embarrassed to be seen crying out of sheer emotion.

In the dark he saw mostly the glitter of the waves, Gretel, porpoise-like, diving and coming up again. For a few seconds she stood on her hands in the shallows, her legs and feet sticking out straight, toes pointed like a ballerina's. There was a breeze across his chest and shoulders and he threw his weight backward and floated on his back, water skirting his bare chest. He could not help but think of sharks and other predators, sluggish and ominous beneath him. Awakening. Tendrils or tentacles or rows of sharp teeth . . .

Above him he saw the moon, but not with clarity; just a blurred scoop of white. He closed his eyes. It was reassuring to have Gretel nearby. Nothing would befall her. No shark would dare. By extension he was also safer. Wasn't he?

Something brushed against his back from beneath and at the same time he panicked and he knew it was her. Her sleek, wet head emerged beside his own and she was spitting seawater on him and laughing. He sank down a little, coughed and sputtered and righted himself, feet searching for the sandy bottom and sinking in.

Without warning she kissed him. Their bodies were touching all over, under the water and above it, solid and inflaming. Her nipples were against his chest. At once he was both frozen and pulsing with current. Even as it happened, and then continued to happen, it was completely impossible.

He would have to pay for this, he was thinking. And he would pay. He would pay. Gratefully.

6

They were clean-looking guys with brush cuts, looking intently ahead of them and carrying the smell of fresh sweat and what he suspected was pine-scent deodorant. The armed forces weren't as Caucasian as he'd imagined them, more Latino and black, but just as muscular and young. He stood in the sand beside the dock watching as they filed past, he in his shorts and tattered old sneakers, they in stiff uniforms and bulky black boots. He felt unarmored, a tiny pale civilian.

They dismounted from the dock in rapid succession, boots thumping into the sand, and ran past him and up the beach, leaving their two powerboats tied to the dock. A few hundred yards out on the water the mother ship was anchored, a line of flapping flags flying over her gleaming white bulk. He recognized only the Stars and Stripes.

"*Nantucket,*" he read, off the side. "Wow. She's big."

Hans, a few paces off with his hands clasped behind his back, shook his head with a *tut-tut* noise. "Smallest patrol boat in the fleet, except for the Barracudas," he said. "A 110. Island class. 155 tons full load. Two diesels, two shafts, 5,820 bhp and about 30 knots. For guns, a 25-millimeter Bushmaster low-angle and two 7.62-millimeter MGs."

"I have no idea what you're talking about," said Hal.

Hans laughed joyously, as though Hal had told a good joke.

"I thought you did airplanes," Hal added.

"Tactical sensor networks," said Hans. "I like boats though. Kind of like a hobby." He waved at a man standing on the powerboat's massive bridge. Hal squinted to see him better; he was a small stick figure.

"I don't get it," said Hal. "How did you manage this?"

"They were already here. Humanitarian assistance," said Hans. "This mission falls in the category of hurricane casualties. Even though technically it was only a tropical storm. Your friend is an American citizen, no? And an important businessman also. An asset. I impressed them with this. They are based in an operations center in Miami. The ones in light-brown are the Belize Defence Force cadets. They are just here to learn."

"I didn't think anyone would show up," said Hal, still stunned and failing to adjust. "I really didn't."

"Of course," said Hans, and grinned. He put his hand up for a high-five.

Dazed, Hal slapped it compliantly and then felt stupid.

Hans consulted his waterproof digital watch, which he had worn diving the day before and of which he seemed to be quite proud. "We weigh anchor at 10:00 hours," he said. "So you have exactly ten minutes for preparation."

"Oh. I'll go get my shit, then," said Hal after a few seconds, and struck out for his room at a jog.

He was dizzy and almost trembling from too little sleep and too many margaritas and lying awake in disbelief remembering the recent past—Gretel's mouth, thighs, and hands all over him. They lay on their shucked clothes on the sand; they had to be careful not to get sand inside her, between them where it counted. He brushed it off her thighs and stomach, off himself . . . but she was lighthearted and playful so he had tried to seem lighthearted too, though he was dead serious.

After they finished he had walked her to the flight of stairs outside the room she was sharing with Hans and the cornboys. Salt-encrusted and shivering, he had gazed up at her back and legs, flashes in the dark as she went up. Probably he had been beaming the whole time, he thought. He had felt like beaming. The room door had closed softly behind her and he had almost run back to his own room, bounding forward giddily. Like a kid.

He was not without pride, lying there, he had to admit it. He even fell asleep proud.

Then first thing in the morning Hans found him at the lobby coffeemaker and rushed him outside to watch the patrol boat cruise in.

Back in his room he drank thirstily, a whole bottle of water he found standing on the dusty metal lid of his air-conditioning unit. He grabbed his green backpack and a baseball cap, filled the water bottle again from the sink and took a fresh one from the shelf. You weren't supposed to drink the water here but there were filters on the taps in the rooms . . . he should feel guilty in the company of Hans, he thought, but curiously he discovered his conscience was more or less clear. Maybe it was Hans's automaton quality.

The armed forces were present; he had flown down here on a whim and somehow now there were armed forces to do his bidding. Fortunately Hans would lead them, Hans would manfully take the reins. Hans would assume the armed-forces leadership. He, Hal, had no interest in armed-forces leadership.

He checked himself in the mirror. He had a tan, he noticed. Would Gretel come with them today? Would she see him by daylight and cringe?

He could hardly blame her. He had seen her as in control, seamless and perfect, mostly because she looked that way. But in fact she had been as drunk as he was, if not more, and she had the upper hand—laughably so. She was far younger, far better-looking, and married to a kind of Germanic Apollo who also happened to be an avionics genius. She must be regretting her rash act, her fleeting impulse. He could almost imagine the knot of remorse in her stomach.

He would respect that remorse. He would comport himself with discretion. Lowered eyes, deference.

•

But she was not there. It was only Hans, the armed forces, and him. The two of them stood with an officer on the forward deck of the *Nantucket*.

"Gretel is spending time with the boys today," said Hans when Hal asked. "They are going to see manatees. In the lagoon."

"Manatees," said Hal, and nodded.

"It is also possible to observe dolphins, crocodiles and sea turtles," recited Hans dutifully, as though from a brochure. "There are hawksbills, green sea turtles and loggerheads."

It was high above the water, which Hal was not used to since the few boats in which he had been a passenger before this were small boats. Except for a ferry once, past the Statue of Liberty. In the ferry there had been kids running and eating hotdogs, gum stuck on the undersides of benches and vomit in the bathrooms. Overall it was none too clean. The *Nantucket*, by contrast, smelled only of bleach. And she was moving fast. Easy to see how in the armed forces, wearing a clean authoritative uniform with a machine like this beneath you, you might come to believe you ruled the seas.

On Hans's other side was someone named Roger, who was apparently in charge.

"Now in the event we get a Medevac situation," Roger told Hans, "that's going to be at least an hour out for the Dolphin. Minimum. Sorry we couldn't bring reconnaissance airpower on this one. Woulda been nice to have all the new toys to play with. But you know how it is. All dollars and cents. With UAVs, too much bureaucracy."

Hal moved away from them, stood at the portside rail and gazed out over the ocean, the white-blue curl of froth rolling away from the ship. He could see fishing boats dotting the waves out toward the atolls, though they were too far away for him to make out the fishermen. But he imagined all their faces were turned toward him, in awe of the leviathan. Or resentment, if the engine noise was driving off the fish.

He was finding it hard to relinquish his doubt. To get past his own skepticism that this was real—the vast boat, the gunmen—he had to remind himself he did not need it to be real. Accordingly he could take it lightly, as though it might easily be nothing more than a drunk or a delusion . . . if the hurricane had brought humanitarian relief, for instance, in the form of these men, such relief seemed to have missed Seine Bight with its muddy field of shanties. He recalled the light-brown earth dried in right angles where it had flowed around the corners of buildings that were now gone. He thought of sheds the size of closets whose particleboard walls were held to the plastic roofs with what looked like duct tape—sheds that apparently housed whole families, because half-naked kids were running in and out of them in every appearance of actually living there.

He had not seen any sign of officials or their vehicles, a vast white prow looming on the water or brand-new supplies being offloaded into eager hands. Maybe the humanitarian assistance had gone to settlements up the coast. Or maybe the humanitarian assistance had been the duct tape.

But clearly his information was incomplete. He glanced over his shoulder at Roger, who was nodding, close-mouthed and sanguine, at something Hans was saying. He had a humble, sunchapped face with a beaklike nose. Such a face was homely and workmanlike. It seemed trustworthy.

Appearances were often deceiving.

The engines thrummed beneath Hal's feet. Their noise was deep and steady, their vibration relentless. He was silenced. He felt he had left his personality on dry land. He should ask Hans how to address the men; their uniforms flummoxed him. When he felt the urge to ask a question his instinct was to preface it with "Officer," timidly and with a sycophantic tone, as on the rare occasion when he had been pulled over for speeding. He did not like policemen; neither did he enjoy the company of soldiers, but he felt more respect for them. Many came from poor backgrounds and were lured by the GI Bill.

Safer to say nothing.

When one of them walked past him he received an impression, in the quickness of the step and the forward-looking, dogged progress, that the walking itself was in the service of a greater business; the detail, the formality of personal transit was a small machination for the sake of general welfare.

And the bodies of the men were budding, strong, confident.

Yet Gretel. Gretel had picked *him*.

Maybe she was simply unaware that there were other options. Much could be ascribed to ignorance, in the world.

And anyway the fitness of these bodies was only partly a reflection on the men themselves. It was a fitness achieved by the state, in a sense, or at least the cost of the fitness was borne by the state. Also the state-sanctioned deployment of the fit and muscular bodies (which were in no way similar to Hal's body, sadly for him) was further augmented by a wide variety of complex and powerful weapons, explosives, and multimillion-dollar, high-tech delivery systems for same. When the state chose to spend roughly the same on its military as on all other things combined, the owners of these now-fit and muscular bodies were the beneficiaries.

True, their occupation could also bring sudden death. But so could many occupations. Sewage work, for instance. No one wept for the sewage workers. Or the electric-light-and-power men. Life insurance companies hated them. Were they needed? They were. Were they acclaimed as heroes when they died? They were not. Same with miners, truck drivers, roofers, all the guys with high premature mortality rates, or PMRs, as the insurance industry called them. Even doctors had a high PMR, the cause being suicide.

In Hal's line of work, which was also conducted in defense of the state, a fit, muscular body was not required. As a result employees of the Internal Revenue Service often suffered from a wide range of their own work-related ailments, including migraines, coronary artery disease, chronic obesity, and carpal tunnel syndrome. These were admittedly less glamorous than battleground injuries. Yet the discomfort was real. And like the sewage workers and the electricity guys, if Hal were to be killed in the line of duty he would not be mourned as a fallen hero. Despite the fact that he had toiled not for private industry but in the unflagging service of his country and all that it stood for, no Taps would play for him.

IRS service did not, however, happen to carry a high PMR.

But finally it was hard to sustain resentment toward the Coast Guarders. Armed forces personnel were not as bad as cops, when it came to the aggregate probability of antisocial personality disorder. They had a different makeup. They were not homicidal so much as Freudian; they liked to feel the presence of a constant father. And their fringe benefits included fit and muscular bodies.

Still, one or two might be behind on their taxes.

He smiled privately at the horizon, a hair-thin line between two shades of blue.

•

The armed forces took small powerboats from Monkey River Town, loaded with personnel so that they lay low in the water. Roger was not coming with them. There was a Coast Guard guy of lower rank, in blue, whose name Hal did not catch at first. Hans told him he could call the guy "Lieutenant."

There were others in camouflage, some in berets, all wearing mirrored sunglasses through which it was impossible to establish eye contact. His fellow Americans were bedecked in chunky black equipment, belts and holsters and field packs and canteens and knives; they wore headsets and spoke to each other in clipped undertones, as though everything they said was both highly confidential and extremely important.

The sheer weight of their accessories, Hal thought, could capsize the boat if they all moved at once.

The local cadets had no veneer of soldiery and hardly any gear either. Their beige uniforms hung loosely on them and Hal thought they looked eighteen or younger, thin and lost.

"How come they need all those guns? We're just looking for someone in the jungle," he whispered to Hans.

They rounded a curve in the river, which was so brown it looked more like mud than water.

"They are active-duty military. Of course they have guns."

"What are they going to do? Shoot the trees?"

"They're treating it like an extraction. For training purposes."

"Uh huh."

"By the way," said Hans, close to his ear, "no photographs are permitted. This is an unofficial mission."

"I didn't bring a camera," Hal protested, though at the same time it occurred to him that he probably should have. Documentation; proof. For Casey and Susan. "Are you kidding?"

Then the men hunched around maps, Hans among them. They appeared to be tracing routes on the maps with markers and pushing buttons on their watches. The Americans took a paternal air with the local cadets, who nodded eagerly at every directive. Hal tuned them out and gazed into the foliage growing over the stream banks. It was bushy and disordered, thick, unruly—it could hide anything. A wave of dismay rolled over him. There was no way they would find Stern.

That was all right though, in the end. Wasn't it? He would have made an unimpeachable showing. If these Rambos could not locate Stern, Susan and Casey would never think to be disappointed in little old him.

•

After a while they tied the boats to some trees at a place in the river where there was a muddy embankment. It looked like a dirt path of some kind, mostly overgrown.

"This is the trailhead," said Hans, and pointed at a place on the map. It was where Dylan's brother had directed them.

"So we're all getting out here?" asked Hal.

"There are several groups," said Hans, as the Coast Guarders surged around him off the boats. "You will go with the BDF group. The trainees. It will be less strenuous."

"Oh, good," said Hal. He was being babied, but he could care less. "Little hungover, sorry to say."

The Americans were using their black radios, or walkie-talkies, or whatever they were. Static squawked out of them, and nasal tinny voices. All of them huddled on the bank, nodding and talking; Hal grabbed his pack and stepped off the boat with barely room to walk between the broad impervious backs and the hem of reeds and bushes along the water. He stepped too far into these and soaked a foot, swearing, then skirted the crowd.

He felt lost.

"Mr. Lindley?" called one of the young cadets. He had a scar from a harelip. "Right here, sir. Just a moment, then we're going."

The cadet had an accent, but what kind Hal couldn't say. Maybe he was a native Garifuna. Light-brown skin, dark hair, like all of them. Hal didn't feel like getting to know anyone. Small talk, names and places, details. He wanted to trudge in peace, passively. Just let them do their duty. Whatever the hell that might be.

He found a low flat rock in the shade and sat down. It was all shade, just a few feet from the riverbank it was all trees, tall and thin-trunked, most of them. Underfoot was mud and tree roots, a few dead leaves. Young backs were turned to him, blue and beige and camouflage shoulder blades. He let his head flop back and stared into the green overhead, barely moving except for his toes in the clammy, wet shoes.

No sky through the treetops to speak of, only leaves. Strange how the green of these tropical places seemed so unvarying—as though every tree had the same color leaves. Was it the brilliance of the sun, washing out their difference? The quality of the light as it beat down on them? But in the shade they were all the same too, the same bright yet curiously flat green.

Then the men broke their huddle and were jogging past him down the path, a group cutting off along a trail to the right, another group getting into a boat again and gunning the engine upstream. The lieutenant was in charge of the cadets, apparently—the once-harelip motioned to Hal and they were striding after him up the trail.

Hal hoisted himself off the rock and followed.

"We got monkeys," said the once-harelip kid, turning back to him and grinning. "You might see some of the howlers. Way up. Black things. They're not so cute monkeys. They got big teeth. Kinda ugly."

Hal nodded and smiled.

•

It was a long march, a long, hot, wet, relentless, rapid march, it seemed to him, and three hours in he was bleary with exhaustion. He couldn't believe he was there, couldn't believe that no one had warned him. Hard to keep up—more than hard, actually painful: a form of torture. Long time since he'd had this much exercise and it was practically killing him. It was all he could do to stay in earshot behind them. He was far past embarrassment; he was past even humiliation. He had no pride left at all, nothing left but the strain. He had to struggle just to put one foot in front of the other. Every now and then, from in front, came the sound of voices or a branch snapping. Sweat had wet his shirt through and through, and it was making him cold in the shade of the trees; his water bottles were almost empty.

Take pity on me, he thought, and shortly afterward they stopped for lunch.

They had reached a rough campsite, he saw, coming up behind them, a small muddy clearing. The lieutenant kneeled at a fire pit ringed with rocks, touching the ashes or some shit. Sniffing them? Hal wiped his dripping brow with the back of his hand

and sat down heavily on a log. Not watching. All he wanted was rest. He had no interest in them or what they were doing, except insofar as it caused him direct physical distress.

Maybe if he asked they would just let him rest here, let him lie down in the mud and sleep, sleep, sleep while they kept on marching.

He put his head on his arms.

"A watch," said someone.

Hal raised his head. It was the lieutenant, holding out a wristwatch.

"Do you recognize this?"

Hal took it, flipped it over. It was a cheap, bulky digital with a plastic band—no brand name, even. Dried mud between the black plastic links.

"No," he said. "He wouldn't wear one like this. He's more of a Rolex type."

"Could belong to the guide," said the lieutenant, and turned back to the others.

They were passing around sandwiches, eating them standing up. Hal's damp log was the only seat in the house. Someone offered him a sandwich, the cadet with the harelip scar, and he took it gratefully. Maybe after he ate he would be stronger, maybe it would invigorate him. He wolfed it down inside a minute, barely registering the contents. He drank the rest of his water and someone gave him a can of juice. It was quiet for a while as they all ate, hardly any birdsong, until a radio squawked and a low murmur of conversation started.

He got up to pee in the woods, picked his way over tree roots and ferns for privacy. Staring at a thin, light tree trunk with thorns up and down the trunk, ants traveling up and down between the thorns, he noticed movement far off, in the shadows—what? A dark shape—a long, low animal, roughly the size of a dog. Were there dogs in the jungle? It moved more like a cat, though. Jumped from a stand of bamboo to some trees and was gone. He wiped his eyes, which ached from tiredness or dryness or something. Hallucinations, now. He should go back to the boat. He was sick, possibly. In the tropics, viruses thrived.

He was no better than the neurotic bohemians.

•

The trail continued on the other side of the campsite but it was more overgrown. There were vines, and now and then a cadet took out a machete and hacked at one.

Hal dragged after the column, defeated. Sometimes he had to climb over a down log, encrusted with fungus, and pieces of rotting bark got into his shoes and irritated his ankles and heels. He had to stop to pull them out and then catch up to the others, who waited for him. There were biting insects, so he slathered on some bug juice a cadet handed back. He did not bother trying to hear their exchanges; anyway they were mostly lost up ahead.

After a while a light rain began to patter on the leaves and his shoulders. The cadets had ponchos on now. He had nothing. But his shirt was already soaked and he found he didn't mind the rain; the insects bit less. Not too much rain hit the ground, anyway, it seemed to him, much of it trapped above them in the canopy.

It was late afternoon when they turned around. Hal wasn't sure how it happened, but they turned, and he was so grateful he smiled as he stood watching them file past, waiting to bring up the rear again. The lieutenant told him they were headed back to the boats.

"That's it?" said Hal.

"We've been walking six hours give or take," said the lieutenant, nodding. "We got no sign since the campsite. We're tracking thin air. We got a timepiece, that's it. Plus there's a storm moving in. And we don't want you collapsing on us."

"Me?" asked Hal weakly, and as he fell into step behind them wondered if they were turning around for his sake. He wanted to weep with gratitude.

•

It was night when they got back to the boats, dark and raining. Hal could barely see—was so blurry with fatigue he blundered along the trail, slipping, with his eyes on nothing but the back of the man in front of him. That was his fixed point, that was his everything. He heard greetings in front of him, saw the shine of water beyond the light of the boats, but registered nothing more in the dark except the fact that he could sit down now, he could sit down. His legs shook violently as he sat and someone put something on his back, a blanket, then put a hot drink in his hands—a hot drink. How? But he did not think, he only drank and rested his bones. It was hot chocolate, possibly. Sweet and thick.

Hans was beside him, sitting in the boat, a clap on the back.

". . . sorry," said Hans. "But C Team believes it located a guerrilla training camp. In that sense the mission has been an exceptional success. And they have you to thank."

"Gorilla?" asked Hal, barely above a whisper.

"Guerrilla. Guatemalan guerrillas. Possibly Mayan."

"I see," said Hal, and something vague went through his mind about Rigoberta Menchú and the Peace Prize. The killing of civilians; the Guatemalan refugees, straggling to Mexico . . . but he was tired, too tired. He couldn't think of it now. He drank, half-dropped the empty cup at his feet. He wanted to slide down, lie down on Hans's lap. Maybe he could. But no. Other side: a clean slate.

Fumbling, he spread out the blanket on the seat beside him, where Hans was not.

". . . in troops," Hans was saying. "Possibly airpower."

"Humanitarian?" asked Hal weakly, but he was already lying down, arranging the side of his face on the blanket. He felt the hardness beneath it against his cheek, but it did not stop him.

• • • • •

As he trudged up the dock to the hotel he had the dawn at his back, bands of pale pink over the sea. Exhaustion was making him woozy, unsure of himself; it took over everything. He might still be dreaming. There was a crick in his neck. *Old man*. The palm fronds dipped a little in the breeze off the ocean, almost bowing . . . he and the palms deferred together, it seemed to him, his bent neck and their dipping fronds.

The beach was deserted except for a short wide guy in a baseball cap, raking sand. Hal went by him and pushed up the hill, passing beneath a coconut palm. A falling coconut could kill you if it hit you on the head. The neurotic bohemians had said so. Everywhere there were hazards, waiting.

He turned and looked back at the sea but there was a mist above the surface and he could barely make out the powerboat anymore. Was he losing his vision? A ridiculous thought. But there was something unreal about all of it. As though eyesight could be stolen, like an object . . . he felt a sudden panic and rubbed his eyes. It was a mist, that was all. Fuzzy whiteness.

He kept going toward the buildings. He'd been jolted awake a couple of minutes before by the harelip cadet, who put a small, hesitant hand on his shoulder as the engine throttled down in the shallows. He was groggy, having slept, almost reeling from it, but at the same time there was an edge of anxiety. If he lay down in the hotel bed he was afraid he would toss and turn and have to get up again. The morning light might seep in.

He wanted to talk to Casey, but what would he say to her? His exhaustion, the blur of it . . . first he needed more sleep.

Passing a fence he heard the light, plastic *tic tic tic* of a ping-pong ball hitting the table. He knew who it was. The cornboys were early risers, and this did not surprise him. He would not talk to them, though, he would avoid them neatly. No question. Their English was limited to single words they pushed out with a kind of belligerence. The last time he'd encountered them all they did was jab their fingers at items they were holding or wearing and assert the brand name. "Coca-Cola." "Swatch." "Nikes."

The more he pondered it the eerier it got.

He brushed past clusters of pink flowers on vines growing over a white trellis—*stapled* there. Wait: he leaned in close and saw the tendril of vine was *stapled* to the wood. Was it plastic? He had the suspicion the whole place was fake, was a façade—now that he thought about it, the cornboys in their eeriness were a little unreal, as all of it was turning . . .

The *tic tic tic* of the ping-pong ball, no one at all on the beach but the man raking sand, *scritch scritch scritch*. If not fake, the place must be abandoned. There was only a silence behind those faint sounds—like everyone had filed out of here in the night, faded away and left it empty in the gray of early morning.

Even Gretel was fading from him, the best part of it by far, by far . . . receding already like smoke, a wishful invention. But he would always have the shine of the memory. And a shine was all it was, a glow. No one could see it but him.

Still it shone.

At the moment he would actually be comforted, he realized, to run into the bohemians. He knew they were real. The way they got on his nerves would be a reassurance at this point, make the world more solid. With the bohemians complaining and bickering he was not, finally, far from all that he knew. It was too early for them now, however. Unlike the Germans they did not rise with the sun. But later they would be up, drinking their black coffee or espresso or whatever it was they drank . . . it would be good to see them. Ground him. Something like that.

Until then, pass the time—past the dreaminess, how it unsettled him—maybe he should lie down by the pool.

There were clean white towels in a cart on the deck, beneath a blue-and-white-striped awning. He helped himself to two, then another. He lay down on a chaise and covered himself with them.

•

"Excuse me. Sir?"

Coming awake again he realized the sun was higher in the sky but hidden, shedding a cold metallic light from behind the grayness. It was overcast. The towels had fallen off him and he was shivering. He sat up, dizzy. Wretched.

"Sorry, sir."

"Sleeping."

"I apologize. But they said you are looking for me."

Hal stared at the interloper. It was the man raking sand. The unreality . . . as though he would look for this man, as though he went around looking for sand-rakers.

"Who?"

"The manager. Mr. Lindley, right? My name is Marlo."

It was a fog. He sat tiredly on the side of the lounger. Marlo. Yes.

"Right! I was looking for you. Before the armed forces."

He leaned down, wanted to touch the water in the pool and splash it on his heavy face, but then the edge was further than he could reach. He let the arm fall, defeated.

"He said you wished to talk to me?"

"I was trying to find Thomas Stern. You worked for him."

"You are his lawyer?"

"Lawyer? Never. Friend—friend of the family."

"Please. Come with me."

Hal stood up unsteadily.

"Please. This way."

He was missing his belongings. What had he done with them? Wallet in the back pocket. Otherwise . . . he felt unmoored. He was floating. Why not: follow some guy named Marlo.

They went down a path from the pool, through a gate and a yard where the sand-raker said something to another yard guy, an unshaven youth in overalls with a lawnmower. They trudged on through the service area, where guests were not usually welcome, past bags of fertilizer on a pallet, ladders against a wall, rusty tools on a bench, boats turned upside-down and equipment under a tarp. Maybe it was the lack of sleep, but he had to watch his feet to keep from stumbling. Needed something.

A Bull Shot, was what came to him—he needed a Bull Shot, beef broth, vodka and a shot of Tabasco. His mother used to drink them. During a certain era she drank Bull Shots and served cocktail sausages.

"Here. It takes ten minutes, maybe fifteen. OK?"

He must have nodded because now Marlo wanted him to help push the boat off the sand, a small boat with an outboard motor. The man was already wading out, the bottom of his white pants swirling around his legs in the water. In the boat, nothing but wooden benches—no padding and no shade.

He didn't have it in him to object, so he bent down and grabbed the back of the boat and heaved. Then he took his shoes off and stepped into the water after it—his pant legs were soaked right away and he sat down heavily on the back bench, feeling the wet material and the grains of sand against the skin of his calves. Marlo was beside him, pulling the cord, so he groped his way to the center bench.

Head spinning, he was on the water. Again.

Neither of them said anything over the noise of the motor and the thump of the prow against the waves. Hal felt thirsty—a throat-cracking thirst came on him in an instant. Afraid his throat would crack he found himself looking under the rough benches for water bottles—anything!—and seeing nothing but an oar and a plastic bucket, he closed his eyes.

His mother stood at the corner of a bar they had in the rec room in the basement, a basement that opened with sliding doors onto the backyard patio. He remembered trays of the miniature sausages in pastry wrappings, toothpicks stuck in them with colored flags of cellophane, flags of yellow and orange. But something thirsty about it—the dry air . . . his father in a Hawaiian shirt, standing over the barbecue.

"Nadine, dear. Here. Have a Bull Shot," he heard his mother say. Nadine was the lady from across the street. She was getting a divorce, he had heard his parents whispering about it. She wore bright, aqua-colored eyeshadow, far too much all the way up to her eyebrows, which Hal, nine at the time, fixated on until his mother told him to stop staring. Hal had firmly believed the eyeshadow was the reason for the divorce. He remembered his conviction on this point, asking his mother why Nadine didn't just stop wearing it.

Even now he recalled the texture of the eyeshadow, how it made him notice the lines beneath the turquoise sheen on the lady's skin, their fine cross-hatchings.

Susan had gone with him to the funeral—his mother's, not the eyeshadow lady's—shortly after their own wedding, twenty years later. He had held her hand at the side of the grave, which was surrounded by a carpet of something like AstroTurf. He held her hand and felt this contact was the armor worn by the two of them. Armor was what it was, the pair bond, marriage: something enclosing them that offered protection. But it was not metal, finally, it was far too flimsy . . . at different moments in a life you had these companions, blurring around you like figures in stop-motion photography: mother, father, friends of his youth, wife, daughter. Gone.

Not one of them forever.

He was riveted by the pain of this flashing away, this dimming. He would die from it, die from being alone.

He opened his eyes.

"I am so thirsty," he said to Marlo over the engine noise, in the vain hope he might be able to help. But the man only nodded and smiled, probably no idea.

Then they were sputtering to a slow glide. Glancing down he saw the boat was over the shallows again, simple sand beneath them through the light water. No coral, no seaweed. He turned around—he had spent the whole ride facing backward, facing where they'd come from. There was a small beach, some trees—an island, he guessed. A small island.

"Where are we?" he asked Marlo.

"Mr. Tomás's property," said Marlo, as the boat cruised in and the hull scratched over the bottom.

Hal looked up the beach. He could make out what seemed to be piles—piles of what he did not know.

"You go," said Marlo, and gestured.

He had no idea what he was doing here but got out of the boat anyway, waded up the slope of the beach still clutching his shoes. He tried to cross the sand barefoot but there were sharp things in it, little sticks or twigs or something, that hurt him. He had to stop, wavering, hopping to keep his balance as he put the shoes on. Off balance, he almost toppled. The sensation of his wet feet inside the shoes was unpleasant: cold toes and gritty sand.

All he could do was walk toward the piles. Nowhere else to go; there was nothing else here. He felt a prick of fear. Maybe Marlo had brought him out here to kill him. Why? A good question. Still. Hal was middle-aged, exhausted and weak—a natural victim. It was just the two of them.

He turned around and gazed back at the boat, where Marlo stood cupping his mouth with his hands. He was lighting a cigarette.

Up the beach a little further were the collapsed walls of a building, its concrete foundation. What was Hal supposed to be noticing, for chrissake? He was too tired for games. Tired and stupid. He wasn't a forensics investigator. He was no Sherlock Holmes. He noticed nothing, did not even want to have to pay attention. Splintered plywood, chunks of plaster, waterlogged Sheetrock with yellow stains browning at the edges. That was it.

Then someone came out of the trees, a man zipping his fly. A dark, lean man with a full beard, shirtless and half-emaciated, his ribs showing over a concave stomach. A mountain man or hippie. His white painter pants were filthy.

"Who the hell?" said Hal, not meaning to. Then it struck him: this was the man on the boat, the bearded man on the boat he had seen from the scuba island.

"Wait," said the man. He was American. Small mercies. "God! I know *you*."

Hal gazed at him. His eyes were a startling blue against the brown of his face. The beard was brown but blond strands were woven through it; the nose was straight and peeling across the bridge from the sun.

He heard himself laugh nervously. He clutched his arms around himself, then let go.

Yes: he had seen this man standing up in a boat, the day of the scuba dive. It was him.

"T.," said the man, stating the obvious, and stuck out a brown hand. "You're Casey's father, aren't you? The tax man!"

Hal hesitated to take the hand, recalling how it had recently zipped the fly, and was startled when Stern clasped him into a warm embrace.

He felt a tinge of hysteria, then confusion.

"I'm tired," he said, drawing back. "But I'm really thirsty. Do you have some water?"

"Sure, come with me," said the newly brown, bearded Stern.

Wary of where he put his feet—there were rusty nails in the disintegrating Sheetrock—Hal followed droopily over the piles of debris, back through the trees. A sandy trail had been cleared, just wide enough for single file. Thin trees on each side, shiny miniature leaves. A minute later they were in a small clearing. Ahead of them was an unfinished structure of wood built around a tree; Hal saw a camp stove, a tent, a dark-green metal tank. PROPANE, read a red label on the side. There was a folding chair and he sank down into it. Stern was already handing him a cup.

He drank it down, all of it, with closed eyes. His blood was rushing in his ears.

"Have more," said Stern. He took the cup from Hal, filled it and handed it back.

Hal drank the second cup and realized his head was aching again but that he felt better. It was water he had needed, water and sleep.

"Is your head hurting? Your eyes?" asked Stern.

"Yes," nodded Hal. "Yes."

"You're dehydrated. It's a dangerous condition. Just keep drinking, small sips but steadily."

"They're afraid you're dead," said Hal, after a few seconds sitting there nodding and dazed, stroking the near-empty cup with a thumb.

"Dead? Oh," said Stern. "I kept planning to call. I needed someone to look after my dog for a while. I was just about to call."

"We picked her up. She's OK," said Hal.

"I knew the kennel would take good care of her. Place costs a king's ransom."

"She's at my house," said Hal.

"Oh, good," said Stern. "That's great."

"But they've been really worried," said Hal.

It was a letdown after everything to be sitting with Stern, the plastic water cup in his hand. Stern took it to fill it again, leaned over to a jug, a five-gallon plastic jug with a spout. Water gurgled as Stern tipped it forward.

Hal sipped and felt himself shiver and then laughed, a bit wildly. He could hear it but not stop it.

"We had the armed forces looking for you," he said. "It was a search-and-rescue. Organized by Germans."

Stern looked surprised and then barked out a laugh of his own. Hal laughed harder. They were fools, laughing. Uncontrollable, stupid laughter. Hal bent forward, tears running from his eyes. He shook his head to stop himself laughing. Eventually it petered out.

"I miss them. I miss Casey," said Stern, nodding to himself. "Susan too."

"She's having an affair," said Hal. It slipped out.

"Casey?" asked Stern.

"Susan!"

"I see," said Stern, and glanced at him sidelong.

"With that paralegal who works in your office. That young, preppy guy named Robert."

"Robert? Huh," said Stern, shifting in his seat and turning his face upward. He squinted a little at the sky. "Well. I never liked him."

Hal felt a surge of gratitude.

"You know, it wasn't so long ago that your daughter told me," said Stern, "that I should avoid wearing those shirts with the blue pinstripes on them and the solid white collars. You know the kind I mean?"

"Those are bad," agreed Hal. "She was right about that."

They sat quietly, Stern gazing into the distance with a kind of enraptured tenderness.

"And here you are," said Hal. "You're not wearing one. Are you."

They smiled at each other again. A bird squawked.

"I do need a shirt, though," said Stern, musing. "I ran out of them."

"I see that."

"I've been working," said Stern, almost apologetic.

"But," said Hal, "I mean—what happened to you?"

"I'll tell you," said Stern. "You should rest first, though. I'm serious, I think you're pretty dehydrated. Come with me."

He got up, gesturing for Hal to follow him. At the wooden hut built on the tree—a kind of tree-house, Hal guessed—he lifted a piece of coarse cloth that was serving as a door and put his hand on Hal's shoulder, guiding him through. Hal saw a sleeping bag on the rough floor.

"Lie down there for a while," said Stern. "You need to be out of the sun. It's cooler than the tent. I'll get you something for the headache."

Hal did what he said, lay down on the sleeping bag, which smelled a little of mildew but not bad, exactly. A few seconds later Stern was back with two small pills in his dark hand. Hal took them.

"Thank you," he said, and slowly crumpled sideways.

• • • • •

When he woke it was dark out again. He had slept through the morning, slept through the afternoon. He could barely believe it. Time was wrong for him now, out of kilter since the invasion of the armed forces.

He scrambled to his feet. He felt better, almost normal, though there was still a dull throb at his temples. The ache was less urgent. Through a window in the tree-house, if you could call it that—a gap between the planks—he saw the glow of a campfire in the dark and the silhouetted figure of Stern standing a few feet off, back turned.

He lifted the cloth and went out.

"Thomas," he said. "Did the boat go? Marlo?"

"Call me T.," said Stern, turning. He was standing in front of his camp stove, a two-burner thing, Hal noticed, connected to the propane tank by a thin tube that snaked out of it, curling . . . it was balanced on an empty crate. T. held a large spoon, with which he was stirring something in a saucepan.

"T. OK then," said Hal, reluctant. "I didn't mean to sleep the whole day. I can't believe it."

"You needed it," said T.

"So where's my, uh—Marlo?"

"Marlo left."

"He left? He stranded me?"

"I wouldn't put it that way," said T. "You're with me. He had to get back to work. We thought you needed the rest. Dehydration, if it lasts long enough, you know—it can have serious consequences. How'd you get that far gone?"

"I don't know," said Hal. "I think—I wasn't paying attention. Basically."

"Making chili," said T. "From a can, but it'll do. Got a kick to it. Want any?"

"Sure. Thank you," said Hal, and made his way around the fire to the folding chair. He was starving, he realized. Also thirsty again. He looked for his plastic cup. It was back in the tree-house, so he went to get it.

"Make yourself comfortable. There's a bottle of wine sitting on the cooler," called T. as Hal came out again. "Cheap and red.

Probably not the best idea if you're still feeling the dehydration, though."

"I've been drinking too much lately," said Hal. He downed another two cups of water before he reached for the wine.

Slopping cup in one hand, the folding chair in the other, he went around the propane tank and the cooler and plopped the chair down in the sand to sit facing T. It seemed polite, though awkward.

In the trees around them there were the slight sounds of birds, maybe crickets. An insect landed on Hal's arm, a mosquito, possibly, and he slapped at it. He could hear the faint plash of waves through the screen of trees. They were low, scrubby trees not much taller than he was—more like overgrown bushes, really. He let his head fall back on his neck: above him the sky was huge. The stars were more visible tonight. They went on and on.

"So how did you end up down here?" asked T. He was slicing an onion.

"I should be asking you the questions," said Hal. "Are you kidding? I came looking for you, of course. To help Susan. And Casey. You vanished into thin air. Your business, you know—it's not doing so well. You're losing money. For starters. What gives?"

"You know," said T., and shrugged, "the usual."

"The *usual*?"

"Change of priorities. I went on a river trip."

"I know all that, the Monkey River. That guy who you were with? The guide or whatever? Dylan? His brother is worried sick about him. We found his watch at your campsite, maybe."

"Delonn. Not Dylan. But yeah. That's—I need to talk to his family about it, sooner or later. I've been keeping myself to myself. Marlo's brought me some food and supplies while I lay low. Maybe not the best idea. Tactically. It looks bad, if anyone's looking. But what happened was, our first night out, he was in his tent, I was in mine—we each had our own tent, you know?—and I must have been asleep when it happened."

"What happened?"

"He died."

"He *died*?"

T.'s face was in shadow. Hal tried to make out its emotion.

"A heart attack, I think. A stroke, maybe an aneurysm. Something quiet, while he was sleeping. He was an older guy, Delonn. Maybe in his sixties. Still. There'd been this—earlier he had problems breathing, but he didn't seem worried about it."

"Jesus!"

"He was a tough guy, you know, pretty rugged. Carried more weight in his pack than I did. I found him in the morning and what I ended up doing was, I dragged the body back to the boat. I was in shock, I think. I panicked. The boat's propeller broke after that and I ditched the boat. And the body with it. I tried to hike out on foot. Stupid, but that's what happened. I got lost for a while. Finally I made it down to the coast. I don't know if it was days or weeks, honestly. From there I hitched a ride to Marlo's place and he brought me here. Short version."

"It wasn't in the boat, though. I mean, the body."

"I know," said T., a little vaguely. "I noticed that. Yeah. That's a complication."

Hal sat for a second, waiting. He wondered if T. was lying to him. Here, though, he seemed better than he had before. Hal liked him more. Maybe only because he was familiar—after all, Hal had practically even been willing, just a few hours back, to cozy up to the bohemians.

In a strange land you found yourself seeking. Afloat among the aliens, your standards were relaxed.

Anyway, like him or not, T. could still be a liar.

"Shouldn't you probably tell someone?"

"Marlo was going to meet with whoever there was," said T. "He was going to say I was recovering, that I would talk to them soon. I didn't know . . . anyway, but. It should be me. I should go talk to them, I should face the music. You're right. Of course."

"And you didn't call anyone. How come you didn't at least call Susan?"

There was a pause. T. seemed distracted, pondering.

"You like onion? Because I can chop it fine or leave it in these big chunks."

"Whatever."

Hal watched as he tossed the onion into the tin frying pan, pushed it around with the spoon.

"My wife," said Hal a bit stiffly, "is devoted to you."

"I'm sorry for letting her down. Hard to explain. Call it a mid-life crisis."

"But you're what," said Hal. "All of, like, twenty-six?"

He took a slug of his wine. It was nice. The guy looked older at the moment, that was true, with the deep tan, the crow's feet at the corners of his eyes and the uneven beard that gave him the look of a homeless individual. He could pass for forty, if you didn't know.

"I've always done things too early," said T. "When I was seven I was already thirteen. When I was in college I was already in my thirties. Youth passed me by."

"Please," scoffed Hal. "Give me a break."

"It's a mind-set, is all I mean. Partly."

"My age, now," said Hal, "that's when you have a mid-life crisis. Fact I may be having one as we speak."

T. poured the chili out of the pan, dividing it between a bowl and a can marked CHILI.

"I only have the one bowl," he said apologetically, and held it out. "Here."

Hal took it gratefully. He was ravenous. T. was eating too but more slowly, spooning his chili out of the can with a deliberation that seemed incongruous to Hal—almost graceful, even. He looked underfed but apparently was in no hurry to remedy the situation.

Gnats landed on Hal's neck, or maybe they were sandflies—they bit lightly—but they were nothing to the hunger. He polished off the bowlful inside a minute.

"Bit more left, if you like," said T., and handed over the frying pan.

"So what are you, uh, actually doing here?" asked Hal, after he'd scraped it up. "On the island?"

"I was having a hotel built," said T., putting down his can and crossing his legs, leaning back. He held a scratched plastic mug with a coat of arms and some writing on it; Hal squinted to read it in the light of the lantern. There were four yellow lions on a red background. Faded words read CAMBRIDGE UNIVERSITY LIGHTWEIGHT ROWING CLUB.

He rowed for Yale.

"You didn't row for Cambridge, did you?" Hal asked him after a few seconds, and quaffed.

"What? Row?—Oh, this? This isn't mine. This, actually, was Delonn's. It was in our camping stuff. I ended up with it. I didn't really mean to."

Hal was feeling the wine already.

"You go to Yale?" he asked.

"I went to a state school. Where my father went before me."

A relief. Somehow it had seemed to Hal, back in L.A., that Robert the Paralegal was a pale imitation of T.—that maybe Susan saw in him a reflection of her employer, to whom she gave such fealty. Maybe Robert was only a stand-in for T., had hovered at the far edge of his suspicion. Now he found out even T.'s WASP credentials were nothing much. Somehow it was consoling.

In point of fact he himself was a WASP, if he wanted to be literal about it, and specifically a WASP with some recent German background. His mother, long ago, had flirted with genealogical research and once told him the branches of their family tree sprouted nothing but Englishmen, Germans and a few glum, dead Swedes.

Still, it was the WASPs and the Germans that most alarmed him.

"Sorry," he said, "digression. You had a hotel here?"

"It was under construction. The storm destroyed it, though."

"Oh, wow."

"Half-destroyed it, technically, but it was totaled. So I've been demolishing it."

Hal watched as T. poured wine into his plastic mug, emptying the bottle. Luckily Hal's own vessel was still nearly full.

"Didn't know you were quite so hands-on," he said jokily. "What Susan said, you were mostly the brain trust. Not so much on the brawn side of things."

"I've been giving it to the ocean. Piece by piece. I figure it could be an artificial reef. You know, like the old tires they sink in some places, or the wrecks, and then the fish come and inhabit them."

Hal looked at him. He seemed sincere, but maybe there was something absent about him. Maybe he wasn't all there. Like mother, like son, finally. It made perfect sense, of course, with the sunburnt castaway look and the whole tropical island, spurning-society deal.

"Wait. So this is why you haven't called anyone? This is what you're—you know, with your business losing money and all that this whole time? So you can personally, like, lug the wreckage of your hotel into the water?"

"Well, when you put it that way," said T. lightly, smiling, and then gazed past him. "I mean, losing money—so yeah. It's OK, finally. All my life I thought that was the worst thing that could happen to you."

"Uh huh," said Hal. He waited.

"I thought money was real."

Poor guy.

"Well, I tell you," said Hal mildly, as though speaking to an infant. "Admittedly I'm biased, being an IRS man. But I can't think of a lot of things realer than money. I mean, to most people money is life and death."

"So that's two things right away. Life. And death."

"I don't really follow you."

"They're both more real. Living for money is like living for, I don't know, a socket wrench. Unless you're going to do something specific with it, it's a complete waste of time. Obvious to some people, I realize. But I just now figured it out."

"Sure. Hey, I get it. You're talking to a civil servant here. So obviously I'm no high-earning capitalist. I've seen what money can do, though. Take income tax revenues. Social programs."

"That's not what income tax revenues do," said T. softly. "Social Security has its own—"

"Not primarily, maybe—"

"Primarily, taxes pay for weapons. Weapons and war. Always have, always will."

A straw man. Statistically, it was far more complicated than that. Hal could break it down for him. Basic protester stuff.

"Well, tech—"

"I know. Weapons, war, and please don't forget the D.O.T."

"As a percentage of—" started Hal, but the guy was shaking his head.

"Hey. Can I show you something?" he asked. "I've also been building the tree-house. I'm using some of the hotel materials for that. This is an island caye, palm trees and sand, which is what made it buildable in the first place. You know, some of the cayes around here are only mangrove, no real ground to build on. Mostly water. This one is island but it has a lot of mangrove vegetation too, kind of a mangrove-swamp thing on the east side, and the west side is solid ground. Right here we're phasing into mangrove, and those are mostly scrubby. But I found one tree that was tall enough, that was it. Come here," and he rose and Hal followed him, both with their cups of wine in hand.

There were rough steps up the tree with the lean-to beside it, pieces of wood hammered clumsily onto the narrow trunk. Whatever else the guy was, he was no carpenter.

At the top there was a platform, several layers of plywood with holes cut in them for the topmost limbs, which stuck out like grasping arms. Hal pulled himself up behind T., unsteady.

"Is this thing safe?" he asked.

T. shrugged. "Enough."

They both stood looking out over the mangroves, over the low tangle of vegetation eastward to the open ocean. Nothing around them but air; at only twenty feet up they were the highest point for miles.

Hal saw a huge ship far out on the water, dazzling with light.

"Cruise ship, huh," he said.

"You can see from here to the utter east," said T. softly. "All the world ends in sea."

The wind picked up the branches of the trees that ringed their clearing, swept through and subsided again.

"Right," said Hal.

So the guy was maybe not doing too well, mental-wise. It happened. He had been in an extreme situation—lost in the jungle, pretty much. He had a little breakdown, or maybe an epiphany; he found God, he saw the error of his ways, he renounced the accumulation of capital. Good, fine, and even excellent. More power to him. Let him become ascetic, live in a small hut with zero Armanis. At last Susan could stop working for him.

Hal's new fondness was a pleasant enough sensation. The man

who used to be Stern had a gentle demeanor now, or that was what it felt like. Maybe Hal could even serve as his advocate with the Belize authorities, if it turned out he had committed a crime. If he had, for instance, murdered the tour guide, say, and that was why he had spiraled out of control and was building tree-houses and forgoing personal grooming. Hal could stand beside him like a brother.

He drank his wine and felt the cool breeze on his face and the warmth in his throat.

"Not a bad place to be," said T. "Is it?"

But wait, maybe this was why Marlo had asked if he was a lawyer. When he first woke him up by the pool, Marlo had asked if he was a lawyer. Maybe the guy knew he needed a lawyer. Maybe Marlo had already called for one.

"Not at all," he concurred, and looked up into the dark blue. It was light up here, the wind lifted you as though you could soar or fall, and let it, you wouldn't mind. Stars were visible, but soft and washed out by the water in the air, not like infinite separate pinpoints he'd seen once in the desert.

They had gone camping in Joshua Tree one weekend, Susan and he, not so long after the accident, because they had to get out, they had to go anywhere, they had to escape, and it was the closest empty place they'd heard of. Casey was in rehab then—the physical therapy kind, not the drug-using. They'd driven east on the interstate out of L.A., through the miles and miles of industrial sprawl and car dealerships flying their advertising blimps in the gray, smoggy sky along the crowded freeway. Finally they pulled up outside the visitors' center and sure, there was concrete, just like at home, the concrete parking lot; but beyond it there was sand and sand and mountains and sky, and there was air all around them, plenty of room to breathe. The spiky cactus-trees were everywhere, the low mountains, the campsites with gigantic boulders.

What he remembered now from that trip, besides the stars, was how they hardly spoke, he and Susan, they hardly talked at all. But it was not bad, it was not a measure of distance, or it hadn't been back then. It was restful and good, peace in the wake of a long struggle.

Their borrowed tent had a transparent window in the top of it. He had lain there on his back at night, on top of his sleeping bag, and gazed out at the stars while Susan slept beside him. He thought they'd never looked so clear, and there had never been so many.

Casey would like this tree-house, he thought; Casey would love it here. She had looked into flying, flying in a glider. There was a program that could take her up in the sky. She hadn't done it yet, but she still could. He would call her and say do it, do it. To know that lightness . . . it was not the running, not a vision of her once in a race, say, her slim young legs flying, though there had been times like that and he remembered them well enough. Field Day at school, when she was in the hundred-yard dash: he loved to watch her but she complained both before and after the race, even holding her purple ribbon. She did not like running. Hard to believe while he was watching her go, it so closely resembled joy . . . or flying a kite once, on a beach in Cape Cod, her feet kicking up sand on him. There were cliffs near them and the water was far too cold for swimming.

But that was not what distressed him, the memories of running. Only the simple memory of her face—her face without tension, without strain or grief.

"My daughter would like this," he said.

"She would," nodded T.

"I wish I could just take her—take her anywhere," said Hal, with a rush of agitation. He saw Casey in flight, swooping. "Anywhere she wanted to be."

He was staring out at the cruise ship. Its lights were like the lights of the ballroom in the resort—was it last night? No, the night before—dancing with Gretel. The nearness to the water made the lights blur and shimmy, part of the very same liquid.

"You know," said T., and Hal realized T. was looking at him, reaching out to rest a thin hand on his arm, "she's going to be all right."

"I don't know," said Hal, but it came out like a sigh. Something about the guy's bearing reassured him—his confidence, his certainty. He said Casey would be all right. So she must be.

"I promise."

No need to move.

Only around the cruise ship was the water dappled with light; other than that it was blackness. Hal did not want to take a step, in case the platform broke beneath him or he fell off the edge, but this was fine for the moment. This was where he was now.

7

The boat was anchored on the east side, where no one would see it coming from the mainland. There was no dock there, only a narrow sandy path through the tangles of mangrove.

After a breakfast of instant oatmeal and water Hal followed T. along the path, ducking between branches. T. carried a canvas sack of his belongings slung over one shoulder. They had swum in the shallows on the other side of the island but the saltwater bath had not made T. seem any cleaner. He was still wearing the filthy painter pants, on which the pockets bulged.

"I have a razor, you can shave at the hotel," said Hal to his back. "Before you get in touch with anyone. Because the cops, I mean if they see you like this, you know, the credibility issue."

"You have to wade out," said T. over his shoulder. "I recommend just leaving your shoes on. There are branches just beneath the surface, things that can cut."

They emerged from the bushes with their feet already in the silty water; the roots of the scrub reached below the surface, long, thin vertical brown lines like wooden drips. Hal felt their knobbiness through the soles of his shoes. The cool water was around his knees now and his feet slipped in the mud beneath. He could see the boat ahead, a long, simple white shape with peeling paint.

"Here we go," said T., and dropped his sack in. He climbed over the side and held a hand out to Hal. "Help?"

"I'm fine," said Hal, and stepped in awkwardly, the boat rocking.

•

As the motorboat throttled down, nearing the beach, Hal realized they had an audience: Gretel. Gretel and the cornboys.

She was watching them from the swimming dock a few hundred yards away, standing on the sand in her blue bikini and shading her eyes as she looked out over the ocean toward them.

The cornboys, in overlarge sunglasses and a hot-pink double kayak, were paddling toward Hal and T.

Gretel raised her arm and waved.

"One of the Germans," he told T., who was easing them into a slip. He waved back at her, trying to seem casual, which luckily was not difficult in the wave format.

Did she regret it? How deeply? Was she kicking herself? Seeing him now she would probably feel repulsed. Then again, maybe she would not notice him: he had T. in his company, the prodigal son. T. would demand her attention by not being dead.

"The Germans?"

"With the whole Coast Guard search thing? Looking for you? Her name is Gretel. The pink kayak? Those are her kids."

The cornboys were bearing down. They paddled fiercely, their small mouths clamped into grimaces that indicated they were trying desperately to win. Yet there was no competition.

"Hey, guys," called T., throwing his rope over the piling. "How's it going?"

"Their English is rudimentary," said Hal.

"My father went to get the airplanes," called one of the cornboys proudly, slowing the kayak with his paddle.

"Yes," nodded the other. Hal was still unclear as to whether in fact they were twins.

"Sounds pretty good to me," said T., bent to his knot-tying. "The English."

"I never heard them say that much before," admitted Hal.

"Airplanes!" repeated the second cornboy.

"Gotcha," said Hal. "He went to get the airplanes. Good to know." No idea what the kid was talking about, but who cared. Wanted a shower, actually; wished he could have had one before he ran into Gretel. Not that it mattered: he expected nothing, or less than nothing. But just for the dignity.

T. was climbing up onto the dock; Hal followed him. The cornboys were staring at them in that way children had—staring with no goal in mind, just like it was normal.

"This is the man your father was helping me look for," said Hal.

"The dead one?" asked the first cornboy. He tended to speak first; probably the Alpha. Possibly he was older, but they both looked the same.

"Exactly," said Hal, and hoisted himself onto the dock after T. He wanted clean, dry clothes, and the sun was making him squint.

Gretel stood at the end of the dock now, one hand on a hip, smiling quizzically; she was curious about T. already.

"Hi there," she said as they approached.

"This is the guy," said Hal. "This is him. Thomas Stern."

"No way!" said Gretel, and leapt into T.'s arms, hugging him. "Oh my God! You're alive!"

"I feel bad to have caused all this trouble," said T., and pulled away gently.

"*Doch*, the important thing is that you are *safe*," said Gretel, beaming joy as though he was a long-lost friend. Hal stood by with his arms dangling, awkward.

"Well, thank you," said T. "I am. Thank you."

"I'm going to get him cleaned up," said Hal apologetically. "We'll see you a little later?"

"Yes, please," said Gretel. "I want to hear the whole story!"

"Of course," said Hal.

"OK," said T., and they left her smiling at their backs.

"She actually means it, I think," said Hal.

"I can tell," said T.

•

Hal lay down on the hotel bed while T. took a shower. The sound of its steady falling was a hello from the civilized world. *Welcome home.* He listened with his head on the soft pillow, his body on the long, solid bed. What a relief. It was so good to have them. The pillow and the bed. The lights, the air-conditioning, and the running water. He was no nature boy. T. could keep his tree-house, no matter how good the view. There was a reason their hominid ancestors first stood upright and started beating smaller creatures to death with cudgels. It was better than what came before, that was why.

The whole atavistic thing was overrated at best.

There had been a shaving kit in T.'s suitcase, which the manager had handed over to Hal several days ago now—a shaving kit and clean clothes, and T. had taken them both into the bathroom with him. But still Hal worried he had failed to impress upon his new friend the importance of a mainstream appearance, when dealing with authorities in a third-world country, and when there was the corpse of a local involved.

Sure: in the past the guy had been Mr. Mainstream. In the past the guy wore Armanis and refused to get behind the wheel of anything but a Mercedes. Once Susan had been forced to rent him a Lexus, when his Mercedes was at the shop for service. To hear her tell it the guy had suffered a martyr's holy torments.

But he was not that guy anymore. No indeed. Now he was a guy who ate chili from a can, had long toenails and a wiry beard that almost grazed his nipples, and apparently sported a well-worn, formerly white baseball cap—now sitting humped on the nightstand next to Hal's bed—whose inside rim was ringed with a crust of brown stain best regarded as a potential disease vector.

He had to call Susan, of course. He was still tired, felt almost waterlogged with a fatigue that wouldn't lift off, but he had to call her. Duty.

He raised the receiver, then remembered he needed the phone card from his wallet and rolled slowly off the bed to reach for it. As he typed the digits, it occurred to him that she might be in flagrante with Robert the Paralegal—she might not deserve this prompt, nay servile attention. Then the telephone rang on her end, rang and rang until he hung up before the answering machine clicked in. He had to tell her this himself, wanted the clamor of it in person—his reward in the form of her stunned amazement, her astonished gratitude at the good news.

He tried Casey's number next, but the line was busy.

She was probably working.

Lying flat on his back, waiting for the shower to cut off, he considered the likelihood the authorities could be bribed to overlook the problem of a dead tour guide. Of course, to offer a bribe would imply guilt. Were they corrupt? Were they righteous? And where were they, in the first place?

He called the front desk to ask. The nearest police station, said the receptionist, was twenty miles up the peninsula to the north. It was connected to an outpost of the Belize Defence Force, apparently. The cops and the military, in an ominous conjunction. But maybe the young harelip cadet would be there, take pity on them, and intercede with his superiors on T.'s behalf.

Was there a problem? asked the receptionist, still on the line. "No," said Hal, "none at all, thanks." He hung up.

Possibly they would be ill-advised to contact the police after all. Asking for trouble. If T. told Delonn's brother how the guide had had a heart attack, probably the brother would not bring charges. He wasn't the suspicious type. And anyway what motive could T. have for murder?

He must have dozed off then, because when he woke up T.

was standing over him with light around his thin, nut-brown face. The eyes were a piercing blue. Cleaner, wearing a white collar shirt and gazing down at Hal with what appeared to be compassion, he also seemed sanctified. Beneficent.

But he had omitted to shave, just as Hal feared. The long beard still stuck out stiffly from his chin like a useless appendage. He looked like one of the Hasidim. Or even a saint or Jesus.

Although Jesus was seldom pictured in collar shirts. They had not been popular at the time.

"Sorry," said the Jesus-T. softly. "I didn't mean to wake you. You can go back to sleep. I'm taking off for a while."

Hal sat up, jolted.

"Taking off? Taking off where?"

"Headed to Monkey River Town. With Marlo. Sit down and talk to Delonn's brother."

"Good, right," mumbled Hal, rubbing his eyes. "You're coming back here after, right?"

"Should be back by sometime around dinner," said the Jesus-T., nodding. "Don't wait on me though. Time runs slow in these parts."

"All right then," said Hal weakly, and lay back as the Jesus-T. receded. The room door closed softly.

The Jesus-T. left the scent of soap and toothpaste. At least he had used them.

•

A short time later Hal made his way to the hotel restaurant for lunch, himself freshly washed. He was spooning up soup and halfheartedly reading the paper when someone jostled his elbow: a cornboy, probably the Alpha.

Both of them were hovering, shirtless and dripping, in wet shorts. They held fluorescent boogie boards under their arms.

"Hey," said Hal, wiping his mouth with a napkin.

"Where's the dead guy?"

"He went to a meeting."

"You finished?"

"You mean—my lunch? No," said Hal, mildly astonished. "I just started it."

"My mother wants to see you."

"Uh . . ."

"You talk to her. OK? Then we go snorkel."

The waiter leaned down and removed his soup plate.

"She gets bored. She likes friends. You talk to her."

"Where's your father?"

"In the airplane."

"*Im Hubschrauber,*" intervened the Beta, shaking his head.

"Yeah, right. A helicopter," said the Alpha. "He took a helicopter to get to the airplane."

"Dolphin HH-65A," nodded the Beta, enunciating perfectly.

"I'll be happy to talk to her," said Hal. His club sandwich had come. He took a sip of iced tea. "Right after I eat. OK?"

"We are in front. We are by the ocean."

"OK," said Hal. "I'll come find you. Promise."

He watched them jog away, picking up a fry and dangling it over the small paper cup of ketchup. Were they actually concerned for their mother? Or was the snorkeling more the point? Or had Gretel sent them? Hal thought not. Their expedition had seemed self-directed. Gretel would have come to talk to him herself, if she wanted to. He might go over to her and then she might not be glad to see him. She might not want to talk to him at all, at least without T. in the mix. Possibly he could tell her T.'s story to cover up the awkwardness.

When he finished he took a chocolate-mint from the dish next to the cash register, popped it in his mouth and made a side trip to the bathroom in the lobby, where he splashed cold water on his face and combed his hair with his fingers. Nothing between them, in a linear sense: no future, no expectation. But still.

And he should call Susan again. Soon.

In the sun his eyes smarted. He had left his sunglasses in the room. He walked through canvas beach chairs, umbrellas, both with white and blue stripes, matching; hammocks were strung between tree trunks, his fellow hotel guests lying on them unmoving, fleshy and naked like human sacrifices. Mostly fat. Or fattish. He saw brown bottles of lotion with palm trees on them, dog-eared paperbacks splayed open on towels. One man had on a Walkman, and a tinny beat issued forth.

Shading his eyes, he looked for the cornboys. They were easy to spot in a crowd, typically.

"Hal!" cried Gretel. She was still excited, apparently, about the nondeath of T. She smiled happily.

She wore an orange and brown sarong below her floral bikini top and looked beautiful, though maybe a little older, he was noticing, or more tired than he had thought previously. Her face was shaded by a straw hat. She held her arms open. He leaned into them. She reminded him, suddenly, of people who mourned celebrities—celebrities they never knew, of course, people who were nothing but symbols to them. Fans at Elvis's grave, for instance. People swaying with candles, or gathered at monogrammed gates holding armfuls of flowers. He had never understood it. The mourners had not even met the celebrities, never seen anything of them but a constructed public image, yet they wept, they swayed, some did violence to themselves.

Clearly the celebrities were symbols to them, and these symbols carried weight. He knew about symbols and their weight, their mystical eminence and power to enthrall. But that did not explain it. If the famous people were symbols, why did it matter when they died? Symbols went on forever.

Gretel had not known T., did not know Susan. How could she care, really? Her beaming happiness. For all she knew T. was a swine, yet she was visibly rejoicing.

"Tell me how you found your friend!" she exhorted, and pulled him underneath her umbrella. The cornboys were in the water. He plumped down on the canvas beach chair beside her, which turned out to be wet. The seat of his pants was instantly soaked and clammy.

"I went to an island," he said, wondering how much credit to take. "An island he owns. He was building a hotel there, before the storm hit."

As he told the story she gazed at his face attentively, nodding and smiling eagerly as though he, too, must feel overjoyed and brimming with triumph. In fact he felt unsurprised, he reflected; T. being dead had never been a foregone conclusion to him. It was Susan who had been so convinced of the worst-case scenario. To him the question of T.'s deadness had been, in fact, basically a matter of indifference—which shocked him, now that he thought of it. His former indifference rattled him slightly, he realized.

Now that he liked T., now that he had appointed himself T.'s protector and ally, how automatic, how thoughtlessly callous the former indifference seemed.

At the same time he was noticing Gretel's breasts, a caramel, tanned color, the scoops of them smooth and perfect where they emerged from the fabric of the bikini. He regretted his former indifference to whether T. was alive or dead; he was mildly astonished to recognize it. But he was more astonished at the beauty of the breasts, barely covered. They hid their light under a bushel. Men were not queued up beside Gretel's beach umbrella, for instance, rubbernecking for a gander. The breasts were here, and yet their presence had not been widely broadcast, though it would clearly be of interest to the general public. He thought of crowds along city streets, waving and straining for a look at the Pope in his Popemobile.

Not so in this case. The breasts were unsung heroes.

Incredible that his own hands and mouth had been on them such a short while ago—a few hours, a couple of days' worth of hours, anyway, many of them passed quickly in sleep. In geological time, it was a second ago—an instant. The sense memory of it . . . no one was mentioning this. Neither he nor Gretel said to each other, right away, we are people who fucked, you fucked me and I fucked you, or made-fucking-love, or whatever. Instead it was as though this fucking had never taken place, and here they were discussing the status of a third party, one basically irrelevant to the fucking and its memory, in a separate compartment. Neither of them was bringing up her tits, her ass, how he had been all over all of them and also in the deep interior of her personal and individually owned body, to which he had no right at all but had been granted, for a few fleeting minutes, a provisional entry.

Neither of them was bringing up this list of items, these glaringly real items whose reality was greater, in fact, than most other realities, at the moment. At least for him. While genuinely regretting his callousness—which no one else knew of, and which was therefore a secret even more than what had passed between him and Gretel was a secret, because in that case she, at least, knew of it also, whereas no one at all knew how indifferent he had been to the alive- or deadness of T. (he was so grateful, as always, for the privacy of the mind)—he was far more interested in the fact that he did not want to escape from any of them, Gretel's tits, her ass, even the softness and sweet, almost babyish smell of her inner-thigh skin. He wished it had not all happened in the dark, so he could have better recall, could see things as well as remember the feel of them . . . but now the tits and the ass, the soft, musky thighs with their hideaway—or at least the darkness that had surrounded all of these during his only contact with them—were added to his list of regrets. Which was ridiculous. Regretting his indifference, which had actually hurt no one, and now regretting the darkness, which he had not chosen.

"I hope you don't think badly of me," he blurted, interrupting his own droning and semi-vacant narration of the events associated with T. He was bored of it.

"Of course not!" said Gretel. "What do you mean?"

He shrugged, awkward. Maybe there had been a tacit pact between them never to mention the sex, the adultery, whatever you wanted to call it. Now broken.

"Your friendship is important to me," he said, lying. It was a lie, and yet not in spirit, because *she* was important to him—just not her friendship, per se, which was, given the logistics of their situation as well as the marital pairings, unlikely to the point of sheer impossibility. Could they be friends in theory, separate but aware? And what would be the point? "That's all."

"You don't have to be embarrassed," she said, and put her hand on his knee.

"It's not a problem, then?"

"No problem," she said, and smiled. She squeezed the knee lightly. It was as though she had nothing to hide, and nothing immoral or illicit had ever passed between them.

But the touch of her hand made him want to have sex again, with sudden desperation.

"*Mutti! Mutti!*" called a cornboy, and the two of them were running toward the umbrella, kicking up sand.

Gretel removed her hand, but not too hastily. Somehow her every movement was both graceful and casual. He wondered how she managed it.

"*Der hat eine grosse Qualle gefunden!*"

"A jellyfish," she explained to Hal, and turned back to the boys. "Use your English! Did it sting anyone?"

"No." They shook their heads.

"Good."

"Coke please."

"Me too."

"How many Cokes have you already had today, Stefan?"

"Two."

"Three," tattled the Beta.

"That's enough, then."

"Please?"

"Please?"

She sighed.

"Look in my bag, then."

They rummaged for money in her purse while she laid her head back and stretched her gleaming legs out beyond the umbrella's shadow. "We haven't lived in the States for that long, you know? They are still learning."

"T. thought their English was very impressive," said Hal, as the cornboys ran uphill again toward the poolside bistro. As he said it he felt the dynamic between them returning to normalcy, to the politeness of regular behavior. In the shift whatever had been intimate was lost, the raw, open thing between them was covered up and buried.

Which was an ending, but also a relief.

• • • • •

He tried Susan again from the telephone in his room, and she picked up on the third ring.

"Susan? I found him," he told her, in a voice that was carefully solemn. Suspense.

"Oh my God," said Susan, low. He heard her fear and felt a remorseful pang.

"He's fine," he said quickly.

"What?"

"He's fine. He's grown a beard."

"You're kidding."

"No. Really."

She screamed on the other end. It sounded like she'd dropped the phone. It was a minute before she came back.

"I can't believe it," she said breathlessly. "Hal! I can't believe you found him!"

"Seems he had an experience," said Hal. "He has a new opinion about capitalism. He's a changed man."

"But he's in one piece. He's all there?"

"He's physically fine. Thin though. You can see his ribs sticking out."

"But so, so why didn't he call me? What is he *doing*?"

"I think he had a breakdown, or something. He may need help. In the readjustment process. He's been living in the middle of nowhere like a hermit. No running water. Or electricity."

"*T.*? My God. I can't believe this. So when is he—is he coming home soon?"

"We haven't got it worked out yet. His tour guide died—"

"My God!"

"—is what happened. He was on a backpacking trip and he had to hike out alone. He got lost. It was a near miss, sounds like."

"God! Get him to call me, then, Hal. Get him to call me right away. There are things I can still salvage, if he calls me now. I mean finances, legal situations. He would want me to, I know it. If I still can. I should try. Would you please?"

"I'll try. But he's not all there, Susan."

"Just get him back here then. Get him back here. We'll take care of him."

It irritated him somehow, the assumption that T. would prove malleable in her hands and she could automatically mold him into his former shape.

"Who will? You will? You and Robert?"

There was a pause.

"I'm saying we need to have him taken care of, Hal. With access to services. Expertise and—and medication, if he needs it. It wasn't so long ago he had his loss, you know. This is still fallout from that, I'm guessing. You know, his girlfriend—her dying was out of the blue. But he never did any bereavement counseling. None."

He felt resistant to answering.

"Hal?"

"I'll do what I can," he said finally.

Selfishly she dwelled only on the functioning of her office, the linear track of returning to normal. As though normal was all she wished, all anyone would ever want to secure. It did not occur to her that normal might be flawed, might be wrong through and through—that maybe T., unbalanced or not, did not wish to be normal, did not want to go back to the steady state she apparently required for him.

"When you get back we should have a talk," she said, softening. "I know you're not happy right now. And it means so much to me that you did this."

"I saw you," he said. "On the floor of the office. In front of the file cabinet."

Silence.

He hung up.

•

Lying on the bed with the television on in front of him, not watching it exactly (it was not in English anyway and seemed to be a Mexican game show involving a tacky, glaring set and flashing lights, whose sound he had muted), he mulled over the various possible effects of his words. She might be considering the option of divorce, whether he wanted it, whether she did, whether this constituted, for the two of them, a divorceable offense; she might be cold to the very core or gleeful and exhilarated, terrified or relieved. She might already have called Robert the Paralegal with the news of their discovery, might have told him what Hal had said, or might never have thought to call him. Among all these, what were his own feelings?

It came to him gradually that he was not angry. His anger had dissipated. He had told her what he knew, and now he was not angry. There was still a sense of disappointment, of letdown—maybe for the unchangeableness of the past, the stubbornness of his unpleasant memories, which were now implanted within him permanently. Maybe for the fact that their marriage had been, in his mind, a pure union, and now it was adulterated. That was what adultery did.

He had wanted it perfect, he thought, but wasn't that a false want? What was perfect anyway? Possibly this new, sullied marriage was in fact more perfect than the previous innocent one, more perfectly expressed the state of lifelong union or the weather of affection. Possibly the previous, innocent marriage, uncomplicated by disloyalty, had in fact been inferior to this one, more superficial. Maybe they were achieving maturity.

On the other hand, it could be simply that the thrill was gone, that it had been eradicated and would never return.

Then again, he was assuming that, just because this was the first time he had caught her in an act of unfaithfulness, this was the first time such acts had occurred. But what if she had been practicing free love down through the years, ever since the Frenchman? (And Casey not his biological—paranoid crap.) What if the marriage had in fact never been what he thought it was? The real instability, real liquid . . .

Someone was knocking; someone looked in the window, through the crack between the frame and the curtain. Gretel.

He had forgotten about his own infidelity in all this. But his own infidelity was of a lower order, or a higher order, depending how you organized your judgment hierarchy. He would never have slept with Gretel were it not for the condom wrapper fragment on his own bedside table, the bad lesbian song playing on the shower radio, Susan and Robert on the floor of the office and his subsequent unmooring. It was a kind of post-traumatic stress disorder that gave him permission for misbehavior—even a broad series of permissions, airy and limitless as the sky.

It was second-order adultery. That was it.

He opened the door.

"Come for a paddle with me and the boys. Won't you?" asked Gretel, cocking her head and smiling.

It was late afternoon. Hans had not come back yet and neither had T., clearly: and Hal was sick of the silence of the hotel room, the static of his own body laid out on the bed.

He turned around, grabbed his sunglasses and bottled water, and followed her out of the room, down the stairs and onto the beach to where the hotel's bright kayaks were arrayed on the sand. They pushed two of them into the placid water, the cornboys in a double kayak ahead of them, and scrambled in.

They were going to head out toward a mangrove caye, said Gretel, and pointed to it. A quick trip before sunset. It was about a half-hour's paddle to the southeast, and on the other side there was supposed to be a small reef. She had extra snorkeling gear, if Hal wanted to use it. She handed him a hat to wear—one of Hans's, no doubt. It was emblazoned with the single word BOEING.

The two of them lagged contentedly behind the boys, who raced ahead, locked into their perpetual battle of speed and strength. Once more they fought an imaginary opponent. Hal paddled at a leisurely pace.

"They have found some kind of rebel camp," said Gretel after a while. "Hans did what they call a flyover. In a plane with someone from the Marines, or something."

"Rebel camp?" asked Hal.

"Guatemalans, I think."

"Correct me if I'm wrong," said Hal, mildly alarmed. "Isn't the army the bad guy, over there? Doesn't it do genocide?"

"I don't know about the politics," said Gretel apologetically. "Hans just said they were guerrillas. He said it was an armed camp of guerrillas that came from over the border."

"Over the border is Guatemala, right? And if it's the Mayans, they're probably escaping a fucking massacre! I mean there are official refugee camps for them in Mexico. You haven't read about this? There was a genocide going on, a couple of years ago. Civil war. All this shit with the CIA propping up the military there, the generals that are smuggling cocaine through to the U.S. from Colombia or somewhere—remember that woman who won the Nobel Peace Prize? Rigoberta Menchú?"

Gretel shook her head.

"What the hell," said Hal, and mulled it over, making deep, slow strokes with the paddle. What were they up to after all, those toy soldiers? Rigoberta Menchú: in all the pictures she wore bright, printed clothing. Cloth tied around her head, typically, and she had a brown, broad face, smiling. The smiling face was at odds with the reports of various family members of hers, shot dead or burned alive. He only half-remembered.

The Marines, or the Coast Guard, whichever branch of the armed forces they had been: while he was with them he had been pathetic, reduced to childishness. They were strongmen; he was nothing but a victim. What felt like a death march to him had been a pleasant day hike for them. You could be brought down to that—to contests of strength, to the brute force of physical superiority, if you put yourself into the situation. And it was a plain situation, a simple one, the situation of survival. That day, on that walk, nothing but the basic, primitive unit of the body had mattered. His unit had failed him.

But now he was thinking of those same Marines with condescension, as they must have thought of him, because their subjugation was permanent and far worse than it had been, briefly, for him. They were muscular windup dolls, forced to do the bidding of men of greater ambition. It was their job description.

The cornboys pulled ahead, further and further away from Gretel and him. There were powerboats on the water, though none were close at the moment. He thought of the jellyfish the boys had seen, the sharks, the rays—a great sea beast rising from the depths and lifting their kayak from below, capsizing it. Their small bodies splayed and sinking . . . but Gretel was relaxed. He looked over and saw her bronzed limbs, lazy but perfect in the sun, as she lifted and tipped her paddle. She looked up and smiled at him. He felt lulled, the awkwardness between them evaporated. They had started in water, in the cool blue, and here they were on the water again. It was all right. Gretel had her boys up ahead of her and him by her side—a temporary companion, sure. But then they all were.

That was it: that was it. She let her sons go ahead, and she was not worrying. He too had freedom, a strange freedom in this adultery, this strange and half-lonely honeymoon. The dissolution of everything. Because he had forgotten Casey this trip, he had been emancipated from her—Casey, who since he arrived in this foreign place had not, for the first time in years, guided his every impulse. For a time he had left her behind; the weight of carrying her had been released.

But for the years before that, what had he been doing? He felt a sudden panic. Wasted. He had wasted them.

He had lost them, and only realized the loss now, like a bolt, shocking. Like a nightmare: time shifted and the years of your life were gone. The light shimmered sideways over the water.

He had forgotten his wife, mostly. He loved her, but all this time he'd practically forgotten she was there. Susan had been left to her own devices, alone and in the cold while he dreamed his soft dreams of regret. That was what had happened to the two of them, nothing mysterious. He had drifted away to his memories of his daughter as she had been, the cycles of blame, remorse, longing. He had been somewhere else all the time, in spirit if not body—not with his actual daughter, for the time he spent with her in the course of a day or a week was normal, regular time, not a nightmare or dream, but the daughter he once had, or the daughter who might have been. He was like an enchanted man. That was who he had been, all these years, a man under a spell, a man absent without knowing his own absence. He had been gone, but he had not noticed. He had not noticed himself or Susan, had noticed neither of them. All he had known was remorse. He spent his life knowing it.

And so Susan had disappeared too. Of course. Even her job was a form of her disappearance. The job, her allegiance to it, the affair—it was all the stuff of her life, while he was not.

Susan had vanished for a simple reason: she had nothing better to do.

It was his fault. And here on the long, blind road he had been blaming her.

• • • • •

He used Hans's snorkeling equipment, his blue mask and fins. Putting them on he thought fleetingly that he was borrowing everything from Hans.

But Hans did not register its absence.

The corals were not so bright here as they were further out, toward the barrier reef—dying, he suspected, some of them dead already. He had read at the hotel that this year, suddenly, corals were quickly bleaching in Belize. But fish still moved among them, their bright bodies flashing among the worn gray humps like the Mohawks of teenage punks drinking in a graveyard. He saw small fish, mostly, but it felt good to follow them for a while and watch them disappear.

Gretel decided they should go up when the sun began to sink

and the water was darkening around them. It grew harder to see. After they surfaced he held her kayak steady for her while she clambered in, treading water with his free hand, and then she leaned over and held his.

The cornboys, blue-lipped, were already waiting, eating half-unwrapped chocolate bars and jiggling their legs, feet braced against the footrests. Without a wetsuit the coldness of the water had sunk in; Gretel's golden skin was goosebumped. The end of day cast violet shadows on her, on all of them. Quickly the surface seemed almost black.

•

When they put in at the hotel beach again people were eating dinner at the outdoor tables, beneath the bistro's palm-thatch awning. Citronella candles were burning on the tables and Hal could smell their bitter lemon edge as he walked up the beach.

"Bring T. and join us for dinner, won't you?" urged Gretel, and he said he would, as soon as he showered and changed.

But T. was not in the room, and there was no message light blinking on the telephone. He took his shower quickly, anxious, and was bent over his open suitcase with a towel around his waist when Marlo knocked at the door.

"Mr. Tomás had to go with the police," said Marlo. "He wanted me to tell you."

"Go with them?" asked Hal. "What do you mean?"

The towel fell as he lurched forward. He grabbed it and held it up tightly.

"They took him to detention," said Marlo solemnly.

"Detention? They arrested him?"

"First to Dangriga, then Belize City."

"I mean—why? Is it serious?"

"Because of the death. You know?"

"But it was an accident!"

Guests passed behind Marlo, a family with long-haired young girls. Self-conscious, Hal stepped back and waved him in.

"The brother, you know? He did not want to press charges. But then there was a neighbor who asked them to come. This lady—she does not like Americans. The soldiers, the other day, I think one of them was rude to her daughter, you know? So then they came. There will be an investigation."

"Jesus!"

Central American jails did not boast a good reputation for client services. He would have to leave right away for the city.

"I'll go up there. I'll pay his bail, or whatever. I'll get him a lawyer. Can you get me a car to the capital? Or a plane?"

"Tonight?"

"Tonight. Right now. I mean he's in jail, right?"

"They are taking him there."

"Then I need to go right now. I have to get him out."

"The flights from the airport in Placencia? They go in the daytime."

"Can't I charter one or something? It's what, to Belize City—a half-hour flight?"

"I will see. I can see."

He dressed in a hurry after Marlo left, stuffed his clothes messily into the suitcase with a sense of growing urgency. Anything could happen. The guy was *non compos mentis*, and they had arrested him. It often happened to the mentally ill, even in the U.S.—since Reagan anyway. They were let out onto the streets, wandered there, and were promptly arrested for the crime of existing. Then jail, insult added to injury. He would not let prison violence happen to T. Just when the guy was acting human for the first time in his life and abandoning his Mercedes-Benz fixation, they went and arrested him.

A man turned away from the path of Mamm on and that was what he got—thrown into the hoosegow.

In the lobby Marlo was talking to someone in Spanish, a bald guy in a satiny red windbreaker. The guy was shaking his head—a bad sign, surely.

"Is it going to happen?" asked Hal, and thankfully Marlo nodded, consulting his watch.

"He will drive you to the airfield," he said. "Five minutes."

He had to say goodbye to Gretel before then. Who knew if he would ever be back. He headed to the restaurant and stood in the doorway looking, but could not see her at the tables. No cornboys either. Their white-blond hair was a beacon. He would have to go to the room. It disturbed him, but it could not be avoided. Up the sandy cement of the stairs—was it 323? 325? He knocked at the first one. He had three minutes left. He hoped Hans was not there. He had no time for avionics experts.

A cornboy opened the door, video game in hand.

"Your mother in?"

The door opened further and the cornboy faded. Gretel had her hair twisted up in a towel but was fully dressed. Thankfully.

"Listen, I have to go," he said. "They arrested T. The local authorities. They took him to Belize City. I have to go get him out. I'm flying."

"My God," said Gretel. "Arrested? Him?"

"Because of the tour guide dying. The heart attack. Remember? But now they want to investigate it, apparently. I have to fly to the city, try to meet them. Post his bail or bribe someone. We can't have him in there."

"Yes!" said Gretel, nodding hastily. "Of course. You should go."

"So," he said. "I guess, goodbye?"

He leaned forward to embrace her, awkward as usual.

"You'll get him out. I know you will. You are a good friend," said Gretel with her arms around him. She smelled like cinnamon.

"Thank you," he said. He was late now, for the driver.

He smiled at her again. Should he ask for her phone number, or something? Cheesy.

"Wait," he said. "In case you ever come to Los Angeles." He slid his messy wallet out of his back pocket, slipped out a business card. "This is me."

"Thank you, Hal," said Gretel softly.

He backed out of the room, turned and took the stairs two at a time. When he glanced over his shoulder she was braced against the railing of the balcony gazing down at him, face in shadow, the towel standing tall on her head like a crown.

•

The airport was a small trailer with a dirty linoleum floor, fluorescent lights overhead and a desk at one end with a few papers piled on it, an olive-colored metal lamp on a bendable arm and a stained paper coffee cup. The lights were on but no one was around, yet Hal was supposed to meet his pilot. He went to the bathroom, the size of an airplane toilet, and when he came out he saw a light through the building's glass door.

On the airfield—all grass and weeds with a single thin, short runway that looked more like a driveway—sat a small plane. He pushed the back door open and walked over the grass toward it, suitcase in hand, slapping against his leg. It was almost completely dark out; a couple of lights on the runway had halos around them, and then there were the small lights of the plane itself and the squares of yellow that were its windows. The plane was small and white with a blue stripe on the side—a four-seater, he saw when he got close.

Its propeller was already whirring, there was a door open, and the pilot was seated, wearing a bulky headset. Hal put a foot up on the rim of the door to step in.

"Here, here," said the pilot, and gestured for him to sit up front. It was tight, barely room to move.

"This?" asked Hal, raising his suitcase.

"Back there," said the pilot.

Hal was sure they would skim the trees on takeoff. The night outside was daunting from the tiny cabin of the plane, its bottomless dark; he wore the headset the pilot had given him, but they hardly spoke. He recalled a phrase an FAA guy had once used with him on a commercial flight, discussing Cessnas just like this one: *single-point failure.* No backup systems in case of malfunction. As they taxied and rose up above the runway he willed himself beyond the plane, out of the frail and shaking capsule into the rest of his life.

L.A. was spread out far to the north, gray and blond and spidering everywhere—its fastness, its familiar blocky strip malls and wide boulevards with their unceasing traffic and smog and the glamorous jungly hills that rose above and housed the royalty. Everything was the same; his house was the same, even, full of the mundane objects he knew so well . . . by now Susan had told Casey T. was alive. They would both know by now, and Casey, at least, would feel affectionate and grateful. But Susan's gratitude he had foolishly squandered. By accusing her at the very moment of triumph, the moment of revelation, he had squandered all his credit. Such as it was. It should have been a pure gift, the culmination of a gesture that quietly knighted him; instead he had revealed his petty nature, his real motivation for leaving and coming here, thus giving the lie to any idea she might have had about his minor effort at heroism.

He had to get T. out of the hands of the Belizean cops. It was imperative. Both for Susan and Casey and for him, T. himself, because actually he did not deserve it.

A short time ago, before he went to the island, if someone had told him Stern was in jail Hal would not have objected too strongly. Only mildly, for the sake of politeness. He might have held the private opinion, in fact, that a few nights in a Central American hellhole could benefit the Armani-wearing shithead. But not anymore. Now he wanted to get the guy out, partly because he seemed a painfully easy mark, now that he had gone hippie. Hal had always had a weakness for hippies, despite their free-love tendencies. Between them and the libertarians, he'd take hippies. Now—a benevolent-seeming, almost submissive individual—T. was without defenses. He would be instantly victimized, by either the thugs in the police force or his fellow inmates. It was ugly to contemplate.

Often people prefaced a stupid remark with the words "There are two kinds of people in the world," and Hal had always been annoyed by this. The words tended to introduce a false dichotomy, an infantile reduction. At the same time he, too, felt the urge to divide and categorize, the satisfaction of separating the world into discrete parts that could be identified. If T. had once been a person who thought chiefly of himself and his shining Mercedes, he was now something else—if only on a temporary basis.

For it was entirely possible, as Susan had suggested, that he would revert to his usual form once the trauma of the hiking misadventure was past. People tended to settle back into their old routines. Returns to form were standard. Fundamental character change was all but impossible.

Still, for now he more closely resembled the pet lovers, for instance, than Donald Trump or Leona Helmsley. He was like the post-hippie nomads that drove around in painted vans, let their children grow dreadlocks and lived on pennies. He had the beard and the hygiene, anyway. But the key distinction was this: he had gone from being consumed with his own life and advancement to looking outward. Whereas Hal himself, once youth had passed, had gone the other way.

For there had been an interval, while he and Susan were both young, when he too had thought of the rest of the world quite often. He had often thought of justice and liberation, of the good of mankind, etc. But then he had forgotten it.

Except for his job, he had argued to himself over the years, but he had to admit it: even the job had become little more than a sinecure. He could not argue that in going to work every day he made a sacrifice of himself. It was more like a well-fitting shoe that was worn all the time but was never noticed.

If there were in fact two kinds of people in the world, those who faced inward and those who looked out, he had been the latter and turned into the former, whereas Stern, or T., had been the former and turned into the latter. It was T. who was taking the road less traveled, whereas Hal, with all his ideas about a government that protected and sheltered the people, with his lifetime of civil service, had in fact become a typical domestic drone, a man wrapped up in the details of his own life and only his own.

He had acquired the habit of blaming the accident for this. And yes, the accident had made it easier to shelve the concerns of the world, to relegate them to the back burner. But if he was honest, the patterns had been worn into him years before the accident, possibly even from the time when he manipulated Susan into abandoning her commune. He had manipulated her away from her youthful Eden Project ideal out of a sense of desperation, true, but that did not excuse his cynical calculation. He had been desperate to keep her and had reassured himself that love was enough reason for manipulation. But it was selfish and nothing else. Love had been an excuse, more than anything, for greediness. Love and self-interest had coalesced.

And separated from her Mendocino ideal—from the future of fresh air and the fields of organic strawberries—in time she had given up public high-school teaching, with its long hours and low pay and frequent disappointments, and become an assistant to a real-estate guy. This was after the accident, of course . . . she had taken an office job, become an office worker. He himself was an office worker too, nothing more than a glorified clerk, really, but still: who knew what she might have become if, back in 1967, instead of manipulating her he had just let her go?

And it might still have worked out between them. In due

course he might have sought her out again, might have followed her to the commune, gotten down on one knee, and humbly asked Rom to give him a free lute lesson. After a potluck dinner, around a bonfire, Susan might have played the tambourine and sung songs about the giving spirit of trees while he and Rom accompanied her on twin lutes.

And Casey: Casey might have been born in a yurt with a midwife attending, instead of by emergency C-section at the UCLA Medical Center. When she was seventeen she might not have gone driving at all, in that snowstorm in the suburbs of Denver. She might have had different friends, might not have even have decided impulsively that she wanted to learn to ski, wanted to take her turn on the baby slopes, and therefore never have asked Hal and Susan if she could go on a Colorado ski trip with her L.A. friends, who in addition to skiing enjoyed drinking games and fast driving. She might have been, say, more of a horseback-rider type, competed in horse-riding meets in a black velvet cap and tall boots, and had different friends entirely, who knew, friends who did Outward Bound courses or line dancing, friends who won prizes at the county fair for growing outsize tomatoes.

But instead he had followed one urge, a single urge. What was an urge but a quick pulse of energy through the brain? He had followed a jealous, self-protective urge and consecrated his behavior to persuasion. For two or three weeks his attention had been focused entirely on preventing Susan from leaving—on preventing his future wife from realizing her dream.

And that petty urge of self-protection, that small urge that passed through him in seconds, had determined the future for all three of them.

8

As soon as his taxi pulled up alongside the curb outside the small police station he saw the building was locked up tight as a drum, lights off. He got out to check the sign on the door—a paper clock with the hands stuck at seven and twelve—while a streetlight above him flickered and buzzed.

"I don't understand," he said to the driver as he got back in. "What about the jail, then? There has to be some kind of holding cells, at least. Supervised by police. Do you know where that would be?"

The driver shrugged and shook his head.

"But what if there are crimes committed? And someone, you know, a criminal does something and needs to be arrested? I mean, no one commits crimes after the end of the workday?"

"You come back in the morning," said the driver, nodding. He had an accent like the harelip cadet: maybe Garifuna. "I take you to a nice hotel. Your friend be OK. Don't worry."

The hotel had iron gates and a fountain playing in the front garden; its lobby was empty save for a clerk at the long counter, who found him a room right away.

"Maybe you can tell me," said Hal. "The police. What do you do if you have to call the police in the middle of the night?"

"We've never had to call the police," said the night clerk, smiling. "We have a quality clientele."

"I'm sure you do. But let's say something happened—a break-in. Something like that."

"Yes sir, I would report it first thing in the morning," said the desk clerk.

Hal was exasperated. There was no way. Was the man ill-informed, or was it Hal who was wrong? There was no way to know.

In his room, which was small and so cloying he had to open a window immediately, the clock radio read 1:15. He sat down on the bed and took his phone card out of his wallet, keyed in the long sequence.

She picked up after a single ring.

"Hal?"

"Sorry to wake you."

"Actually I couldn't sleep. I called the resort and they said you guys were gone, both of you."

"I had to charter a flight to the city. They arrested him."

While he explained what he thought had happened he was preoccupied with himself—himself and the free love. What to say next, about the rest of it, the rest of their lives and whether there was a future? He was bound up in the saga, his own concerns.

"Suze," he said suddenly. "I know it's my fault. I don't blame you."

"Your fault?"

"I realized, this trip, how I've been preoccupied for so long. I'm always feeling regret. I go around in a daze . . . years now, Suze. For years. But I know it at least. I've seen it now. I mean I already knew it, rationally, but I hadn't . . ."

"It's all right, Hal. You don't have to apologize. Please."

"But you've been . . . I mean, I think somewhere in there I may have left you alone."

She was quiet. He had the window open, and a palm was waving. Outside he heard a car swish down the empty street. Had it rained? They were both alone now. She was alone because years ago he had left her for an idea of loss; he was alone because he had chosen it, without even knowing. He was afloat in the world, its vast and empty spaces . . . far away from his wife and his little girl, in a foreign city where not one person knew him. A silent, sweltering city in a subtropical country, toward the equator, toward the South Pole, toward the black place in the sky around which all the stars seemed to spin.

He was awake in the warm night, alone, while everyone else was sleeping.

The walls of the room felt closer than they were, covered in a dark-red-and-white-striped wallpaper like Christmas wrapping. Beneath his legs, the bed's coverlet was scratchy. Susan always stripped the coverlets off hotel beds as soon as she got into the hotel room. She said they were unhygienic—that hotels never washed them and they were the repositories of bodily secretions and pathogens. In the main she was not too uptight about germs, but when it came to hotel coverlets she made no exceptions.

"We'll talk about it when you get back," she said gently, after a while. "OK? I mean the phone isn't the best for this, you know. This kind of conversation."

"I just want to know if we're going to be all right. If we're going to get through it." He waited for a second, then got up restlessly, holding the receiver. The red wallpaper was closing in.

The cord barely stretched but he made it to the window, gazed through the silhouettes of fronds onto the dark street. She was not answering. The silence was ominous. His stomach turned. "Or if you want to, you know, leave me. And be with that . . ."

He let it trail off. Damned if he would say more.

The wait made his stomach lurch again.

"Be with—? Oh. No, no, no, it's nothing like that, sweetheart. It's not, you know. Anything important."

"I see," he said, nodding invisibly.

He felt lighter, though at the same time his skin prickled with a faint annoyance. It was not important to her, yet for it she risked everything: for a trivial fuck, or series of fucks, she had done this to him. But he should count his blessings. They were still married. It seemed they would probably continue to be. His home was still his home, his wife was still his wife. She was not trying to get away from him. On and on, as always, it would keep being the three of them, him and her and Casey.

"I mean, that's a relief to me. Of course."

He felt almost off the hook, now that he knew. Now that he knew, the familiar was coming back. Already—he felt it—already the strangeness of life was receding. He heard something in the background—was it here or in the background in L.A., across the many miles? No; it was here, it was outside the window. A siren, but different from the sirens he was used to, slower and tinnier. No surprise: in a foreign country the sound of a siren was bound to be a variation on the familiar theme, not an exact replica.

It was amazing, astounding, come to think of it, that even the idea *siren* was replicated throughout the world—and the idea *traffic lights*, for instance, wherever you went: red, yellow and green. (Although in the United States officials insisted on calling the yellow lights "amber," for some consistently aggravating nonreason—like a tic, like an officially sanctioned form of Tourette's. If you had to go to traffic school, say, or take a test for your driver's license at the Department of Motor Vehicles, it was a sure bet the yellow lights would be referred to as "amber," as though the word *yellow*, in this official setting, was somehow regarded as obscene and therefore required a euphemism. It made him glad he did not work for the Department of Transportation, which needless to say had a checkered past anyway. For while the Service was guilty of many things—many bureaucratic complications of a Kafkaesque nature all too easily lampoonable by opportunistic politicians who irresponsibly advocated for harebrained schemes like the flat tax—at least it had the cojones to call yellow yellow.)

The world seemed to be in opposition and even turmoil on many subjects—who would claim the rights to its riches, for instance, who would hold sway from year to year or decade to decade when it came to the rule of law, dominance and extraction, trade or sales or production. On the other hand it presented a more or less united front on who should do the fighting and dying, whose children should starve or die of malaria by the tens of millions. In these matters there was the polite appearance of dispute, in diplomatic and academic circles, but in fact a stasis of hardship on a massive scale that could only reflect, in the end, a kind of global consensus.

And when it came to details like traffic signals and sirens the human population might even look, from outer space, like a single race of peaceful, compliant men.

At first he did not register the siren's significance. Susan was saying something about *emotional rollercoasters,* a term he flatly, privately rejected.

You had aversions, in this life, aversions to foods like granola and terms like *emotional rollercoaster.* You wished to excise these items and the terms for them. But a woman like Susan, despite being highly intelligent, did not know that intuitively nor, if she did, would she necessarily respect the aversions. Instead she ran roughshod over them. In fact, few women respected his aversions.

Men also failed to respect them. People, you could almost say, did not respect the aversions.

Maybe, when all this was behind Susan and him—call it the free love, call it adultery—they could sit down and have a conversation on the subject. He could talk about the importance of aversions, and why the term *emotional rollercoaster* should be, as the Germans said, verboten.

Then the car went by, a light-colored car, its red lights flashing. A squad car, surely.

He should go! He should follow it. Sooner or later it had to take him to some outpost of the police, to what he needed to know.

"I was, at first I was so excited," Susan was saying. "When you told me it was like the best gift I'd ever had, but that, you know, that euphoria of relief—it passes so quickly and regular life comes back. With its own kind of normal and boring pace. You know?"

He had his eyes on the police car's taillights as the car made its way up the street. It had slowed down, it wasn't going that fast. If he ran, he could catch it. Maybe it was right nearby, the police emergency. He should drop the phone and run. He should run up the dark street after it.

Now. Now. Go.

"And now it's just like, I take for granted he's alive and I'm back to worrying about these petty details . . ."

He stayed where he was. It seemed unrealistic, impossible to catch the car. Of course, he would never know.

Standing there, watching the taillights disappear and holding the phone, he felt this had happened to him over and over. He never jumped out windows, never moved suddenly, with a jolt. The lights faded as he stood still and looked at them. He did not leap, did not give chase. It always seemed unfeasible and rash. But there was a defeatism in that, clearly, a submission to ease, a cowardly risk avoidance. The same force that had bound Susan to him through manipulation rather than honesty.

T. would have his night in jail, that was clear. He would spend the whole night in a cell while Hal lay sleeping in the soft hotel bed. Albeit with scratchy coverlet. He pictured a medieval torture chamber, the rack, a rusting Iron Maiden. Then burly sailors.

"You'll find him in the morning. Make sure you get a good night's rest," said Susan.

She did not know, of course, about Gretel, spinning now in a topless dirndl in his memory, German and gold forever.

There was no need for her to know. He could tell her, but it would be selfish, a small and petty revenge.

The private sanctum of the mind . . . he fell back on it gratefully. What a freedom it was, what a perfect freedom. In the future, if he felt lonely, he would have to remember this, remind himself of its benefits—the unending and sweet privacy of thinking. How no one else, no matter how great or powerful, could ever enter here. This place was truly his.

Because if it was painful to be alone, not being alone would be torment. A mind that was invaded by other minds could be nothing more than prison. And yet there were people out there who wanted to believe in ESP, who fantasized telepathy. Maybe what they had in mind was a kind of selective mind-reading? No one sane would want to walk around reading minds in some kind of flowing, open exchange.

Did an ant have a mind of its own? A bee? Uncertain. They seemed to operate differently, dying by the thousands for the sake of a queen and all the time never stopping their work. An ant, a bee, neither seemed gripped by doubt, typically. Doubt had to be a requisite of the private mind. It was a perk of being human: your mind was your own, always and forever a secret territory.

"You too," he echoed softly. "You too."

• • • • •

In the morning he walked out in front of the hotel and got a car to Belmopan, about an hour away.

It was a small town, the capital, and nothing else—grass, palms, scattered pastel-colored buildings. Less slumlike than the city, but with a feeling of vacancy. The embassy was a two-story white, wooden edifice with a porch all around, columns in front, palm trees, a flag and a bright-green, well-kept lawn.

Inside a woman rose from her desk when he came through the door.

"There's an American citizen who was arrested," he told her without preamble. "A businessman. Down in Placencia, but they brought him up to Belize City last night. I have to find him. Get him immediate legal aid. He shouldn't be in there."

"Give me his name," she said. "I'll make some calls."

The secretary went into another room. While he waited he sat in a teak chair and jiggled his leg. The floor was wood and a wooden fan turned on the ceiling; beside him sat a shiny, tall plant whose leaves brushed against his shoulder. He heard the sound of a fax machine dialing. Then the front door opened and two red-faced men came in wearing loud, floral-print shirts. They seemed to be familiar with the premises and moved past him into a back room, talking about sportfishing. One said he'd caught a wahoo, the other a snook.

After a while the secretary came back. She had a man with her, thin and balding, with glasses.

"Jeff Brady," he said. "Public affairs section chief. We don't have staff attorneys, but we do refer out. Not clear yet whether we need a lawyer though. Need to appraise the situation, put out feelers. Be on our way?"

"You found him?"

"We know where they're holding him, yes. Taking my own car, Sarah. Binadu's got the VW. Later."

He drove a small, open jeep, making swift, jerky turns until they got out onto the highway. Hal held onto the door handle. The exhaust of other cars made him cough.

He resolved to act as T.'s staunchest ally. He would tell the diplomat a story that would raise his sympathies.

"He was obviously deeply affected by the death of his girlfriend. I'm not saying he's in great shape emotionally. But he has no history of violence or anything like that. Not even a misdemeanor or an unpaid parking ticket."

"Uh huh?"

"He's a conscientious boss-type guy, my wife's devoted to him. Right now, you'll see, he's unshaven, he looks like a mountain man, but the guy I know wears three-thousand-dollar suits and drives a high-end Mercedes. So yeah, was he depressed when he came down here? Sure. Anyone would be. But that's it. He needed a change. Decided to do some backpacking, so he hired a local guide to take him up the river. I think they were headed for some trailhead near the jaguar preserve."

"Ways up there. Cockscomb? Past the confluence with the Swasey Branch? You can drive there in an hour. Tourists don't tend to take the river route."

"Their first night out the guide apparently died. Out of the blue. He suffered a heart attack or something. Stern said he found out in the morning, because they were each sleeping in their own tents. He went into shock or something, the death of the guide really threw him."

"I bet."

With his left hand on the wheel, Brady fumbled with his right to shake a cigarette from his pack and light it off the dash. He seemed distracted. Hal needed to get his attention.

"I mean here he was, this young guy from L.A., up a jungle river with just this one person who was his lifeline. And that lifeline suddenly disappears. Plus the fact, this guy Stern, over the past few months, is like a death magnet. Everyone close to him dies. Or gets debilitated. My wife told me the father left the mother—this aging frat boy left the mother, you know, his wife of so many years, to be a gay stripper in Key West. Then the girlfriend dies, of some heart condition he didn't even know she had. This woman, by the way, was twenty-three and ran marathons. His mother tried to O.D. but ended up losing her mind. She's got dementia or something. His dog gets hit by a car. Even his business partner ditched him."

"Rough year."

A spark of interest. Either the cigarette or the drama was putting Brady in a better mood.

"So anyway, after he found the guide dead Stern went into shock I guess, and eventually he dragged the body back down to the boat. We're talking, for miles. I did that hike, looking for him. It was exhausting even without a 200-pound dead weight to haul. I guess he wrapped it up in the tent and got it all the way down to the river, where he put it back in the boat. But then later the boat's propeller snapped and he ditched it against the bank, body and all, and tried to hike out. He almost died too. It was a close call for him."

Brady nodded, negotiated a pothole. The car jumped.

"The guide was older, in his sixties I guess? It was a freak thing, but there's no way it was anything other than natural causes. A couple days later the boat floated down to the ocean, but by then there was no body in it."

"No body," said Brady. "At all? Huh. Problematic."

"The guide's brother, I met him, I mean he isn't bringing charges or anything. It was called in by some neighbor lady or something who has a beef with Americans. I don't even know what they're holding him on."

"We'll find out. Don't worry."

They drove in silence for a minute or two. Cars were smaller here than at home, smaller, older, more banged-up. The road was called a highway, but as in Mexico there was no fencing alongside to keep out stray animals. The corpses of roadkill appeared every few hundred yards, here a dog, there what seemed to be a raccoon.

"You know anything about a military incursion into the jungle down there, by the way?" he asked Brady.

"Come again?"

"A military incursion."

"Whose military?"

"Ours."

"When?"

"I think maybe yesterday. Or the day before."

Brady laughed abruptly.

"Uh, that'd be a no."

"I think there was one, though."

"I'd know. Trust me. This is a very small country."

"I heard they were doing a flyover. Some alleged guerrilla camp of Mayans, from over the border."

"There's no such thing."

"If you say so."

"Who told you this, anyway?"

Hal looked away from him to his own side of the road. There

were flat, ugly fields stretching out beside him to the east, while to the west rose the low mountains.

"A German schoolteacher," he said slowly.

"What?"

"Long story."

"I'm all ears. We still got half an hour to go."

Hal told him about the armed forces, the boat trip, the hike. He told him what Hans had said as he lay down on the boat's bench at the end, his stomach full of warm liquid.

"Aural hallucinations. Fatigue can do that to you."

"You think so?"

"I know so."

"But then what about what his wife said? Yesterday?"

"Guy sounds like a weapons hobbyist. Maybe he likes to spin tales to impress the little lady."

"Huh," said Hal. "I don't know, Jeff. I mean he did bring the Marines to me."

Then it struck him that this discussion might be impairing his credibility. He should change the subject.

But Brady did it for him.

"What do you do, anyway? Stateside?"

Hal was surprised. He was sure he had mentioned it.

"IRS."

"Kidding."

"Why, you delinquent?"

"My brother works at the Service Center in Austin."

"Government service runs in your family, huh?"

"That and gallbladder problems."

"Sorry to hear it."

By the time they got off the highway and headed into Belize

City he felt reasonably confident that Brady was won over. He had recognized, in Brady, the cynical posture of high-waisted Rodriguez. And by treating Brady essentially as he treated Rodriguez—as though they were brothers-in-arms, jaded yet hearty mercenaries in civil service's trench warfare—he was in the process of securing Brady's confidence.

He coughed, breathing exhaust fumes as they made their way down a narrow street behind a rickety pickup full of bags of garbage.

"No unleaded gas around here," said Brady. "Not yet. Pity. OK. Not far now." He pulled into a parking space abruptly and braked. "Here we go. Follow me, and don't speak unless you're spoken to."

"Draconian."

"Only because I've been in the situation. Trust me."

As it happened Hal was made to wait in the lobby, near a uniformed guard standing beside a young woman's desk, while Brady was ushered into the interior. The chairs were uncomfortable, the walls gray and the ceilings low. On a bulletin board was a picture of a wanted man with a banner above his head: FBI TEN MOST WANTED FUGITIVE. Beneath, three headings: DESCRIPTION. CAUTION. REWARD.

For a second it seemed to Hal that Belize was an outpost of America. It had been British Honduras, previously. But the British were nowhere.

An overhead fan whirred, the blades ticking monotonously against the dangling chain, but did little to aerate the room.

He wished he had a glass of ice water.

Finally Brady came out again, a portly man in shirtsleeves beside him, sweat stains under his arms.

"Hal, Jorge Luis. Hal Lindley, U.S. Internal Revenue Service."

They shook. The man's hand was faintly greasy. Hal's own was probably just as bad.

"Mr. Stern is not here yet," said Jorge, in English that was unaccented and fluent. "He's being transported overland. They should be getting in a little later."

"We can come back," said Brady. "We'll have our interview then, and talk to the detective."

"Do we know—"

"We'll get the details then," said Brady, smiling. "No problem." He turned and shook Jorge's hand.

Out on the street he told Hal not to seem overeager, that a casual attitude was best. Hal stopped on the sidewalk and turned to him, incredulous.

"Casual? Casual attitude? An innocent man's languishing in prison! Who knows if the rule of law even holds? I mean do we even know if they have grounds for arresting him?"

Brady took him by the shoulder.

"The key is not to get overwrought. Trust me. Keep things low-key, unless we get indications there's a hidden agenda. In that case, we'll go in from a whole different angle. But there's no sign of that yet. Best way to get him out quickly is to act like the stakes are low, like there's no official anxiety. Act like we're all on the same side. Because we are, basically. Walk softly, carry a big stick. Trust me."

"Poker face. That's what you're saying?"

"More or less. Let's go get some lunch. I know a nice little place right around the corner. Family runs it. Shall we?"

•

Lunch was jerk chicken they ate off paper plates on cheery red and green vinyl tablecloths. They washed down the chicken with tepid half-pints of watery beer, and afterward Hal retired to his hotel room, a relief. In the thick air the beer was making him feel heavy, his limbs difficult to lift.

He lay down on the coverlet, then thought of the bacteria Susan would assure him were writhing there—possibly even parasites such as crabs, which would take up residence in his pubic hair.

All right! Jesus.

He stood, pulled the coverlet off and lay down again on the cool top sheet. He was logy, but he was also restless. He missed Casey.

When she picked up the phone he felt drunker, suddenly, than he had since Gretel. It seemed all things were transparent, and who was he to pretend otherwise?

"I know about the phone sex," he said.

"Shit," said Casey.

"Yep. I do."

"Huh," said Casey. "What can I say. Sorry?"

"You're not sorry," he said. He was curious, actually. "You said you liked it. In the kitchen, to what's her name. Who crochets the hideous multicolored afghans. And the baby booties."

"Nancy."

"You don't have to lie to me, is my point. I'm your father."

"Come on, Dad. You don't want to know stuff like that. I mean really. Do you?"

He felt clean, miraculous. As though the details had no power over him. Everything was the idea of itself; everything was the shape of itself, not the texture—the shadow it threw or the light it cast, the arc of its traveling. Not the trivia, not the variables, no: the great sweep of feeling, the adventurous gesture.

"If it makes you happy, that's good enough for me. Whatever. I mean not everyone wants to work for the IRS, either."

"Nice try, Daddy. IRS, phone porn, same thing."

"Anyway, sweetheart, I don't need to know the details. But that doesn't mean I need to be lied to. I'd rather get the respect of hearing the truth and having to deal with it."

"I thought, you know, no one wants to think of their crippled kid doing phone porn for a living. Sordid. You know—do you really need the ideation? It's like seeing your parents have sex. Right? Pretty disgusting. No offense, but who wants that? Come on!"

"The truth will set us free."

"Speak for yourself."

"OK, the truth will set me free. That's what I'm seeing, since I've been down here. Or wait. What I'm seeing is more: I want to know the truth, but I don't want to have to *tell* the truth. See? You want to have the truth available to you, but then you also want the freedom of never having to tell it yourself. That's the deal with truth. It sets you free when you hear it, but if you have to tell it, that's pretty much a non-freedom situation. Get it? People should tell the truth to me, if I ask them for it. But I should be able to hide the truth whenever I want to."

"Are you drunk?"

"I resent the implication."

"Uh huh. Mom said you'd been hitting the sauce. It's not like you. So what is this? A mid-life-crisis thing?"

"I did have two beers with lunch. With the guy from the embassy. Beer in the middle of the day knocks me out, though. It's humid here."

"She also said T.'s in jail."

"It's more of a holding facility. Don't worry. We're gonna spring him. We'll bust him out. I'm working closely with the U.S. embassy."

"He killed someone?"

"Of course not, honey. A guy just happened to, you know, die next to him."

"Just die?"

"Hey. It happens."

"And there's no, they don't have any evidence against him, or whatever?"

"There's no body, even. Don't worry, Case. Hey, listen. What about Sal? How's it going with him?"

"Oh, you know. It's not anything, really."

"Good to hear."

"I bet."

"Hey. Case."

"Uh huh."

"So I've been wondering. What happened with you and T.?"

She was silent. He was overstepping, but he couldn't help it—there was a carelessness to him. Or he was carefree.

"In a nutshell? He condescended, Dad."

"He condescended?"

"He condescended to me."

There was nothing more. Casey was not one to step into an

awkward pause, to take up the slack. The static buzzed between them. He let it rest.

"That's all?"

"That's all, Daddy. So when are you guys coming home?"

After they hung up he lay back on the sheet, content. It always made him feel good to talk to her. She always sounded like herself, whole, confident, abrupt. Her matter-of-factness was comforting, her cheery pugnacity. When he went to see her, or even heard her speaking to him on the phone, it reminded him that she was not gone at all—not gone at all and not miserable, at least no more so than the rest of the humans. She was warm, she was there, she was not the specter of a miserable daughter that lived alongside him. That specter could be dismissed.

It was irrelevant.

•

When he met Brady outside the jail there was another man with him, a younger Anglo in a seersucker suit. It turned out he was a lawyer.

"You said there was nothing to worry about," said Hal, alarmed. It was beyond his control after all. It had run away on him. "You said walk lightly, not to show we're worried!"

"A basic precaution. Cleve's an old friend of mine from Miami. Jorge knows him too. He met him last year at a pool party. Remember that, Cleve? After the ribbon-cutting? At the new youth hostel?"

"With the—that woman with the grass skirt? The supernumerary nipple?"

"Right. Right! Who kept showing it to everyone."

"Jesus," said the lawyer, and shook his head. He turned to Hal. "She was an entertainer I guess? Something to do with the music? But she had this extra nipple. It was, like, right under her clavicle." He tugged his shirt collar down to display the area in question.

"It was weird, though," said Brady. "It was little."

"Almost like a big wart."

"But with an areola."

"So this won't, this won't make the cops think we're adversarial?" asked Hal. "Marching back in there with an attorney?"

"It's just a formality. Don't worry. After you, gentlemen."

Brady opened the door for him.

"She kept going, 'my supernumerary nipple,'" said the lawyer. "That's what she called it. I never forgot. 'Supernumerary.'"

"Made it sound official," said Brady.

"Bureaucratic," said Cleve.

After a few minutes' wait, with Brady and the lawyer still talking about the pool party—apparently a man had walked through a plate-glass door and been airlifted to a hospital in Mexico City—the stocky, sweat-stained man from before came out and ushered them in. It seemed to Hal that the security guard looked askance at him as they passed, as though Hal posed a security risk.

Inside they went down a brightly lit corridor and the stocky man opened the door to an interrogation room.

There was T., seated at a Formica table. At his elbow was a bottle of water.

Hal bent down and held his shoulders, then stepped back. He did not look upset.

"Are you OK? How are you holding up?"

"Fine, thank you," said T., and smiled.

"Where were you sleeping last night?"

"We were driving for some of it. There was a rest stop. I didn't get that much sleep."

"Man. I'm so sorry. This is wrong, T."

T. patted him on the arm and then looked past him, polite. "Tom Stern. Please call me T. And you are?"

Hal introduced Brady and the lawyer. On the other side of the table the stocky man arranged chairs.

"One moment," said Jorge the stocky, and left them.

"Have they accused you of anything?" asked Hal impatiently.

"No, nothing," said T. pleasantly.

"But so—on what grounds are they keeping you?"

"They have some questions, is what I've been told. They want to know what happened. Get it into the record."

"You haven't been interviewed officially, I assume," said the lawyer.

"No one's really asked me anything," said T. "We were in a car, then a transport van with a couple of prisoners, then we stopped at a rest stop . . . I'm tired. But nothing's happened."

"They'll be taping this now, then," said the lawyer. "Wish we had more time to prepare. Key is, you don't want to disclose more than the basic facts. You ever been deposed?"

T. shook his head.

"You have nothing to hide here, I'm sure. But keep it brief. We want to avoid even the suggestion there's anything you could have done to stop this man from dying."

"If I had EMT training, maybe . . . ," said T. pensively.

"That kind of speculation is exactly what we don't want. Just the basic facts. No emotional statements, for instance. You think you can do that?"

Then Jorge was back, and a woman with glossy lipstick and a tape recorder.

"Excuse me," said Jorge. "This is our stenographer. Could she—?"

There was little room. Hal saw he was motioning to the chair beside Hal, in which he had not yet sat down.

"Sure, sure," said Hal, but then, in the ensuing arrangement of persons as they settled, was left with nowhere to sit. He leaned against the wall, arms folded.

"You can just tell us what happened, your version of the events," said Jorge, and T. nodded. Jorge narrated some protocol in the direction of the tape recorder—who was present, the date, the date of the guide's demise. T. began to tell his story, which Hal had heard before, in an even, pleasant tone. It was as though he was unaffected by stress.

Hal himself was sweating. There was no air in the room, no windows and no air. Not even a ventilation grid, he saw, looking around. Maybe if he could crack the door open? Even a few inches would offer relief. But then there would be background noise, he guessed. Ambient sound on the tape recorder, compromising its integrity.

He was wet beneath the arms. Disgusting. And the ceiling, it seemed, was perilously low, pocked with little pinpricks in what looked like white cardboard.

Yet none of the others seemed to be noticing. They were not bothered by any of it. Except for Jorge they were not even perspiring, as far as he could see. He felt a tenuous bond with Jorge. They were the only ones with armpit stains.

Possibly he was slightly claustrophobic. Before his venture into this small, subtropical and foreign country, he had never thought of himself as a wimp. Yet it seemed he was often in discomfort since he got here, uncomfortable, exhausted, or alarmed. He had turned out to be a hothouse flower—a hothouse flower from the first world that wilted in the third. An American hothouse flower, adapted only to the United States. And within the U.S. only to Southern California, or more restricted still—adapted to the unchanging mildness of West L.A., where the worst weather you encountered was gray.

"By the time I dragged myself back down to the coast," T. was saying, in his low, well-modulated voice, "I was in a state of exhaustion. My body weight had dropped. I went to my foreman, Marlo. Later he said I was starving. But my own worry had been thirst, you know, potable water. The river water I'd been avoiding as much as I could. I was afraid of illness. Possibly giardia. Delonn had told me there were cattle upstream. So I used the filter, but I didn't trust myself. I was afraid I was using it wrong. By the time I saw the tourists—it was a family taking pictures of a toucan—I wasn't thinking clearly. And the recovery was slow. This is what accounts for my delay in contacting Delonn's family. I regret . . ."

The lawyer shook his head in a small, tight movement, but T. ignored him. Neither Jorge nor the stenographer, who seemed to be doing nothing other than keeping one hand on the tape recorder, noticed either.

"I regret that my recovery prevented me from contacting them earlier," he went on. "I do think Delonn's problem on the boat, the possible arm pain and mild distress he appeared to be having as we came up the river, were an early warning signal."

The lawyer shook his head again, but T. was not looking at him.

"But he chose not to turn back. At that time, as I said, I asked him if he was OK. He was an older man, but he seemed to be in good physical shape. He was active. My recollection is, he said it was probably heartburn. He had no interest in turning back, so he dismissed my concern."

The lawyer nodded, as though to affirm: good. Good. Blame the victim.

"Mr. Stern. What is your opinion," asked Jorge, tipping his chair back onto two legs, "about what happened to the body? Go over that one more time, please."

T. was drinking water from his bottle. He recapped it and set it down carefully.

"A couple of days after I abandoned the boat," he went on, "I was at my campsite at night. I saw the boat drifting downriver. I ran into the river and tried to climb over the side, but I was too slow. I slipped off and the boat kept going. But while I was still hanging on I saw the inside of the boat, and the body wasn't there. The tent, you know, that it was wrapped in?—was that bright yellow of raincoats. Even at night I would have been able to make it out. But there was nothing."

"You're sure?"

"He already said so," said the lawyer.

"My guess was—"

"You don't have to guess," said the lawyer. "That's all you saw."

Hal felt heat rush to his face, and a suffocation. He closed his eyes and lights pricked at the darkness.

"Excuse me," he said.

The hallway was slightly less stifling but not enough, and he kept going past the security guard and the reception desk, out the front door. The sky had clouded over and a cool breeze was up, and he relaxed instantly.

The guard would probably not let him back in by himself, but he was indifferent. The lawyer was his watchdog. The lawyer was being a lawyer. There was nothing Hal could do to help, past the fact of having brought him in, Brady and him. He was unsure of their competence, but what could he do? Nothing. These were guys who spent their spare time discussing women with extra nipples.

He sat down on a deep window ledge, feet planted far apart on the sidewalk, and raised his face to the sky. He took a deep breath and then looked level again, gazed in front of him. A car or two passed. Across the street there was a store that seemed to sell things made of ugly plastic. The objects festooned the windows brightly but their nature was unclear . . . he had always thought of himself as competent, but then he came down here and had to do everything through proxies—all he did was delegate tasks to those who were more qualified. His own qualifications, it turned out, were limited to Service business. He had no qualifications outside those narrow parameters.

And yet back home, day in, day out, he walked around like a competent man.

That was what his country did for people like him. It specialized them. They knew how to live, day in, day out, in one highly specific undertaking. They thrived in their tunnels, however narrow. Manual laborers knew more. Manual laborers, many of them, could perform myriad tasks if called upon to do so, but white collars like himself knew only one thing.

He was a surplus human, a product of a swollen civilization. He was a widget among men.

When civilization fell and government went with it, his people would die off, replaced by bricklayers, plumbers and mechanics—replaced by farmers, weavers, and electricians who could forage through the ruins for generators and fuse boxes and wire. There would be no more use for his kind.

Could he adapt, given time? Possibly. Although with some difficulty. His former mantle of confidence would fall away; losing authority, he would become a kind of beggar. He and the bohemians. Clearly they were even more useless than he was. This was why, no doubt, he partly identified with them. The presence of other broadly useless humans offered a certain comfort . . . more comfort even than Gretel, in fact, who had been so kind to him, because the young and beautiful were in their own privileged category. They would always be needed, or wanted, at least. The young and beautiful were an end in themselves. Even in the postscript to civilization, the young and beautiful would seldom be forced to beg. Plus they were good breeding stock.

In any case civilization was not quite falling at the moment. It was on its way down, collapsing in slow motion, but it had some good years left in it yet. Chances were he would continue to be what he was, live out his life as a widget, and never be called upon to learn to, say, butcher a calf.

There was Brady, coming out the front door. He nodded briskly at Hal, shook a cigarette out of a packet and lit it.

Brady, too, was a human widget.

"My prediction," said Brady, after a first inhale, "is they keep him in overnight. Maybe one more night for good measure. I don't think we're looking at a serious situation."

"Jesus," said Hal. "That's great to hear."

He didn't quite trust Brady. Brady was not smart enough, he suspected. But still it offered some relief.

"Can I talk to him by myself? Or do the cops always have to be there?"

"Give 'em another five minutes," said Brady. "You should be able to get some face time then."

Bail was not an option, apparently. T. had not been arrested, he told Hal, sitting in the interview room again with the door wide open. He was being detained, but no charges had been brought. He was staying on a voluntary basis, until they were satisfied he was not a flight risk.

"As a courtesy," he explained.

"You're staying in prison as a courtesy? Why be courteous? I don't get it. They have no right to keep you."

"It's all right, Hal," said T. calmly. "Really. They're doing a search for the body, just in case. Mostly the riverbanks, is all they can manage. Manpower issue I guess. But if they don't find anything in the next twenty-four hours, the lawyer said, I'll be free to leave. And if they do find it, they'll conduct an autopsy. Verify my story."

"That's bullshit," said Hal.

"It's OK. Really. It's not a problem for me."

"Do you even know the, you know, the conditions? Have you gone to where they're going to keep you?"

"Not yet. It's just down the street."

"And the lawyer advised you to go along with this? I mean we have money. You know. There's plenty of it. We should be able to post a bond. You could stay at my hotel while they do their search. Their autopsy."

"I don't think they'll find the body," said T. "I think the animals got to it."

He seemed matter-of-fact about the prospect.

"Listen. T. Why not stay in my hotel? You want to—I don't know—have to use the toilet in front of perfect strangers? Eat gruel?"

"My own cell, they said. It's not a high-security thing. There are private showers. And it's just for one night."

"I don't know," said Hal, shaking his head. He felt fretful. T. was not practical; in his new form he had become irresponsible, flaky. Could he be trusted even with self-preservation? "Maybe we should call a lawyer in the U.S. Someone famous. Get a referral, at least. I don't know about this."

"You know how you could help?"

"Just tell me."

"If you could arrange for the flight out, a couple days down the road, that'd be great. I was thinking of walking, but now I have other plans."

"Ha ha."

"No, really. I was going to try to walk home, at one point."

"In delirium, I assume."

"I just wanted to do it. But now I think we should maybe go ahead and get back, if that works for you."

"Good thinking."

"Mr. Stern?"

Jorge was at the door.

"We can move you on now, sir."

Hal stood, scraping his chair back.

"I'll keep close tabs on you," he told T. "That's for sure."

"I appreciate your concern, Hal. I do."

"Tomorrow," he said.

"See you," said T.

9

The young lawyer had told Brady about a party, and Brady told Hal. There was always a party, apparently.

Brady called the hotel room and invited Hal to join them. He himself was not driving back to Belmopan, but staying overnight in Belize City. It was a party held by a company, a company that had just opened a Belize location and was looking to make friends.

This meant, Brady explained, there would be ample libations. Hal was welcome to come with them.

Could they promise, asked Hal, a supernumerary nipple?

But he had nothing better to do. He was waiting for them in his room, bored, freshly showered, flipping through channels, when the telephone rang.

"I talked to T.," said Susan breathlessly.

"They're letting him make calls, then," said Hal. "Good sign. Glad to hear it."

"Hal, he's crazy. Do you know what he said to me? He wants to dissolve the corporation. He wants to give away everything."

"I told you he would need some adjustment time. Didn't I?"

"*Adjustment* time? He's delusional. Hal! I don't know what to do!"

"Just wait till he gets back. There's nothing you can do till then anyway."

"He wants me to start right away. He wants us to pull out of everything. I mean it's crazy. I don't even know if it's going to be possible. Or legal. Seriously."

"Just sit tight till we get back, OK? He's being detained. He needs to get home and get his bearings. Regroup. I warned you about this, honey. Right? Just try to be patient. I have us on a return flight the day after tomorrow."

"You do? When?"

"We get in late. Evening."

"I can't believe this. Hal, he's raving."

"Actually, he seems fairly rational to me."

"Are you kidding? Hal! Seriously. Are you *kidding*?"

"Different, but rational. In his way. I mean, he can still string a sentence together. He doesn't foam at the mouth or anything."

"Well, but you don't even know him. I mean, from before. Hardly. You wouldn't know the difference. You said yourself, he had a breakdown. He had a near-death experience!"

Someone was knocking at the room door.

"Just a second."

Brady, holding car keys.

"Phone with my wife. Give me a minute," said Hal, and stood back to let him in. "Susan? I should go. The, uh, the man from the embassy is here. I need to talk to him."

"He was going on about *animals,* Hal. Wild animals dying? I'm worried. What if he does something to himself before we can get help for him?"

"He won't, Susan. It's OK. Just sit tight. Can you try to do that for me?"

Brady patrolled the hotel room, picked up the remote and flicked off the TV. There was something overbearing about him, it seemed to Hal. He carried himself as though it was his own hotel room.

"I'm worried. He just doesn't sound like the same person."

"Maybe he's not, Suze. Maybe he's not. But does that have to be so threatening?"

"I'm talking about mental instability. You remember Eloise? Her son went down to the Amazon on a photo safari and took some malaria drug? He was like twenty-five and getting a Ph.D. in biology. Anyway the drug or the sickness drove him crazy. Forever, Hal. *Forever.* He had a psychotic break. He dropped out of grad school and his girlfriend left him. Now he wanders around Malibu carrying sand in his pockets and calling people 'nigger.'"

"In Malibu?"

"White people."

"You should chill out, honey. Stop worrying. There's nothing you can do, he's safe and sound, we're both coming home soon. And listen, I promise. He's not going to call anybody 'nigger.' I'll go out on a limb and guarantee that."

Brady was impatient. He was not paying attention. He stood with the room door half-open.

"OK," said Susan, in a dissatisfied tone.

"OK. I'll call you in the morning."

•

As they drove to the party, Hal in the passenger seat wrestling with a broken seatbelt, it became clear that Brady had an agenda for the evening. It was unclear to Hal what that agenda was, but clearly there was one. He was purposeful in his movements. He drove fast. He was out for more than just a good time; he had a mission.

"You think T.'s doing OK in that place?" he asked, as Brady lit a cigarette at a stoplight.

It was already dark and the streetlights were on, surrounded by circling insects. Staring at a single light, he could see hundreds of them, possibly thousands.

His eyes smarted with the brightness. He turned away, blinking, and saw stubborn afterimages.

"He'll be fine, he'll be fine," said Brady dismissively.

Hal found him irksome. Most of his smoke went out the window, but not all of it.

The afterimages of the streetlights were fading slowly.

"You ever spent the night in a jail around here?" he asked.

"It's a holding facility," said Brady, accelerating with a jerk.

"But how can we know what the conditions are? There's no transparency! What if it's a whole, you know, bitches-and-shivs kind of situation? Bend-over, rusty-razorblades-in-the-shower-type scene?"

Brady looked at him sidelong, one eyebrow raised.

"Relax. He's going to be fine. You know, you seem a lot more uptight about it than he was, you realize that? Guy didn't seem that worried to me."

The cigarette dangled and jumped precariously as his lips moved.

But it was true, seemingly. No argument there.

Hal should have had something to drink before he met up with Brady. He didn't like him, he realized. There was something sharp about Brady, something sharp and rancid.

Suddenly he longed for the company of Gretel. He liked Gretel. She was nice.

Germans, he reflected, were possibly not so bad. Even if they were a super-race, maybe they didn't mean to be. After all, as national arrogance went, in his recollection from traveling, the French were far worse. And people often forgot that it was the Frogs, not the Krauts, who invented fascists. When people thought about the French, they thought of wine, the Eiffel Tower, the fatuous berets and painters on streets. They forgot these were the same guys who invented the whole fascist deal in the nineteenth century, then let the Germans run with it.

It was easy to be sucked into the thrall of a European. That much was true. German or French, English or Italian, even quaint, poor and Irish, there was something superior about all of them. They valued education, for one thing, which gave them a bit of a head start. They did not cherish ignorance like his own countrymen. For that reason—recently, at least—they were less destructive, megalomaniacal and brutal, for instance. Which might be seen as an advantage for them. On the other hand, their maturity could also be somewhat boring. In America adults acted like children; in Europe the children acted like small adults. Even the cornboys, though boyish enough in their activities, were more like miniature engineering students than carefree ten-year-olds.

Also, the lack of childish, wanton destructiveness failed to stand the Europeans in good stead when it came to world domination. Being smart, educated and civilized, and having learned some fairly significant lessons from their history, they had pretty much retreated from the world-domination forum over the past half-century and now were like a small band of AARP members watching the carnival from a distance and drinking nonalcoholic beer.

But as far as super-races went, the German women, at least, were warm and generous. He liked them.

The one he knew, anyway.

"Here we go. Bit of a walk. Nice beach house. No parking any closer."

"Your friend Cleve coming?" asked Hal to fill the space as they got out of the car.

"Should be. Yeah. You know, see most of the same people at these things. Whole city's what, sixty thousand bodies. You got a small expat community, you got your local figures. Same old. Except for the help. The help changes."

Ahead of them was a large, white, blocky house surrounded by waving palms. A nice breeze had sprung up off the ocean. It was good to be here, after all, Hal thought with relief, if only for the breeze. There were people milling on a second-floor terrace, which was strung with lights.

"Pool, too," said Brady. "Jacuzzi."

"I didn't bring my suit," said Hal.

"No worries," said Brady.

He followed Brady into the house, through an atrium full of waxy-leaved plants with huge flowers, up tiled stairs onto the terrace, where the drinks were. There was music, but he could not tell where it was coming from. People around, most of them tanned and quite young. Where were all the geriatric expats? They had to be around somewhere. People retired here, after all. There should be plenty of wrinkled old crones smeared with Coppertone. But instead there were only models and athletic types. Among them Hal would not shine.

A bartender, tables with candles in the center, and there: a topless woman in the hot tub. Already. She was on the other side of the pool, down off the terrace on the first floor, but he saw her. Her shoulders were brown but her breasts floated whitely on the water like twin buoys.

He encountered a lot of nudity, in this tropical location. For years, in his life, almost no nudity, only clothing. Clothing, clothing, clothing. Wherever he went, there seemed to be apparel. Although he lived in Southern California, and not far from the beach either, somehow he did not frequent the nude locations.

Then he came here and suddenly: nude. Nude nude nude.

"Here, have this one," said Brady, and put a drink in his hand. Out of it stuck a parrot fashioned from colored pipe-cleaners: red, blue, yellow.

"So who's our host?" asked Hal, lifting the drink to his lips. As he raised it the parrot swiveled and hit him on the nose.

"The folks throwing this shindig," said Brady, whose own

drink featured no parrot, "are ethanol. They just inked some kind of deal with BSI. The sugar monopoly."

"Huh," said Hal. If he took the parrot out it would stop falling on him when he drank. But in his pocket it would be crushed. He liked the parrot. He could give it to Casey. She enjoyed souvenirs, especially if tacky.

He held the parrot with one crooked finger while he raised his glass. That was the trick: restrain the parrot. Keep the parrot captive.

"Toucan's giving you a tough time, huh," said Brady.

"Oh. I thought it was a parrot."

"Hey! Jeff!"

There was the lawyer, lifting himself out of the pool. He wore a Speedo. He reached out and grabbed a silky bathrobe, mounted the stairs and came up to them, nodding and waving at others he passed.

"Let me introduce you around," he said.

They walked down the far stairs to the pool area again, where there was another bar. Beyond a wall lined with flowering vines were the beach and the ocean. A DJ played music on a stereo and people danced. They stood next to the dance floor, watching.

"Thanks for inviting me," said Hal.

"Marcella. Marcella, this is Jeff Brady. The U.S. embassy. The one I told you about? The racquetball story?"

A passing woman shook Brady's hand. Hal noticed long fingernails, shining silver.

"Hal Lindley," he said, because the lawyer seemed to have forgotten his name. "Just visiting. Tourist."

A guy on the dance floor bumped into him, sloshing his drink.

"Marcella handles the Canadians," Cleve was telling Brady.

A server brought up an hors d'oeuvres tray. Brady picked up a small food item and shoved it into his mouth.

"What are they?" asked Hal, peering down.

"Sribuffs," said the server, a dark young woman.

"Sribuffs?" repeated Hal. "I'm not . . ."

"Shrimbuffs," she said again, nodding anxiously.

"Shrimbuffs. Huh," said Hal.

"*Shrimp* puffs," said Brady, impatient.

"Oh. Oh, I see," said Hal, and took one, smiling sheepishly at the server. He tried to seem obliging.

"Why they can't hire fucking English speakers," said Cleve, shaking his head. "When the official language is fucking English."

The woman moved off, her head down.

"You'd like her better if she had three nipples, you're saying," said Brady.

"Shit yeah. I would."

Hal wanted another drink. Not to be critical; to suspend his judgment. The second thing he had learned, on this trip—after the fact that he liked knowing the truth about other people and at the same time keeping his own truth to himself—drink more. He should drink more, in general. Not to the point of alcoholism, but enough to float, in the waning part of the day, in a kind of pleasant and light liquid, a beery amber light. Life was better that way. People were softer around the edges, their conversation less grating.

"Excuse me. Making a bathroom run, then a drink. Get anyone anything?" he asked, raising his near-empty glass.

"G&T," said Brady.

"Cognac," said Cleve.

"OK," he said, and moved off. See what the house held. He would have to find a way to keep the toucan in shape . . . on his way in he took it carefully off the straw it was impaled on and slipped it into the loose pocket of his shirt. It should be safe there, unless he crushed someone against him. Manfully.

But that was unlikely. Gretel was absent.

•

In the bathroom there were seashells of all shapes and sizes. They were made by something, seashells. Various organisms. Were they some animals' excreta? He could not remember. He had seen a show on shell-forming animals with Casey. The term *calcium carbonate* came to mind. The animals formed the shells slowly, but how did they do it?

Possibly the shells were like fingernails, protruding suddenly from the skin.

It was strange, come to think of it. He looked down at the back of his hand. Fingernails. They just started up.

They were made of keratin, he remembered that.

They were a form of hair.

He had read this, but frankly he did not believe it. Or simply, he did not agree. They might be made of similar proteins, he accepted that readily, but still they were not a *form* of *hair.* Any idiot could see that.

He finished peeing, washed his hands and picked up a shell that looked like a snail shell, except huge and spotted. There were also stripes. It was attractive. Inside, it was shiny.

He placed it back on the shelf.

The drink was treating him well. No doubt it had been mixed quite strong. They fooled you with the toucan. You thought: child's play, and swigged heartily. Then you were drunk. But he should not complain, not even to himself. It was what he had intended, after all. He had already made the decision. From now on he would be a man who drank. He would stop short of chronic impairment, though. That was the trick; you had to learn to drink the correct amount. It was said two glasses of wine a day improved your health. Surely three could not do it too much harm, in that case. He could become an oenophile. That was the name, if he recalled correctly, for wine lovers.

Wine-loving assholes. Because let's face it, a wine lover was basically an asshole. Like a cigar lover. The word *connoisseur,* in general, was a synonym for asshole.

If it was up to him, connoisseurs of all kinds would be audited on a regular basis, their files tagged and them personally harassed by the Service until forced to surrender their assets. They would be targeted for audits on a non-random basis, if it was up to him. Wine, cigars, old cars, all pastimes of the genus *Assholus.*

It wouldn't be wine, not for him. The point was, he could have three drinks a day and cultivate new fields of knowledge. He could keep more secrets, possibly lead a secret life with secret leisure pursuits. But what kind of secret life could he lead?

Before, when he found out about Susan, he had wanted to lead a secret life to get back at her. Now he wanted one for a different reason: his own pleasure. Excitement.

He picked up his glass. He still had to get drinks.

Because the life he had currently, he reflected, climbing the stairs, was insufficient. It was quite simply inadequate. At a certain point, you had to insist on quality.

A woman he once knew, who lived down the street from them, had said frequently, "I'm going to exercise my rights as a consumer." She had said this often. Then she would call a mail-order catalog, for instance, and complain about a substandard product she had purchased therefrom. She would receive bulk samples of things, or luxury items free of charge—bribes from companies in exchange for refraining from litigation, which she threatened often.

When she was his neighbor he had frowned on this behavior of hers, which seemed cynical and opportunistic. Susan had thought it was funny, but he had frowned upon it. Now, however, he felt a certain grudging admiration.

"Cognac," he said to the bartender beside the pool. He could barely hear his own voice. It was loud now. There was music, coming from who knows where. He did not see Brady or Cleve. There were more people now also. It was as though, alone in the bathroom, he had slept for hours by himself while on the other side of the wall the crowd swelled and gained momentum. Kind of a Sleeping Beauty thing. "G&T."

"What's your gin, sir?"

"Oh, I don't know. It's not for me. Whatever you want to give him."

Two women dancing near him wore hairy coconut-shell bikini tops. He had never thought he would see that, outside a movie context. The shells did not look comfortable. They had to be chafing. Your average breast was not a good fit for half a coconut shell. The breasts would have red circle marks on them, like glass rings on a coffee table.

Maybe he should work on Casey, with regard to the phone-sex problem. Sure, she was an adult, but adults made poor choices all the time and she was no exception. Maybe he should press her harder to go to college. She was still young enough. Was it wrong of him to let her choose her own path? She was his daughter. And she was only in her twenties. And she was doing phone sex. She was going down the old phone-sex road. Where did that road lead? That road was a dead end.

It was all very well to be accepting. Acceptance had its place. But maybe he was shirking his duty. Maybe he should plead with her, or threaten. Did Susan know? She did not, was his suspicion. Maybe he should talk about it with Susan. Maybe they should formulate policy. Of course, he had just told Casey he was fine with it. The downside of drunkenness. But it was true, in a way. That is, he was fine with the sex aspect, in a sense. What sense? Well, in the sense that he could admit his daughter was a female, and—

OK, so he was fine with it in the sense that he could ignore it, if he tried, or maybe chock it up to youthful mischief, risk-taking, or perversity, or also possibly a nihilistic, self-abnegating impulse Casey had been known at times to embrace. But he was not fine with the whole career dead-end thing. Would she feel amused and fulfilled doing phone sex at fifty? No she would not.

When he got home he would hunker down with Susan. They would devise a phone-sex strategy.

•

"What the hell happened to you?" asked Brady, when Hal approached with drinks in hand, finally. He already had a new one, and was talking to a pretty girl. Cleve the lawyer was not around. "You fall in?"

Brady's sharpness and his focus were on Hal, yet Hal sensed it was for the benefit of the pretty girl. She was half Brady's age at the most and quite elegant, with her black hair swept up on top of her head in a chignon style Hal's mother had favored. This, he realized, was why Brady had driven fast to the party.

He put down the cognac and G&T on a table, the better to drink his own whiskey. Behind Brady, against a vine-covered wall, people in skimpy bathing suits were blindfolded and playing Pin the Tail on the Donkey, shrieking with laughter. He drank the whiskey; Brady was leaning in close to the girl, plying her. He was trying to get her to sleep with him. Hal could not hear what he was saying, nor did he want to.

But his whiskey was already gone.

He grabbed up the extra G&T surreptitiously, without Brady noticing, and moved away from the two of them, toward the taped-up banner of the donkey. Tails hung all over it, willy-nilly. He stood there sipping and watching as a plump woman in a tiny, ill-advised purple thong approached, giggling. She was being roughly steered, almost pushed in fact, by a large man behind her who held onto her shoulders. She raised a braided donkey tail, her arm wavering.

"Colder, colder, warmer, colder," chanted other men in the crowd. But they were toying with the woman. They misdirected her and then they laughed.

Abruptly the large man turned her toward the pool, and she stepped forward. She screamed as she fell. But then seconds later she resurfaced, sputtering and annoyed, tugging at her blindfold as laughter resounded. Hal stepped away, thinking maybe she had let it happen—there was something about her, something irritating—but also touched by sadness.

At his elbow was a young man with a brush cut in wet swimming trunks, toweling his buff body.

"Pathetic, isn't it," said the young man.

Hal felt called upon to defend the woman.

"She's the victim," he said. Possibly slurring.

"That's what I mean," said the young man, and shrugged on a T-shirt. "They're pathetic. Not her."

"Oh. Yeah," said Hal, though in fact it was all of them.

"You know anyone here?" asked the young man.

"No one I want to talk to," said Hal. "You?"

"Same," said the young man. "I'm on leave, I don't live around here."

"You in the army or something?"

"Air Force."

"I was just with some Marines," said Hal. "Or something like that. Coast Guard. Green Berets. Shit, military-type guys, what the hell do I know. In the jungle."

"Yeah?"

"Down south, on the Monkey River," said Hal, nodding.

"No shit," said the Air Force guy. "Me too!"

"Get out," said Hal. Was the guy playing him?

"Serious," said the Air Force guy. "We did a raid on a guerrilla camp."

"A raid? You mean like—"

"I'm a pilot."

"So you mean like a bombing raid? A—dropping bombs on them?"

"Limited airstrike. Yeah. Cluster bombs."

"Cluster bombs?"

"CBUs."

"Don't we—I mean don't we have to declare war or something?"

"Hey. Just following orders. My understanding through the grapevine, this was a War on Drugs operation."

Hal felt dazzled. Water splashed up from the pool onto his back, and people were still shrieking. He thought for a second he was back by the river, exhausted. Was it his fault? Bombing Mayans . . . but maybe they weren't Mayans at all, maybe they were drug kingpins. He gazed down at the drink in his hand; he had mixed tequila, whiskey and now vodka. It was dizzying.

"There you go," said the pilot, putting a hand on his back and moving him. "Guy was about to stick a tail on you."

"You mean on this side of the border, right?" asked Hal.

"Wanna get some food? I'm starving."

"Sure," said Hal, but he felt unsteady. "They have shrimp puffs."

"There's a whole table. Follow me."

At the table there was a surfeit of food. The pilot picked up what looked like a kebab.

"Is that meat? Does that look like meat to you?"

"I think so," said Hal, bending to look at it.

"I think so too."

He put it back.

"What," said Hal, "you don't eat meat?"

"Vegan," said the pilot.

"A vegan bomb-dropper," said Hal. He drank from his glass. It was almost empty. He put it down on the table.

"Best thing for you," said the pilot. "Too much dairy clogs the arteries."

"You don't get anemic or anything?" asked Hal.

The pilot was piling fruit onto a plate, fruit and corn-on-the-cob and bread.

"You should eat too," he said to Hal. "You look like you need it."

"I'm not used to drinking," admitted Hal.

"Here, take that," said the pilot, and handed Hal his plate. "Sit down. Dig in."

The vegan pilot was looking out for him. Why? It was a mystery. Kindly people were crawling out of the woodwork, lately—vegan pilots and German women. Nice people and nude people. In fact there was definite overlap. Did being nude make people nicer? Quite possibly. The inverse was certainly true: putting on Kevlar vests, body armor, etc., made you more willing to go around shooting people. It might also be the case that nice people were more willing to be nude. Chicken or egg question, really.

But then technically the vegan pilot had just been on a cluster-bombing sortie, so maybe he was not so nice. A wolf in vegan's clothing.

Hal carried the plate to a table and sat. The bread was good, though there was no butter on it. He would prefer it with a pat of butter. He took a bite of the corn, also. Then the vegan cluster-bomber was back with him.

"So this bombing, did it, you know, kill people?"

"The bombs were anti-personnel, so yeah, that would have been an objective. I didn't do any follow-up though, I was in and out, that was it."

"You don't feel bad about that? Killing?"

"It's not ideal. But we all kill," said the vegan, and forked up a piece of roasted red pepper.

"Not *people*," said Hal.

"Of course we do," said the vegan.

"Me personally?"

"You eat other people's food."

"Not following you."

"People who need it more than you do and die for lack of a pound of corn. It's what we all are, isn't it? Killers. I mean, all that life *is* is energy. The conversion of fuel. And we take it all. A quarter of the world's resources for what, five percent of its population," said the vegan. "That's us."

He patted his mouth carefully with a paper napkin and raised a glass to his lips. It looked like bubbly water.

"That's ridiculous," said Hal. "Talk about oversimplified." He should drink water too, to clear his head. He looked around for a dispenser.

"Yeah well," said the vegan. "Arithmetic is simple. That doesn't make it wrong."

This kind of discussion was pleasing only in a work environment, and only when it dealt directly with taxation. In a party setting it was unwelcome. Hal had the feeling of being caught in a trap by the vegan. Maybe you had to be careful of vegans. The vegan menace.

Although the vegan still seemed friendly. He spoke in a soft, moderate tone.

"Come on," said Hal weakly. "You're talking about what, middle-class lifestyle? At worst it's manslaughter. It's not murder. It's not like flying over a jungle and cluster-bombing Mayans."

But the buttery corn was slipping out of his grasp. It was devious and slippery.

"Manslaughter or murder, the guy still ends up dead," said the vegan. "Does it matter to him how the killer rationalized?"

"Where'd you get that water?" asked Hal. He also needed a napkin.

"Right over there," said the vegan, pointing.

Hal made his way to the table with the water. He was leaning over an array of light-blue bottles when an elbow struck his ribcage.

"You're married, right?"

It was Cleve, with a woman hanging onto his arm.

"Oh hey, I got you that cognac," said Hal, nodding confusedly, and looked around for where he'd set it down.

"Because the guy you're talking to?"

"He claims to be a pilot," said Hal. "With the Air Force. He talks like an earnest grad student though. Do you know him?"

"He's a pilot. Yeah. But he's also a flaming faggot," said Cleve. "What, you didn't notice? He's probably hitting on you."

"I'm old enough to be his father," protested Hal weakly, but Cleve was already clapping him on the back with a smirk.

"Just a babe in the woods," he said, and moved off.

There was still butter on Hal's fingers, or maybe vegetable oil.

He reached for the top of a stack of paper napkins and wiped his fingers, then picked up a bottle.

When he sat down again beside the vegan he looked at him differently, applying a This Man Is Gay filter. He remained unsure, though. The vegan was buff, clean, and ate politely, but there were straight men like that.

"You know Cleve?" asked the vegan.

"Not really," said Hal. "I know someone who knows him, a guy at the embassy. I don't really like either of them. Just between you and me. But he told me you're gay."

The vegan laughed easily.

"Guilty," he said. "Though I doubt he put it that way. Cleve's got issues."

"They let gay guys fly fighter planes?"

"Don't ask, don't tell. Hey, it's not like we're color-blind. Or women."

"Ha," said Hal. He had finished the whole bottle of water. He felt almost sober. "My daughter always wanted to fly," he said.

"She should take lessons," said the vegan, and set his plate down on the table.

"Paralyzed," said Hal.

"I'm sorry."

"Me too."

He was far soberer, yes, but the food was making him drowsy, the food on top of the alcohol.

"I need to lie down, I think," he said to the vegan.

"There's a hammock," said the vegan. "I'll show you."

They walked down the stairs, past the pool, past the crowds

and onto the beach, where there was a small stand of palm trees. A string hammock swung there. Someone had just vacated it. There was a breeze off the ocean.

"Perfect," said Hal, grateful.

Cluster-bomber or not, the vegan had been good to him.

After he settled down in the hammock the vegan patted him on the shoulder.

"Good talking to you," said the vegan, and moved off.

"You too," said Hal.

When he woke up he would tell Brady: You were wrong. The kindergarten teacher was right.

They cluster-bombed and cluster-bombed and told the diplomats nothing.

• • • • •

What woke him up was not the flying dinosaurs but their calls. The calls of the pterodactyls were the same as the hoarse, throaty cries of young men.

He heard them and shifted in the hammock, registering the way the strings were cutting into his back. He was sore along the lines the strings had etched. White light made him cover his eyes.

Struggling awake he saw it was morning—no, midday; the sun was high in the sky—and the monsters were in the sky too but shockingly close to him, red and green dinosaurs with spread wings. He was back with them. Prehistoric. He could smell the salt of the sea and the freshness of morning air. Dinosaurs had been birds, many of them, and birds were their descendants . . . they skimmed along the ocean, over the waves. It must be high tide, because the water was not far away. It lapped at the sand just a few feet downhill. He was between palm trees, so the dinosaurs were only partly visible.

One landed. It had feet rather than claws. It was running.

It was actually a young man holding onto a glider thing. Was it parasailing? No . . . kitesurfers, that was it. He'd seen them before, on Venice Beach. The man hit the sand running, calling out again hoarsely, a cry of triumph. The others were behind him, still over the water. The young man let his red wings go, his red apparatus on its metal struts, or maybe they were fiberglass. It tumbled behind him. How had he taken off? How did they do it?

Another one alit on the water.

Hal struggled out of the hammock as the fliers landed, rubbing his eyes, bleary: the party would have ended long ago. The party had continued without him, leaving him behind. When he was a young man, in high school and college, he had been almost frightened to miss a party, at least any party his friends were attending. He had thought that everything would happen there, at that precise moment, that on that one occasion all friendships, all bonds would be cemented without him. In his absence, he had feared, the best times would be had and he would have missed them.

He did not have that feeling now. Sleep was a good way to leave a party.

His neck was stiff, though.

He patted his pockets. Wallet, check. Something in his breast pocket; he extracted it. It was a mass of tangled pipe-cleaner. Formerly a toucan. He pulled at it, trying to get it back into shape, but no dice. He must have lain on it.

He left the shouting men behind him, the ones landing with hoarse cries of victory. There were more of them coming, more red and green shapes over the horizon. Best to leave before the full-scale invasion. Recover in the hotel room; possibly sleep more there. But first he needed to rinse his mouth.

He walked over the sand to the water, where waves were curling. The wind was up. Behind him the first man landed was grappling with his sail apparatus; ahead, beyond the break, another man was surfing. Hal bent and scooped water into his mouth, jumped back from the edge, gargled and spat. He did it again until his mouth felt salty but clean.

Around him the red gliders were landing. They made him nervous, as though they might land on him. Were they members of a club? They all bore the same pattern, like a squadron of fighter planes. Panels of red, green, orange. The men who held them were euphoric. Their muscles and the wind alone had carried them. Hal felt envious. Yes: when he got home he would enroll in a class, learn to do this. Or windsurfing. To be one of the blown ones, carried.

Today was the day; this very afternoon he would liberate T. He would hustle him onto a plane and take him back to Susan like a trophy.

Slightly dinged, admittedly. Luster dimmed, in her eyes. But still a trophy.

On his return, he would see Susan in a softer light. He owed it to her. And he would be with Casey again.

Climbing the steps to the pool, he looked across its breeze-rippled surface to the aftermath of the party—glasses still on tables, white tablecloths with edges flying up in the wind, flapping across leftover, greasy dishes. No one was around, not even cleaning staff. It was deserted.

Maybe, he thought, he could salvage a replacement toucan from the ruins. He wove through the tables, scouting. Toucan, toucan! He would score one for Casey. He swore to get one for her. It was his duty. Yet there were no toucans.

Still, as he rounded the last dirty table, where a bowl of floating flowers had been used as an ashtray, he saw what seemed to be a green pipe-cleaner turtle sticking out of a margarita glass. They swam thousands of miles to build nests in the sand a few miles south of here, the divemaster had told him, but after they laid their eggs had to return to the water, and poachers tore up their nests and stole the eggs. They had lived 200 million years, maybe more. Maybe even 400. They had outlived the dinosaurs. But now a few beachfront resorts, a few hungry poachers and they were on their way out.

He would accept the turtle, though it lacked the kitsch value of the toucan.

He snatched it out of its empty glass.

10

It was time. At the holding facility T. would be waiting for him. Turned out the place was an easy ten-minute walk from the hotel: the receptionist drew a crude street map on the back of a piece of stationery.

The humid air of the streets was heavy with a gray smog; cars here still ran on leaded gasoline. Simply because no one had yet passed a law to prevent it. As a result children breathed in the toxic fumes every day and gradually lost brain function.

It came to Hal—a curious thought, because he was not given to theories of the supernatural—that their ghosts must linger here, the ghosts of those children before they were impaired. Even as the living children went on, growing into adults of limited intelligence, so must the ghosts linger beside them, pale images of what they might have become.

How wrong Tom Paine had been. Not overall, but in the sound bites. "That government is best which governs least." If only.

Ahead of him a thin boy stepped out of the darkened doorway of a building. Hal felt an impulse to apologize to this boy in case he was one of the retarded ones. Not that Hal himself was personally responsible for the lead in the gasoline of this foreign country, but in the sense that they all were, that individuals were culpable, especially individuals like him, secure and comfortable and well-educated, for all of the rest of them . . . but now the boy must be confused, because he was not moving out of the way. Hal would have to step around him, down over the curb, onto the street and up again.

He moved to step into the street, smiling apologetically in case—since after all he was the interloper here, not the boy—it had been rude on his part not to do so in the first place. He noticed, in the boy's rising hand, something thin and gray. Then the boy stepped up to him, and the boy's hand was on his pocket; at the same time he felt a pain in his side, and was already on his way down to the dirty sidewalk before he could say anything. Falling into sharpness, or the sharpness was crumpling him. It happened so smoothly that as the boy ran away, a small bundle in his hand—a wallet?—Hal was still feeling beholden, as though he owed him an apology.

He was a child, after all. You wanted to protect them despite the bad behavior, knowing that all hurt animals had to flail . . . it was bad, it was surprisingly bad, but the sharpness faded, actually washed itself out a bit. It softened and covered him as he lay, doubtful, stricken by confusion. Was he supposed to be doing something? Was there something he could do about his situation?

He was part of the world's momentum, part of its on-and-on functioning, its inertia that was neverending. The pilot had said it, and it was true, finally. He himself was responsible for the boy, and by extension for this, for the sharpness and the spreading bewilderment. He had played by the rules—he had always played by the rules, even when, for a second, he considered breaking them and then decided not to. His life had been bracketed by rules, enclosed by their tidy parentheses; he had gone along in the forward motion, he had done nothing to stop it.

Warmth flowed over the sidewalk—his own, he felt in a wave of dismay. Had he disgraced himself? But it was thick—blood, not urine.

The sidewalk heated under his side and his arm but he himself grew colder despite the weather, his legs and stomach icy. He had thought it was so cloying in this place, so humid. Just a minute ago . . . how quickly it all flickered. Time was not in step with humans, in the end. It went too fast and too slow: and yet people expected it to guide them and shelter them.

And the boy was gone. Hal was alone and he almost missed him: come back, he thought. Boy? Anyone?

He tried calling out, but lacked the force or the breath. His voice dwindled.

His face against the sidewalk, then turning to lie on his back while the snake twisted in him—he saw the pain that way, an image vaguely inherited somewhere: a black and white snake with a diamond pattern—or no, the diamonds were not white but a sickly yellow. The image flicked past him, a snake slithering through his own blood. He felt a lick of panic, but then he was calm. It wasn't real, after all.

He would have to wait till someone came to help him. That was what happened, with these incidents. People came to help you. All life was based on this, the social compact. It would not let him down, would it? He himself had held up his end. Not that he was a saint. But he was not a bad guy. It was fair to say that, more or less, he had held up his end.

Sometimes you had to wait first. That was all. T. would be fine without him; there was no bail, so all he had to do was walk out. Possibly, even, he would walk out and find Hal. Rescue him, in a role reversal. At this point he was only a few blocks away.

But the flow—he was soaking. Could he stop the flow while he was waiting?

He felt around with his hand, felt his side where the heat was coming from. He tried to block it, pressing his hand against the wet slick, but his arm was so weak.

The boy might even *be* retarded. One way or another damage had been done to him, that was certain. If it was the wallet he'd wanted all he had to do was ask. No show of force was needed. It was Hal's official policy to give up money quickly whenever mugged. He had never had to invoke the policy, however.

If only the boy had asked . . . he felt a twinge of self-pity. Casey would poke at him with affection, needling. He had it all: he had legs. What right did he have to pity?

Above him a streetlamp winked on. He could not tell if the moon was out. When the moon was full you could not see the stars. Once he had seen the Milky Way. When was that? Long ago, he thought, before he got old . . . there was paradise in the Milky Way, in its seeming infinity.

When they came to move him, loading him onto a stretcher,

he would make sure he got a look at the sky beyond the buildings. The stars would be even better, but in a city there was too much ambient light to see the stars clearly.

He heard sniffing. There was a dog next to him, nuzzling his face. The way it tossed its head slightly, nudging with the long wet nose, was endearing. He had to squeeze his eyes closed against the tongue and at the same time he tried to reach out to pet it, but his arm was shaking too much . . . a black dog, a mutt in the Labrador family. Now it had moved down from his face and was lapping at something. He was afraid—yes. Lapping up his blood. He did not blame it for this, though it was a strange sensation: the dog bore him no ill will. We lick what we can, was the motto of dogs. Was it any different from when they licked the salt off your hands or your face?

He recalled T.'s dog, dog on three legs. This one was here, the other was back at home waiting. Dogs all over the world.

It was a comfort. He might be gone, he himself might be gone, but everywhere were the dogs, with their faithful dispositions. It seemed you could rely on them. The dogs were a kind of love, given freely to men. Their existence meant you did not have to be alone. For if, in the end, you found yourself alone, completely alone, and it was chilling, you could look for a dog. And there, in the dog, would be love. You did not have to deserve a dog. Rather a dog was a gift, a gift and a representative. What a dog was was simple: the ambient love of the world.

The dog moved off after a while—or rather, at a certain point it was not there anymore. Hal thought he might have fainted and missed it leaving.

If he still could, he decided, he would get his own dog. When he got home he would go out and get a dog of his own. A dog from a shelter, a dog that needed someone.

He could hear people laughing, possibly in a nearby bar or restaurant. He had always liked going to bars and restaurants; he should go to more of them. Take Susan along with him. Although he might be dying. If so, he couldn't take her to any more restaurants. But he was sorry for his behavior, so trivial and selfish. Whatever made her happy . . . have some paralegals. There, there. Have yourself a paralegal or two.

Really, I mean it, he told her. He would pass out the paralegals like cigars at a birth.

He was so sorry now that he had left her alone, left her alone years ago and never looked back, when all he thought of was Casey, worrying. He had never intended to leave anyone, it was the last thing he would ever have intended, but it turned out he was the abandoner.

This was shocking. It was just like the wound. It was a wound in himself, like the hole from stabbing. Only now did he look down and notice it: he himself did the abandoning.

Of course poor Susan needed company. She should never have been abandoned.

He hoped the laughing people were in a restaurant, celebrating something with lanterns strung up and deep warm colors that were welcoming. He was almost—almost—at the table himself. There were reflections of lanterns on his own glass, which he would raise to the crowd. If they could see him.

He was sorry for the boy, the stabbing boy, but then the boy, he recognized, was also his daughter. Not that Casey had ever stabbed him. He corrected himself, as though someone was listening. It was his feeling he meant, his feeling . . . as soon as they were past, perceptions took on a transparency. There was an impulse, it fled, and then he saw what the impulse meant. He saw through the obfuscations of his own mind, through the dodges of his remorse and his wishful thinking, and behind it all was a vision of his daughter.

It was Casey he wanted to apologize to, not the boy, and it always would be. When you were born, he could say to her, I was born too.

This appeared to him in the light of a new idea, though it was not. I was born then because it was true, as soon as you existed, that I only existed to care about you. From then on I myself was nothing.

And you know what, sweet girl?

I was happy that way.

"It was you who made me necessary," he said.

It came out as a mumble. He wished he could hold her close in perpetuity, as he had wished so often when she was small. He was astonished, when he thought about it, that every man was not a criminal before he was graced with a child, astonished that any man was good at all before that. Many of them were not, actually. Statistics told the story: most vicious criminals, the warriors and ax murderers and gangbangers, were young men. Except for the rare among them who were born nice, they needed a child to civilize them.

And yet, of course, they should not be granted the privilege.

He would tell her: It was you who gave me the reason for my life. Before you I was proud—proud and empty. I had no idea what it was like to beg the world for mercy and not be heard, never be heard at all. But still to go on begging, unheard. I knew nothing.

And then I failed you.

He would say this clearly, making sure she understood how fully, fully acquainted he was with his failure. He had failed to protect her, failed in his one genuine calling, being her father. He did not accept this, in the sense that he repudiated it, but he knew it all the same. You could know something and at the same time reject it, no contradiction there. I failed, he would say to her, I failed at the moment when you were hit and after that moment I would never stop failing.

And it was you who suffered for my failings.

That was the problem of the religion he'd been born into. Christians, he thought: his parents had been two of them, but he could never bring himself. He had lived and now was dying an un-Christian, quite pleasantly godless . . . for the problem with the story of Jesus was simply this: it was a reversal, it was a perfectly backward version of the story of humankind, a mirror image of the world. For in reality itself, as opposed to the holy script, it was not one man who suffered and the rest of the world that was saved. It was the whole world that suffered for the sake of one man.

He could make the stipulation now, he could indulge in bombast now that he was, so unexpectedly, becoming dead. The whole world suffered and bled for all eternity, through all of human history, so that a minuscule, paltry few could have leisure and joy and the liberty of wealth for as long as they each should live. There is no doubt, the poor are the sacrifice, he thought, and he remembered this knowledge like a sight he had seen—all the poor and the untended and powerless. Together they are Jesus on the cross, bleeding so openly, bleeding for all to see, and thin like Jesus too, their arms and veins opened.

And yet the rich, especially the very, grotesquely rich, that fraction of a percent that make up the one man that is saved, blithely deny the truth of this, though it is perfectly obvious and as transparently clear as glass. The rich may worship God or they may pretend to but they are kicking Jesus to the floor daily, kicking him viciously and stepping on his face.

Because the poor are Jesus, in their billions. Plain as the nose on his face . . . and he himself, neither Jesus nor Judas but someone in between, was dying.

But maybe it would be all right in the end, or in the end beyond the end. Maybe somehow a second chance would come for him. And next time he would make sure she was not injured at all. He would take her away to a safe place and there she would be kept separate from accidents . . . there had to be a shelter like that for her, even for both of them. As simple as that bar at the end of the street, beaming its warmth. Was it so much to ask? A safe place for his little girl. If bargains were possible he would give himself up a thousand times before he would let them hurt her. Let them accept him, let them accept his pathetic, meaningless sacrifice. It was paltry. He knew that, for chrissake. But what else did he have, what else could he bargain with?

And this was melodrama, he knew that too, so sue him, who cared, he was dying. And anyway the melodrama did not make it less true . . . all he wanted was to hear the word *yes*. Yes: we will accept it. We will accept what you offer, be it ever so puny. In exchange we will give life back to your girl.

So she will always be young. And she will always be beautiful.

Whatever he did or could never do, in the end it was she who had formed whatever he was that was worth being. It is the child who makes the parent on this earth, he would say to her if she was here to listen, not the other way round. The child was more than father to the man; children were father and mother to the soul, whatever that might be. He did not pretend to know much about souls, or the idea of them. He never had. But once or twice he had thought he could hear a sound, a faint music. The spirit moves around us, falls past us invisible like air through air . . . all we are sure we have, all that we know, is the suspicion of its presence.

And if he did ever see it, if he ever caught a glimpse of this passing soul, it was because she let him: she let him see the world was full of hurt things. The world was made up of these shifting beings, of glancing pain between them as they moved—these solitary worlds that inhabited the total, the millions of small worlds that made up the host. That was where the pain came from, he thought, it came from the friction between worlds, the brushing past, the shiver of contact—the touch of feeling and unfeeling. The pain and grace of the temporary.

She showed him and he got to see, but by then it was already too late. By then his own world had become very small, and in his own world only the one hurt thing mattered.

He had forgotten all the rest. He never even saw them.

Small, my girl, oh small, small, small. You see? The world shrinks around us: we give it all up for you. We close our eyes to it, we shutter them, we give it away though it is not ours to give.

For you we give up the world.

LOOK FOR

a novel
MAGNIFICENCE
LYDIA MILLET
FINALIST FOR
THE PULITZER PRIZE